She had never seen a man quite like Saint before.

The tan complexion of his face and arms continued onto his chest and stomach. Long, sinewy muscles rippled underneath his silky flesh.

He had no modesty.

He had a tattoo on the side of this neck; a simplistic dragon, like one might see etched on an old rune. And on the opposite shoulder, someone had branded him with the image of a cross.

The two markings, coupled with his dark beauty, robbed Ivy of breath.

Here was true insight into who this man really was.

What he had suffered—what he stood for.

Other AVON ROMANCES

Blackthorne's Bride *by Shana Galen*
Bride Enchanted *by Edith Layton*
Seduction Is Forever *by Jenna Petersen*
Sin and Scandal in England *by Melody Thomas*
Tempted at Every Turn *by Robyn DeHart*
Too Scandalous to Wed *by Alexandra Benedict*
What Isabella Desires *by Anne Mallory*

Coming Soon

One Knight Only *by Julia Latham*
To Wed a Highland Bride *by Sarah Gabriel*

And Don't Miss These
ROMANTIC TREASURES
from Avon Books

In My Wildest Fantasies *by Julianne MacLean*
Just Wicked Enough *by Lorraine Heath*
The Scottish Companion *by Karen Ranney*

Kathryn Smith

Taken by the Night

AVON
An Imprint of HarperCollins*Publishers*

This is a work of fiction. Names, characters, places, and incidents are products of the author's imagination or are used fictitiously and are not to be construed as real. Any resemblance to actual events, locales, organizations, or persons, living or dead, is entirely coincidental.

AVON BOOKS
An Imprint of HarperCollins*Publishers*
10 East 53rd Street
New York, New York 10022-5299

Copyright © 2007 by Kathryn Smith
ISBN: 978-0-06-124502-2
ISBN-10: 0-06-124502-X
www.avonromance.com

First Avon Books paperback printing: November 2007

Avon Trademark Reg. U.S. Pat. Off. and in Other Countries,
Marca Registrada, Hecho en U.S.A.
HarperCollins® is a registered trademark of HarperCollins Publishers.

Printed in the U.S.A.

10 9 8 7 6 5 4 3 2 1

This book is dedicated to Nicola Simpson,
who started out my critique partner
and became one of my favorite people
in the world.

To Erika for her trust, faith and belief. It's
so appreciated. To Nancy just for being
her amazing self, and for letting me
know when I'm nuts. And to Tom and
the art department at Avon—thanks for
the gorgeous covers!

And to Steve, because he'd pout
if I left him out.

~~∽∞∽~~

TAKEN BY THE NIGHT

Chapter 1

It was the poorest excuse for a whorehouse that he'd ever laid eyes on.

Saint stood on the doorstep and stared up at the pretty red brick house in Chelsea. There was no cleverly worded sign on the door, no scarlet drapes in the windows, no heavily made-up tart hawking her wares from an upstairs balcony. Rather there were little flowers planted on either side of the clean stone steps, protected from pedestrians by neat wrought-iron fencing. The drapes in the windows were some sort of chintzy, poufy confection that only a woman with too much time and too much money in this decadent age would term fashionable.

In short, what should have been a screaming haven of debauchery looked instead, like any perfectly respectable upper-middle-class home. In a perfectly respectable—although now fashionable with artists and the like—neighborhood.

And for the next thirteen hours this house would be his home as well. Dawn was a growing flush on the horizon, spreading warm and deadly arms toward him. He needed to take cover before the sun raised her brilliant head and made him a smoldering pile of ash on the freshly swept walk. And since he had no desire to meet his end just yet, Madam Madeline's Maison Rouge was his only refuge.

He rapped on the door. It was answered a few moments later by a round-faced woman who looked as though she had been crying. She was dressed entirely in black—an unfortunate color given the paleness of her complexion and rabbitlike pinkness of her eyes.

For a moment, he entertained the notion that he might have knocked upon the wrong door.

"Mr. Saint?"

She knew him, ergo he knew her. He studied her features, the lines of her lovely but no longer youthful face, the graying sable hair. She had the biggest blue eyes he had ever seen, and suddenly he remembered what those eyes had looked like years ago.

"Emily?"

A faint smile lifted her lips as she moved to give him entrance. "You remember."

He did. He remembered a buxom young seductress whose innocent face hid an adventurous nature. Thirty years ago he had shared this woman's bed, strengthened himself on the robust bouquet of her blood and slaked other lusts with her as well. Here she was, back at Maison Rouge and she looked old enough to be his mother rather than his lover.

The realization pinched at his heart, and he wanted to apologize for not aging, for flaunting his everlasting youth in her face.

"Of course I remember, my sweet." He stepped inside the dimly lit foyer, inhaling the scents of incense, lemon, and ever so faintly—surprisingly so— sex. There was no one about and the house was utterly quiet except for soft voices and . . . hushed sobs from behind closed doors. "What is wrong?"

Closing the door, the woman ushered him away from the dangerous dawn. "Oh, Mr. Saint! We've had some awful tragedies. I shouldn't say anything. Madeline will want to tell you herself."

Saint followed Emily down the narrow corridor. The rich, wood paneling and soft creamy wall paper was lit with the warm glow of the new electric light. Anything less than fifty years old was new as far as he was concerned. He remembered when gas lighting was all the rage, and now here they were, bringing light into homes that required nothing more than a switch.

"Has there been death, Emily?" He hated asking, but he had too. He could feel a sense of pain in the house. Low muffled sobs pounded in his brain, coming from more than one person, more than one location within the house.

In the back kitchen, his escort paused long enough to open a secret door in the dark paneling beneath the servants' stairs. "Come, let's get you settled before I burden you."

Her concern for his comfort and sensibilities was endearing if not a touch annoying. He was not some young, nervous fop looking to pop his cherry, as the slang these days put it. However, there was something endearing about her putting his comfort above her own distress.

She lit a lamp—for her own benefit because he didn't need much light to see—and Saint followed her down the steep staircase, lower and lower into the cellar of the house. The air was cooler down there, musty smelling with none of the warmth of the floors above.

Emily didn't have to escort him, he remembered the way, but he wanted to know what had happened to bring such sorrow upon this place. So he followed in silence as she led him to what looked like a simple, abandoned wardrobe. She opened the door, pushed aside a row of clothes that smelled remarkably fresh to Saint's nose, and stepped inside. He waited until he heard a soft click before entering himself. He closed the main door behind him and stepped through the false back into an apartment fit for a king.

And one well suited for a vampire.

It ran the length of the house and extended under the street. No one would notice without careful study that the cellar wasn't as large as it should be, and even if they did, they would hardly suspect a secret room.

There was no smell of dust or mold here. This room had been built with comfort in mind—Reign had seen to that. It was paneled in dark wood, a stark contrast to the whitewashed ceiling. Rich burgundy wallpaper handpainted with delicate Chinese birds glinted in the soft lamplight. The floor was covered with black carpet, also Chinese in design—swirling with gold and red as a massive dragon writhed in rich relief in its center.

Excessive? Yes. Tacky? No.

There were thankfully no windows, but there was a four-poster bed big enough for four adults—Saint knew this for a fact, having had three of Maison Rouge's finest test the theory with him one night lifetimes ago—when such things were still amusing.

There was also a wardrobe, a phonograph on a mahogany table, and a vanity laid out with a full gentleman's toilet. Off one end of the room was a small sitting and dining area. At the other end was the entrance to a dressing room and bath.

Saint crossed the carpet and set his valise on the bed. He hadn't packed much—he didn't own much—but if Masion Rouge kept with tradition, there was a selection of clothing in the wardrobe that would fit him perfectly.

This apartment, and all that came with it was the reason Maison Rouge was a safe house for Saint and his four oldest friends. They had become vampires together and Reign established this house as a place they could come to in order to rest, feed or hide. In return they offered their protection to the women who lived and worked there.

Women such as Emily, who would be looked after until her death.

Saint turned. The little bird of a woman stood in the door frame, swathed in that damnable black. Mourning clothes.

"Madeline will be so glad to see you, Mr. Saint." Was it his imagination or did her voice warble just a bit?

"My dear Emily, tell me what has happened."

"Death." She shook her head, her features contorting as she obviously tried to hold back tears.

"A client?" It wasn't unheard of for establishments such as this to mourn the passing of a wealthy patron, especially if the gentleman in question died while being entertained on the premises.

Another head shake—this time a silent one as a lone tear streamed down the finely lined surface of her face.

"Not one of the girls?"

"Two."

Saint regarded her carefully, noting both her cheeks were now wet and she looked so frail, so . . .

broken. As though her entire view of the world had been irrevocably altered. "How?"

"Murder," replied a voice from just behind Emily.

Saint had been so intent on Emily that he hadn't bothered to listen to the rest of the house, and he hadn't heard this new visitor coming. It was one thing to be comfortable and feel safe in his hideaway, but it was stupid to let his guard down entirely. He turned toward the voice, and the ice he tried so hard to keep around his heart groaned as the usually unassuming organ gave a mighty thump.

Standing just inside the threshold was a woman he guessed to be in her midtwenties. She looked too confident to be any younger, too fresh to be any older. Her tall, curvaceous figure was dressed in a stark black gown, just like the other women. Rich, honey-colored hair was pulled back in a tight bun, leaving the sharp lines of her oval face open and bare.

She had an English-rose complexion—pale with pink cheeks. Her mouth was full wide, her nose long and slightly tilted, and there was something familiar in the slant of her thickly lashed jadelike eyes.

"Mr. Saint, this is Madeline's daughter, Ivy."

He spared the briefest of glances at Emily, who had spoken, before turning his attention back to the striking young woman watching him with little, if any interest.

"Ivy," he repeated dumbly, remembering the

baby who had won his heart, and the blossoming young woman she had been last time he visited. "Good lord, you've grown."

Curved tawny brows rose. "It's been more than ten years. The only one in this room who hasn't changed is you."

She knew what he was—that was plain in the timbre of her voice and the amused way she regarded him. Still, it was a little disconcerting to realize that while time went on around him, Saint was, for all intents and purposes, untouched by it. He could alter his appearance in many ways but the whole of him would always be the same.

Alone.

"You said you suspected murder?" He'd be damned if he'd let this child crawl under his skin after such a brief acquaintance.

"Both of the girls were slain, Mr. Saint," Ivy informed him in a hoarse tone that belied her composure. "Most brutally."

Murder. It was, of course, an occupational hazard for prostitutes to sometimes be brutalized during a night's work, but in a place such as Maison Rouge it was almost unheard of for one girl to be hurt let alone two be killed.

"I am very sorry." Insipid words, but he couldn't bring them back. "If there is anything I can do—"

"Actually," she cut him off without hesitation, "there is."

He had suspected as much. "Of course. What would you like? Payment for the funerals? An annuity for the families?"

"Nothing quite so costly." A hint of a determined smile curved Ivy's succulent lips. As distracting as the sight was, Saint didn't miss the tiny frown creasing Emily's brow, nor the worried glance she shot the younger woman.

Ivy stepped forward, and Saint, a fool when it came to the fair sex, found himself taking a step toward her in response. Her smile grew, but there was no humor in it.

"What I would like, Mr. Saint, is for you to help me catch their killer."

"Help you?" He couldn't keep the incredulity from his voice. "You mean the killer is still at large?"

"I'm afraid so." Her gaze locked with his as she lifted her chin. "You have to help us."

He frowned at her tone. He didn't *have* to do anything. "What I really need right now, Miss Dearing is some rest. I trust you will allow me that before I commit myself to any killer catching?"

She stared at him for at least a full ten seconds, her lush lips compressed into a tight, thin line. Then, without another word, she whirled on her heel and swept from the room as only a pissed-off woman could. Emily followed hot on her heels.

"You'll have to excuse her, Mr. Saint. Miss Ivy and Madeline have suffered a terrible loss."

Saint gave her a tight smile. He knew all about loss and how terrible it could be.

"He dismissed me as though I was a child."

It was quarter past seven in the morning and Ivy was in her mother's bedroom, pacing the length of the burgundy and navy William Morris carpet. She should have let her mother sleep longer—she looked as though she had been up half the night sobbing—but Saint's arrival needed to be discussed.

Her mother smiled as she lay against a mountain of thick, down-filled pillows. She looked like a little doll among the fresh white sheets and wine velvet counterpane. Her strawberry hair was a satiny halo, and despite the amount of tears she'd shed as of late, her green eyes were bright and alert. In the soft light, with the sun still hours from being at its harshest, Madeline Dearing didn't look much older than Ivy herself—much to the younger woman's occasional chagrin.

"You were a child last time Saint saw you," Madeline replied, languorously twirling a lock of hair around one finger.

Ivy's lips tightened, remembering the conversation. "That is no excuse. And I was seventeen, hardly a child." He had looked down that sharp, straight nose of his and told her he was tired—that he would discuss it "later."

Her mother stifled a yawn. "It was dawn. He was no doubt tired and needed to rest."

She stopped pacing and fixed the older woman with a pointed gaze. "We're all tired. Finding Goldie and Clementine's killer is more important than sleep. After all Maison Rouge has done for them you would think the vampires would help us, but Reign is gone and Saint needs his beauty rest." The words left a bitter taste in her mouth.

Just a fortnight ago she had photographed Goldie and Clementine. Laughing and playing in the costumes Ivy had brought, the two young women had been more like children than seasoned prostitutes. They had been all of twenty and nineteen respectively and now they were dead. Murdered by a sadistic bastard.

The expression on her mother's face was sympathetic, bordering on pity. "Reign left before these awful attacks took place, otherwise he would already be searching for the murderer."

Yes. That was very convenient for Reign as far as Ivy was concerned. "How unfortunate that he didn't see fit to leave you with a way to contact him. Not even his own staff know where he is."

"Your face will stick like that if you do not stop sneering."

Which was more maddening, that her mother continued to talk to her as though she was still a child, or that Ivy listened to it? She sighed.

"It is time to face the truth, Mama. We're on our own. The authorities are impotent and the vampires have turned their backs. It is up to us to see the killer brought to justice." Goldie and Clementine had been her friends. She'd be damned if she'd allow the man who slaughtered them to remain free.

"I'm sure Saint merely wanted some time to think about the situation and speak to us when he was more alert."

Think? What was there to think about? Women were *dead*. "You give him more credit than I do."

"I know him."

Were it possible to roll her eyes while scowling, Ivy would have done it. "Ten years can change a person, Mama."

Her mother smoothed her palms over her blankets. "Are you not the one who is always telling me that people don't change?"

Ivy made a scoffing noise when words didn't come readily. She had said that, yes.

Her mother smiled smugly. "What's this, no witty retort? Saint must have made an impression."

The remark hit a little too close to home for Ivy's liking. In addition to being apparently just as confident and selfish as she remembered him being, Saint was just as beautiful as well. In fact, she had never seen a more breathtaking creature in her life. He was almost too sensual. She liked handsome men—men who had a pleasant look about them and who smiled easily. She did not like men who were dark and swarthy and looked at her as though she was a lamb and he a hungry lion. Those dark eyes of his made her nervous; it was so difficult to read the expression in them, and that perfect bow of a mouth curved ever so slightly—almost contemptuously—in amusement.

He would photograph beautifully and she hated him for it. In fact, she was very close to hating him—and for what reason? Because that schoolgirl crush she thought long dead had raised its eager head at the sight of him.

"I always loved his hair," her mother remarked almost dreamily. "Is it still long?"

"Collar length." She refused to remark on how dark and thick it was, or how the soft waves framed the chiseled bones of his cheeks and jaw.

Madeline sighed. "He's cut it then. Too bad. Every girl here wanted to bed him just to play with that hair."

Ivy supposed she should have been shocked by her mother's bold remark, but she grew up in a brothel. As pretentious and fine as Maison Rouge was, she was rather difficult to shock when it came to sexual behavior.

A woman's body was her most expensive commodity, and her heart the most prized, Ivy's governess used to tell her. If she had to barter with one of them—the price had better be worth it.

Ten years ago Saint could have had her heart and her virtue for a smile. He had barely noticed her.

"We're nothing more than food to him! Don't you care about justice for Goldie and Clementine?"

One look was all that was needed for Ivy to realize that she had gone too far.

"Ivy Abigail Dearing." Her mother's voice took that tone that never failed to make Ivy stand up straight. "Only the fact that I share your grief keeps me from boxing your ears. Disagree with me all you want, but don't you dare presume that you care more about the welfare of my girls than I do."

Duly chastised, Ivy nodded. "Yes, Mama. I beg your pardon, but I do not have as much faith in Saint as you seem to."

Why, the vampire's name alone was laughable. Saint, indeed. Saints didn't bed a new girl—sometimes three—every night.

"Darling, I trust him with my life and you should as well."

"In the name of God, why?" She wouldn't trust him with a paper cut on her finger, let alone her entire being.

"Because if it weren't for Saint neither you nor I would be here." As a thick churning began in Ivy's stomach, her mother grinned. "I'm afraid so. That vampire you do not want to trust is the man who saved me and brought me here. You owe him your life."

* * *

Ivy was still thinking about her mother's surprising confession at Clementine's funeral that afternoon, although the fact that her mother had kept quiet about Saint's importance in her past paled in the shadow of her grief.

Why had she never known that it was Saint who saved her mother from a slow and frigid death on the streets of London? He found her alone, weak and about to give birth and took her to Maison Rouge where, after Ivy's birth, she worked, was treated well and eventually became its madam.

Ivy's life wouldn't have been half so comfortable were it not for Saint.

Damn it.

She stood beside her mother on the damp grass, a tiny bouquet of violets in her hand. They were joined by the ladies and staff of Maison Rouge and members of Clemmy's family. Gathered around the small hole in the ground, the damp, clean air smelling of earth and flowers, the group perspired and fidgeted in their mourning clothes as an unseasonably warm sun shone down upon them.

A trickle of sweat ran down Ivy's jaw from her hairline, but she ignored it, letting it flow as the tears refused to. She wanted to weep for her lost friend. She wanted to scream at the newspaper artist capturing the scene from several feet away. She wanted to slap the authorities for doing nothing.

Whores across the city could be in grave danger,

and yet the pimps sent them out onto the streets, not wanting to risk losing one penny of revenue. Did the police patrol those areas of London that "unfortunate" women frequented any more than usual? No. Did they send anyone to Chelsea to watch over her mother's establishment? No.

No one cared if prostitutes died. Foolishly, she had hoped Saint might. That he didn't seem to made her feel all the more stupid for making an idol of him in her youth.

As soon as the thought of him entered her mind, Ivy pushed it away. She would not allow him to take the pain of this moment away from her. She wanted to feel empty and hollow and lost—Clemmy deserved no less.

Clementine's mother stood across from them. She was a handsome woman, but years of hard living had taken their toll on her face and figure. Draped in black and holding a rosary, she stood straight and silent, a steady trail of tears streaming down her lined cheeks.

Watching her, Ivy felt an awful prickling behind her own eyes. What a horrible ordeal for this poor woman, to lose her daughter in such a fashion. To have the newspaper people and morbid onlookers watching her, taking some kind of horrid delight in her sorrow.

Warm fingers twined with Ivy's and squeezed. Ivy squeezed back. She and her mother didn't have to speak to know what the other was thinking. For all the times she might lose her patience or not understand her mother, Ivy loved her with all her heart and knew she was loved in return.

When the vicar concluded, Clementine's mother threw a handful of dirt on the casket. Ivy, her mother and the rest of the Maison Rouge mourners tossed a variety of flowers—mostly violets—into the grave as well. Then, Ivy put an arm around her mother's shoulders and escorted her to where the carriages waited. There were enough for all of them. Madeline had been determined that no one would have to walk home from the funeral—that no one would be alone for the vultures to take advantage of.

They rode home in silence. It wasn't until they were inside the house that her mother spoke. "Ivy, be a love and fetch a bottle of wine from the cellar, will you?"

"I'm sure there is some in the cabinet, Mama."

Her mother stripped off her gloves. "I want one of the good ones."

A sneer threatened. "Trying to impress Saint?"

Madeline sighed. "*Please*, darling."

And so Ivy went. She could not deny her mother, no matter how much she detested the preferential treatment Madeline gave Saint. She understood that her mother felt beholden to the vampire, but what of the arrangement the vampires had with Maison Rouge and all who lived there? The house provided food and shelter, and yes, female companionship to the vampires in return for financial security and protection. When was the last time they had asked their benefactors for anything? And just a few weeks earlier—before the murders started—one of them had been there, glutting himself on practically every girl in the house. They came, they took what they wanted and they left again. They had done it for decades and they always would.

Using the concealed entrance under the stairs, Ivy stomped down to the cellar, her ire growing with her descent. It was directed at Saint, but he didn't deserve all of it, she was woman enough to admit that. Much of her anger stemmed from her own helplessness. There didn't seem to be a damn thing she could do on her own to find justice for her friends.

Not even her good friend Justin would help her. He said he admired her, but when she asked him to aid her in her quest, he told her that he didn't want her endangering herself.

As if he had some kind of right to demand that of her.

Good God, if she didn't find some way to release the frustration inside her she would explode with it. It threatened to consume her. In fact, she was so preoccupied with her own helplessness that she didn't even notice she was no longer alone until her hand closed around a dusty bottle of red wine on the rack on the far wall.

"French or Italian?" a smooth voice asked.

"Bloody hell!" Ivy's heart pounded like it was trying to burst from her chest and run for cover. Thankfully she hadn't lifted the bottle, otherwise she'd have had to explain a destroyed bottle to her mother.

Hand pressed to her bosom, and slightly giddy from the scare, she turned. He stood near the entrance to his secret apartment, looking rumpled and careless and infuriatingly lovely.

"What are you doing here?" It was still daylight. "Shouldn't you be asleep?"

"Good afternoon to you too," he replied silkily, as though she amused him. "Contrary to popular belief, we vampires do not have to sleep from sunrise to sunset. We can wake whenever we choose, just as mortals do. It is only that the day puts us . . . on edge, and the light of it can kill us."

"Only that?" It was no use trying to keep the sarcasm from her voice. "So you thought you'd skulk around the cellar until it was safe to come upstairs?"

The light in the cellar wasn't the best, and there was only one bulb, but still she could see him arch a brow at her tone. "I'm hungry. There's no blood in my room."

She would not feel guilty for forgetting about him, not when she had been at the graveyard burying her friends, but there was a twinge in her stomach anyway.

"We were at a funeral, Mr. Saint," she informed

him coolly. "If you would wait here, I'll see that . . . something is brought to you." He'd have to settle for something bottled because she'd be damned if she'd send one of the girls down after all they'd been through.

She turned to go. Fast as lightning, he moved around her, blocking her path. "So deliciously tart," he murmured, that mocking smile curving the bow of his lips. "And yet you look so undeniably sweet. Which is it, Miss Dearing?"

Ivy's own lips tightened, but she was more annoyed at the traitorous pounding of her heart than his audacity. She did not want to like him—she didn't like him—and yet she could not deny the raw sexuality of him. But she didn't have to respond to it. She wasn't seventeen anymore.

"Are you trying to frighten me?" she demanded. "Because I assure you, it won't work."

Saint's smile grew, revealing sharp, white teeth that were startling in the tan of his face. His fangs weren't extended, but she shivered a little just the same. He raised his hand, brushing her cheek with the rough, warm tips of his long fingers.

"Frighten you? Never." He leaned in, bringing his head downward, closer to hers so that she could feel the warmth of him, smell the spicy scent of his skin.

"What I'm trying to discover, Miss Dearing, is whether or not you are on the menu."

Chapter 2

He didn't mean to tease her, but Saint just couldn't help himself. She had grown from a pretty girl into a delectable woman, and even though she was the last person in this house he'd ever dare try to sink his fangs into, he was an incorrigible flirt.

Tasty little Ivy Dearing stared at him with eyes that glittered like the coldest jade. "I do not work here, Mr. Saint."

Propping his forearm on the shelf above her head, he leaned in a little closer. She smelled of vanilla and nutmeg, with a more subtle trace of musk. "Please don't call me mister. It makes me feel old."

Was it his imagination or was that a flicker of amusement in those cool eyes?

"You are old." She smiled a little as she said it.

If she had thought about her response she might not have smiled. She might have known—courtesy of her mother—that most men would take a smile as an invitation.

Six hundred years of immortality hadn't made Saint any more or any less of a man. He still guarded his own heart and took pleasure in the unexpected moments life had to offer.

And he rarely—if ever—refused an invitation.

She met his gaze with a level one of her own—a gesture that startled him. Most people who knew what he was were afraid to look in his eyes.

"And no, I am not 'on the menu,' as you so charmingly put it."

The smile that tilted his lips was genuinely rueful. "Pity. You could always volunteer."

A little bubble of laughter escaped her. Judging from her expression and stance, she was more annoyed than amused. "Allow me to be perfectly blunt, Mr. Saint. I have no intention of ever offering."

There it was—a subtle quickening of his heart that brought a rush of excitement flooding through his veins. It was very similar to the thrill he used to experience as a thief. The one thing more tantalizing, more tempting than an invitation was a challenge.

Ivy Dearing had just offered him one.

She must have sensed the predator rising within him, because she took a step backward, eying him warily. "I suppose you'll be leaving as soon as the sun sets?"

"Hmm." She obviously wanted him to stay, but not for the reasons his libido wished. It was just as well. "Such questions are generally meant to be asked with a tone of indifference, Miss Dearing. You are not supposed to let me know you care what I do."

"But I do care," she responded, the soft line of her jaw undeniably taut. "I care because two of my friends are dead and no one in this damnable city has done a damn thing about it."

Her anger washed over him, violated and tore at him with its raw power. It was followed by a wave of regret that stung like salt on the fresh wounds.

"Any actions of mine will not bring your friends back, Miss Dearing. It is too late for that."

"I know that." She turned her face away from him and brushed a layer of dust from a bottle cradled on the shelf near her head. "I'm not talking about making them vampires. I'm talking about finding their murderer and making certain he pays for it."

The pain was obvious in her voice. Pain and loss.

Those were two emotions Saint understood all too well.

"Take me to your mother," he commanded grimly. "She and I need to talk."

The drapes in Madeline's boudoir were closed; panels of heavy velvet the only protection Saint had from the late afternoon sun.

He entered the room to find her waiting for him in a small sitting area, as lovely as she had been the last time he'd seen her. Perhaps even lovelier. She sat at a prettily dressed table, looking for all the world like some fine lady about to take tea.

Genuine feeling filled his heart. He would always have a soft spot for Madeline, no matter how many years passed between meetings.

"Hello, Strawberry."

She rose to her feet with a smile, and came to him graceful and light with her arms outstretched. It wasn't until she drew close that he saw the red rims of her eyes and the faint lines around her mouth. She was no longer that young girl he had found in an alley half frozen and in labor. She was a mature woman with a heavy weight upon her heart.

"Saint." Her arms closed around him, engulfing him in the sweet berry scent that was exclusively hers. "I am so glad you have come."

It had been so long since he held a human woman in his arms for a purpose other than feeding or sex. Here was a gentle reminder of the vitality and frailty of the human body. Here was comfort and grace, with none of the pain he often associated with mortals.

"Black is not your color, my dear," he murmured near her ear as he slowly released her. Their gazes locked and the weariness in hers pained him. "Tell me what has happened."

Madeline nodded and took one of his hands in hers, leading him toward the table. "Come sit. You must be hungry."

He was.

"He is," came a dry voice from behind him.

Saint glanced over his shoulder at the seductive Ivy, and allowed a wicked smile to caress his lips as his gaze brazenly roamed every inch of her. "Indeed I am."

He wouldn't say she blushed because that sounded too maidenly for her. It was almost as if she were a succulent peach ripening before his eyes, turning the most delicious shade of pink that said she was ready to be plucked and devoured.

"I have blood," Madeline was saying, oblivious to the tension between Saint and her daughter. "I hope you do not mind that it's room temperature."

The blood was in a crystal brandy snifter on the table. It was all he could do not to grab it and swallow it in one large gulp. "Of course not, but the two of you might have reservations about watching me drink."

Madeline arched a razor-thin brow. "You cannot seriously think I would be so delicate?"

Saint shrugged, but cast a glance at Ivy.

The young woman scowled at him, rebutting his concern with scorn. "I have seen vampires feed, Mr. Saint."

"Have you? Did you like it?"

"Saint, please don't tease my daughter."

"My apologies, Maddie. Miss Ivy." Seating himself at the table, he lifted the snifter to his lips. The blood wasn't as warm as he would have preferred, but it was sweet and salty and it sated his hunger so that a pleasant warmth blossomed in his belly.

Across from him Madeline sipped a cup of tea as though there was nothing bizarre about the situation at all. Her stiff-spined daughter stood a few feet away, her arms folded across the lovely and generous swell of her bosom. Damn this current fashion for high-necked gowns. A woman's throat and breast should be displayed as much as possible.

"Tell me what has happened, Maddie," he urged softly, bringing himself back to the matter at hand.

"Two of my girls were murdered." Her gaze was wet and bright as it locked with his. "Brutally so."

"I need you to tell me in detail, my dear. If it is not too painful."

It was Ivy who answered when her mother hesitated. "They were away from the house. Their throats were slit and their wombs cut out. The authorities are not certain which happened first."

Saint studied her. She tried so hard to be composed and cool, but he heard the tremor in her voice and saw the paleness of her cheeks.

He reached out and covered Madeline's cold fingers with his own. "I am so sorry, Maddie."

She nodded, her lips compressed as though trying to suppress tears. "Thank you."

"Have there been only the two victims?"

Ivy answered. "That is more than enough, do you not think?"

His lips pulled taut in a farce of a smile. "While I find something almost charming in your snippish tone, Miss Ivy, I merely wish to ascertain if there have been any more killings that you know of."

Now she blushed. Good to know she had some sense of manners. "No."

"Thank you." He turned his attention back to Madeline. "So Maison Rouge appears to be our only connection for the time being."

Madeline shook her head. "No one who frequents this house would do such a thing."

Her certainty meant nothing. Madeline was far too good-hearted and trusting. How she had maintained this business and made it thrive was a mystery when she had absolutely none of the callousness needed for business.

He stared at Ivy. "Do you agree?"

She seemed surprised that he asked. "I believe anyone to be capable of a crime of passion, but I do have a hard time reconciling the idea that one of our clients might have done such a ghastly thing."

Saint was much more inclined to trust Ivy's instincts than her mother's. Ivy seemed the kind of woman who trusted no one until they proved themselves worthy of it.

"Why have you not gone to Reign?" The other

vampire who owned Maison Rouge—it had been his idea. Reign should be the one seeing to the well-being of its inhabitants.

"I did go to Reign," Ivy informed him. "He's not in London."

"Where is he?"

"Supposedly in Scotland, but no one has heard from him for a fortnight. We sent a telegram but it has not been answered."

That was unlike Reign to ignore those he felt such a paternal duty toward. But Saint had no idea what his old friend was up to in Scotland—perhaps the telegram never reached him. Or perhaps Reign had moved on to another area for some reason.

Regardless, Reign wasn't there and as one of the Brotherhood for whom this magnificent house was created, the responsibility for Maison Rouge and all who lived there, fell upon his shoulders.

"What do the authorities say?" He glanced between the women as he spoke, uncertain of which to ask.

"Nothing," Ivy responded, her full lips twisting into a sneer. "They've told us nothing. All we know is what we read in the papers, and they are only concerned with selling scandal and terrifying the city. You can imagine the public's reaction."

Yes, he could. A decade ago, when Jack the Ripper was at the pinnacle of his bloody career, the entire city had lived in terror. Everyday the press found something new to print, some new horror to recount or photograph to print.

And then Jack disappeared, and the families and loved ones of those he destroyed never had the satisfaction of knowing he had been brought to justice.

He looked at the faces of the two women with him. They deserved justice. They deserved being able to sleep at night knowing they—and those they cared about—were safe.

"I'll find out what the police know," he told them. "And then I'll find the killer."

He looked up to see Ivy watching him with what appeared to be a glimmer of admiration in the cool green depths of her eyes.

He held her gaze. "I promise."

Ivy followed Saint when he left her mother's room shortly after his surprising declaration.

"Did you mean it?" she demanded, trailing behind him as he descended the stairs. The entire house was in darkness for his benefit and yet he moved. Just how keen was a vampire's sight anyway?

"Yes," he replied, not even glancing over his shoulder as he moved swiftly toward the ground floor. "I do indeed find your snippishness charming." He made it sound both complimentary and insulting.

"Unfortunately I cannot say the same for your

deliberate obtuseness. You know full well what I am talking about, Mr. Saint."

He stopped and turned so quickly that Ivy could not rein in her own momentum. Were it not for the steadying heat of his hands, she would have crashed right into him.

"I do know what you are talking about, yes." His eyes were black in the dusky light. With her standing on the stair above him they were the same height—eyes, nose and lips perfectly on a level with the other.

"Clearly you are a woman who distrusts everyone she meets, so I am trying very hard to not be insulted by you questioning my honor."

"I . . ." She had insulted his honor? Part of her was surprised that he had any. Another part of her felt as duly chastised as she knew she ought, and another, secret part of her wanted to inform him that very few people had ever deserved her trust. "I beg your pardon. I meant no disrespect."

He grinned, the flash of his teeth unexpected and brilliantly white. He could smile the knickers off a nun she'd wager. "Yes, you did, but I accept your apology all the same."

His hands released her and through the light crepe of her sleeves she felt cold where the heat of his fingers had been. She also became very aware of how shallow her breathing had become, her ribs straining against the tight boning of her corset.

Ivy had grown up with these vampires and stories of their adventures. Reign was like an uncle to her, so she knew she was not afraid of this one whom her mother held—perhaps blindly so—in such high esteem.

No, this wasn't fear she felt right now, damn it all. It felt terribly familiar to how she always felt whenever Saint would come to call—that this would be the visit when he realized that she was a woman, not a girl.

"You are so angry." His voice was a velvet caress in the gloom. She could have sworn she felt fingers touch her cheek and yet he never moved. "A young, vibrant woman like you should not be so angry."

His words cut to the very quick of her, touching her with their tenderness and igniting her fury with their careless disregard for the gravity of the situation.

"I am angry because two of my friends have been brutally murdered and no one seems to give a damn." Her voice shook as she spoke. It seemed she had said these words or thought them so often and the pain of them only grew with each uttering.

His gaze caught a glint of light from somewhere in the murkiness; obsidian glowing from within. "I do."

And just like that, with two miniscule words he soothed the rage within her and filled her eyes with embarrassingly hot tears.

"No tears, pet." His command was softened by a roguish grin. "I'm exactly the kind of man to take advantage of them."

As quickly as they had come, Ivy's tears dried. It didn't matter if he said it to save her dignity or if he truly was a scoundrel. "Thank you."

He nodded, and turned to continue down the stairs. "Do not thank me until I find the killer."

She didn't tell him that wasn't what she was thanking him for.

Hiking her skirts, she followed after him. "What is your plan?"

Saint didn't even look over his shoulder at her. "I haven't had much time to formulate one, but I thought I might start by reading the police reports."

"They will not simply hand them over." An officer with Scotland Yard was a client of the house, but he hadn't been able to help them. Ivy thought he could have if he truly wanted to, but she kept that opinion to herself.

"No, I would hope not." He came to a halt in the middle of the hall, beside the statue of Venus, and turned to face her. "I thought I might pay a call this evening and sneak a peek at them on my own."

"You are going to trespass upon the police?" *That* was his plan?

"Yes."

"I want to come with you."

"Impossible."

She braced her hands on her hips. It was either that or try to shake him. "Why? Because I'm a woman and couldn't possibly be of any help to you?"

"Help?" He looked at her as though she were the veriest idiot. "You'd be a distraction of the first order, but that is not why."

A distraction? Her hands fell to her sides. "Then why not?"

"Can you see in the dark, Miss Dearing?"

"Not well, no, but . . ."

Long arms folded across his chest, his shirtsleeves brightly white. "Can you move faster than a man can blink?"

"Now you're talking nonsense. Of course I cannot."

"I can." There was no bravado in his voice, no triumph, just simple fact. "And I can assure my own safety should I be caught. I cannot assure yours. As much as I appreciate your offer, I will not accept it."

If she could have found something in his words to offend, she would have, but she couldn't. He spoke nothing but the truth. She stared at him, flushed and impotent. "I understand."

Saint's hand came up—she caught the glitter of gold on his fingers—and hesitated. Then the warm weight of his palm settled on her shoulder. There was nothing sexual in his touch and yet her blood sizzled with it. Her pulse thrummed, but her soul quieted, drinking in the comfort he obliviously offered.

"You know more about this tragedy than I." He spoke in a low, velvety tone. "When I am done at Scotland Yard I will need you to answer some questions. I will need your help to catch the villain responsible."

Her help.

A hoarse chuckle escaped his throat as he dropped his hand. "A word of caution, Miss Dearing. Do not look at a man with such open adoration when you are alone with him. He might be tempted to take advantage of your virtue."

Cold washed through Ivy's veins. She was thankful to be useful in some manner, not adoring. All she wanted was to find Goldie and Clementine's killer.

"Perhaps you are the one who should have a care, Mr. Saint. You should not tell a woman you obviously want to either bite or bed that you think she adores you after an acquaintance of less than twenty-four hours."

Saint stepped back, obviously startled by her words—and the coolness behind them.

"My dear, if I have given you the impression . . ."

"Don't." She held up her hand. "I've lived in a whorehouse my entire life. I know how the game is played. I might be flattered if I weren't certain you've said the same words to a thousand other women you've tried to charm into your embrace."

He stared at her, his perfect lips slightly parted, his gypsy eyes wide. At that moment she was certain no woman had ever talked to him in such a manner.

"I will leave you now," she announced. "I know you have much to do this evening. I will wait in the library for your return from Scotland Yard."

He swallowed. "Fine."

With just the hint of a smug smile, Ivy turned and started back up the stairs. Halfway, she paused and looked down. Saint was now moving toward the door.

"Mr. Saint."

He stopped, pivoting on his heel to gaze up at her. She knew he saw her better than she saw him—a fact she envied since she sorely wished she could see the expression on his face.

"Yes, Miss Dearing?"

"For future reference you needn't concern yourself with my virtue."

"No?" Was it her imagination or did his voice crack just a little? "Why is that?"

She grinned. "I haven't any."

Chapter 3

No woman had ever challenged him to seduce her. No woman had ever used the word "try" in regards to his success in achieving said seduction.

And *merde*, the man who had relieved Ivy of her virtue was one lucky bastard.

If she sought to punish him for his remarks she had chosen wisely. Her words had revealed to him just how much of an ass he was making of himself in front of her.

Saint by no means thought himself an intelligent man. In fact, he was given to rampant bouts of stupidity when it came to women. But he was smart enough to know when to stay away from one.

He needed to stay away from Ivy Dearing. No matter how appealing she might be physically, she was trouble, and not only because she was Maddie's daughter. She was exactly the kind of woman he adored, and that only made him more resolved to keep his distance.

Resistance had never been one of his strong points. He was a rogue, a cad. A libertine. In the centuries following the death of his docile wife and his own "rebirth" into immortality, he had wooed and bedded thousands of women and then . . .

Well, then he had met Marta. After her death he had gone back to his old ways with a vengeance, ruthlessly seducing any woman he desired. But not anymore. Not this time.

As he quietly dropped from the sky to the roof below, he turned his thoughts away from Ivy Dearing to the task he had undertaken.

Finding a killer in London would be tricky at best. The city had grown over the centuries, as cities were wont to do, but as of late more and more people were leaving the countryside to come to the city for employment as industry spread like a cancer throughout England. The Season was long over but those who dwelled year-round in London made a vast minority of those who based their lives on the comings and goings of Parliament.

And so he would need all the help he could get—including that offered by the lovely Miss Dearing. The police reports might not offer anything, but they would give him the cold facts pertaining to the murders and he wouldn't have to upset Madeline or her daughter or the Maison Rouge staff by asking upsetting questions they might not have the answers to. The police would have to do, for now.

The "new" Scotland Yard was a magnificently Gothic white-and-red-brick building set on the relatively new Victoria Embankment along the north bank of the Thames. The building rose high over the street, imposing in its grandeur. Round turrets rose upward like the smooth barrel of a revolver, dwarfed only by the spire that rose even higher from the dark-tiled roof.

From his perch on the roof, Saint could see the clock tower of Parliament silhouetted against the indigo sky. The moon cast an eerie halo around the formidable structure that seemed to him to watch over the city like a silent father. Londoners seemed to share in Saint's analogy, for the tower had earned the nickname of "Big Ben." Or rather, the bell inside it had earned that moniker—the origin of which no one seemed to know.

Using the dormer windows that adorned the side of the roof as makeshift stepping-stones, Saint deftly made his way toward the row of larger windows just below. On his belly, he stretched across the roof of one window, leaned over and placed his fingertips against the pane. Slowly, he pulled.

The lock inside groaned, stretched and finally popped under the force of his strength. The "Scotties" as he liked to call the police force, would never determine what happened to the lock.

With the window open, Saint slithered over the gabled peak and down. Quick as a blink he slipped inside and closed the window behind him. London was lit better now than it once had been and he couldn't risk having the open window being seen by people driving by or pedestrians.

It took but a split second for his eyes to adjust to the darkness inside. He was in an office of some kind. Ambient light from the city lazily drifted across the floor, almost as a thought pointing the direction for him.

Quickly and silently, Saint moved to the door. This was his first time inside the "new" Scotland Yard, but he had made a few inquiries among the Maison Rouge girls and Mary, whose sister had once worked as a cleaner at the Yard, had known exactly where the records room was located.

He listened at the door before opening it, making certain there was no one outside who might see him. Once in the corridor, he immediately set off in the direction of his target.

He was almost there when he heard voices, accompanied by the sound of footsteps. He could go back, but that would defeat his purpose. There were no doors he could simply duck into and, unfortunately, no windows he could slip out of—without the approaching men hearing.

He went up. Up to the darkest corner of the corridor where the walls met the ceiling. With a foot braced on either wall, Saint dug his fingers into the molding. The plaster gave ever so slightly under the pressure. Someday someone would notice something that looked very much like finger indentations and wonder how the hell they got there.

Two men entered the corridor with a lantern. They were in uniform and laughing jovially as they walked. One had a flask in his hand, the other pulled two cigars out of his breast pocket.

"Fancy a puff, Johnny?" he asked his companion.

The other man snatched the offered cigar from his hand. "Ah, you're a right good lad, Aubrey. Right good."

Two of the city's finest, sneaking off to have a sip and a smoke during a long boring night at Scotland Yard. Drunken police inspired *such* a sense of security among citizens.

They took their time walking beneath Saint. His concern wasn't with his own strength, but with the moldings and the walls themselves. They weren't built to withstand strength such as he exerted for an extended period and he worried that he might actually tear through the molding at any second.

A fine sifting of dust drifted downward, just missing one of the men's shoulders as they finally entered the door just beneath where Saint hovered. He waited a few seconds, then dropped to the floor, landing in a silent crouch. Straightening, he moved on.

Finally, he reached the room he sought. The door was locked. Saint smiled and slipped a black

velvet roll from inside his coat as he knelt on the
floorboards.

Inside the roll was a set of thieves' tools he'd had
in his possession for decades. He didn't have to
look to make his choice; his fingers knew exactly
where to go. Within seconds he had the pick in the
keyhole and he felt the same smugness he always
felt when the tumbler clicked and the door swung
open. Six hundred years and he still felt that little
thrill when he managed to get inside a place where
he shouldn't be—to have access to a treasure that
wasn't his.

Once, a little Jewish doctor living in Vienna—
Freud or something—had told Saint, after indulg-
ing in an interesting substance the doctor perceived
to be a "cure-all" but that simply made Saint want
to fly around the city singing, that his penchant
for lock picking was related to sexual frustration.
Saint hadn't believed him, but he had to admit
there was a certain satisfaction to opening any lock
he wanted to open and finding the treasure inside.

Once inside the room, he closed the door and
turned to survey the stacks before him.

There were row after row of boxes and files,
heaped upon shelf upon shelf. Crime was a boom-
ing industry in London—it always had been and
probably always would be.

There were no doubt several records there con-
taining mention of Saint's own career. Burglaries

that were never solved. He had been quite the thief once upon a time. Made a lot of money at it too, but then Reign had got him investing in businesses and ventures and made an honest man out of him.

Well . . . *almost* made an honest man out of him. A body had to have a little excitement now and again.

And this was just one of those moments. There was something invigorating about creeping through the dark, searching for the object of that moment's desire. The triumph of finding it—the knowledge that he had gotten away with it. It was almost as satisfying as sinking his fangs into the plump warm flesh of a willing woman and hearing her sigh with delight as he drank her into himself.

How would Ivy Dearing taste?

Christ Almighty. What was it about this woman that had him so firmly—and so quickly—by balls and by fangs? He wasn't one to deny himself blood or sex, but he wasn't stupid. He didn't get attached to his fucks or his meals.

But Ivy Dearing refused to leave his thoughts for long. That was not good. He couldn't risk involvement. He wouldn't.

He found the file for Clementine and Goldie in a box labeled *MAISON ROUGE*. There were no doubt copies in a file for the murders themselves, but since no one had told him—and he had no way of knowing—how the police were referring to the murders, the Maison Rouge box would have to do for now.

The police photographer had taken full-length captures of each girl as she looked when the body was discovered. They weren't pretty. Saint had seen a lot of carnage in his days as a soldier and as a vampire, but he never understood how humans could destroy each other in such a manner. The girls both had their throats cut, their abdomens opened and their wombs taken. There were no signs of any other kind of brutality—sexual or physical, although both bore marks indicative of having been shackled or restrained around the wrists and the ankles.

As he read the reports and looked at the photographs, Saint was struck by a feeling of familiarity. These murders reminded him of something, but what?

Then he saw the note clipped to one of the reports. It was a small piece of paper, the handwriting on it neater than that on the report itself. On it was the question, *"Has Jack come back?"*

Bloody hell.

Someone in Scotland Yard believed that Clementine and Goldie had been killed by a monster who had held all of London in fear for seventy-two days more than ten years earlier. A monster who all of London hoped would never return.

Jack the Ripper.

* * *

"Ivy, dearest, you are pacing."

She was too—like something feral and restrained against its will. Her mother's favorite Dresser carpet would have a trench worn in it soon.

"I apologize, Millie. It's nothing to do with you. I am waiting for Mr. Saint to return. He was going out to see what he could find out about the murders." Probably the cad was out stalking his next meal. That she cared amazed her. Twenty-seven years old and she still wanted his attention.

"Ah, yes. Tell me about this mysterious Mr. Saint." Millie Bullock had been Ivy's governess and now remained one of her closest friends. Millie was a dark-haired, pleasant-featured woman of two-and-forty years, possessed of an even temperament and a surprisingly strong will. She had always been patient with Ivy's impulsiveness, but knew when to put her foot down. If she ever minded working in a whorehouse she never said.

But she didn't know about the vampires.

"He's . . ." What could she say that didn't make him sound a scoundrel or herself foolish? The latter, of course, being the more important. "My mother has complete confidence in him." In fact, Madeline seemed positively enamored of the man, a thought that made Ivy's stomach turn. Of course her mother had the right to share her bed with whomever she wanted; Ivy just hoped Saint wasn't one of those people.

Millie watched her with shrewd but kind eyes. "What of your confidence?"

"He hasn't earned it yet."

"Yet, so you think he may."

"I hope he does." Then she added, "For my mother's sake, of course."

"Of course." Millie smiled, looking very much like a sly Madonna. "What does he look like?"

"Why do you want to know?"

She shrugged. "I'm merely curious. Is he coarse? Small of stature? Deformed in some manner?"

"No. Physically he is perfect." Oh, damn.

"Well." Millie seemed poised on the brink of laughter. "That is certainly a more inspired answer."

"Why are you so interested in my opinion of him?"

A graceful lift of her shoulders was all the movement Millie made. "Because he seems to have you discomposed."

"He does not."

"Then you are pacing, agitated and snippy for some other reason?"

Snippy. That was a little too close to what Saint himself had called her. "I've had two friends killed, Millie. Would you expect my mood to be cheery?"

"Of course not, my dear," Millie replied, either oblivious to or undaunted by Ivy's snarkiness. "I would expect you to be sad and angry, but we have not been talking about your friends. We've been talking about Mr. Saint and ever since I mentioned him your disposition has gone from bad to worse."

Ivy couldn't argue with that. "I am not certain I like him."

"Because he is unpleasant? Or because your mother trusts him to do what you cannot?"

Ouch. That was a little too close to the bone. "Finding the killer means more to me than it does to him and he is the one who can actually look."

Millie nodded, her expression sympathetic. "Because he is a man. And can go where you cannot."

Because he was also a bloody vampire and was capable of things no mortal man could dream of attempting. "Yes. Because he can do what I cannot."

The older woman rose to her feet and came to her with an embrace that was as light as it was comforting—a warm, lilac-scented hug that soothed Ivy's ragged nerves and drained the frustration from her soul.

"My sweet girl." Millie released her but kept her hands on Ivy's shoulders as she smiled up at her. "I know how awful it must be for you to feel helpless, but you may want to consider that your presence—your strength—is what makes this ordeal bearable for your mother."

TAKEN BY THE NIGHT

Ivy hadn't thought of it that way. In fact, other than pondering her attachment to Saint, Ivy hadn't given much thought to her mother at all. She hadn't thought of how her mother must be grieving for girls she had known and looked after for years.

Her mother might run a brothel, but she ran the priciest, most prestigious brothel in all of England. Her girls were well paid, educated, examined by doctors more often than demanded by law and given the right to refuse a potential client. The women at Maison Rouge weren't forced into prostitution and they were expected to act like ladies rather than common doxies.

Perhaps that was the reason why the murders were such a shock. No one ever expected something like this to happen there, to happen to one of them.

"It is getting late," Millie remarked, releasing Ivy completely. "I should go."

"I will have James take you home."

"That is not necessary. I'll get a hack."

"Do not argue, Millie. I do not want to worry about you as well."

A soft smile curved her old friend's lips. "I would hate to think I had caused you worry, dearest. After all, it is not as though you ever gave my heart reason to stop beating in the past."

The rebuke was gentle enough to bring a chuckle to Ivy's lips. "Indeed."

Unfortunately the moment of levity was interrupted by the arrival of a guest who made Ivy's heart jump.

Saint entered the room dressed in a black shirt and trousers. He was underdressed by any standard, not even wearing a cravat or waistcoat. His shirtsleeves were rolled up, revealing dark forearms lightly dusted with fine, dusky hair. He was long and lean and moved with the grace and barely restrained confidence of an arrogant tomcat.

Millie went as still as Ivy did at his arrival, and Ivy didn't blame the older woman. Dressed as he was, his dark hair curling around his collar, falling boyishly over his forehead, he was a lovely sight for any woman to behold. He had the devil's eyes and cupid's mouth, and when he smiled at them in greeting, he looked as seductive as sin.

"Good evening, ladies. I hope I am not interrupting?"

"What on earth would give you that idea?" Ivy asked, unable to purge the dryness from her tone, despite the honeyed sweetness of his.

His smile didn't fade, it simply turned into a confident grin. "Because your laughter died a quick death when I entered the room."

"We would have had the same reaction had you been anyone else, Mr. Saint."

"You wound me, Miss Dearing. I had rather hoped that startled gaze of yours was just for me."

She should have been irked. She should have let him know just how annoying his charm and teasing was, but instead she smiled, caught up in his teasing tone. "I would hate to disabuse you of that notion, sir. By all means, believe it if it makes you happy."

Oh, how he looked at her; with his head slightly tilted and his dark eyes glowing. How could eyes so dark seem be so full of light? He was not a man who hid his appreciation of women, and Ivy found herself enjoying being appreciated.

If she gave herself to him he would discard her the next morning, of that she was certain. She was also certain he would be worth it.

The realization gave her pause, but only for a second. If he took her in his arms and told her in all seriousness that he wanted her, she would have him naked in a heartbeat. It seemed her former infatuation with him had matured into something a little more dangerous.

"What did you find during your outing?" she asked, steering her thoughts back to what was important. "This is my former nanny, Millie Bullock. You may speak openly in front of her."

Saint smiled at the little woman, and Millie was not immune to the power of his smile. "A pleasure, Mrs. Bullock."

Millie actually sighed as she offered her hand. Saint of course, kissed her knuckles. Ivy rolled her eyes and fought the urge to make retching noises. "Your findings?" she prompted.

"Other than some poorly written reports, not much," Saint replied as he strode toward the cabinet where her mother kept her personal stock of wine and spirits. "Although there was one thing."

"What?"

He raised his head, his thickly lashed gaze moving lazily between them. "An indication that someone among the police suspects that Jack the Ripper may have returned."

Ivy's knees trembled. As much as she hated being a weak female, that name struck terror into her heart. She'd been young when the Ripper fiendishly murdered those poor women over a decade ago—exactly the right age for it to make a deep impression. The thought of that monster having Clemmy and Goldie at his mercy . . .

She choked back a sob. And when strong arms closed around her, she gave in to the embrace, breathing in the fresh clean scent of laundered clothing and the warm spice of male flesh.

Saint held her against his chest as a mother held a child. No man had ever held her like this and she was a little overwhelmed by the comfort of it. She could feel the slow, steady beat of his heart—too slow to be human—feel his cheek against her temple. "They did not suffer," he murmured. "It was over so fast. They did not know."

She did not ask how he knew. Did not ask if it was the truth, she gratefully accepted his words and took what little solace she could from them.

"If the newspapers print this the entire city will be in terror." Millie's strained voice broke through Ivy's fear and pulled her from Saint's safe embrace.

"We cannot stop that." Straightening her shoulders, she lifted her gaze to Saint's. There was nothing of the predator in him now. He looked at her as though he actually cared what she felt. No wonder her mother and Emily adored him so.

"No," he agreed. "We cannot. But, we can hopefully prevent this animal from broadening his hunting ground."

"How so?"

"As of tomorrow night, Maison Rouge will be open for business."

"No." Did her face look as hard as it felt? "We are in mourning. We will not disrespect—"

"Then he kills elsewhere and some other woman with friends who love her dies." There was no rebuke in his voice, just simple fact. "Right now this place is the only connection we have to the killer."

"How do you know? Perhaps he simply saw the opportunity to kill two prostitutes. Perhaps he doesn't care that they came from here."

It was then—as though they were on a stage and the story dictated it—that the door flew open and Emily came rushing in, her face pale and her eyes wide.

"Did you hear?" she demanded.

"Hear what?" Ivy knew the answer would not be good.

"He's struck again. They just found the body of Mrs. Maxwell in Drury Lane. She was killed exactly as Goldie and Clementine had been."

Were she the sort to swoon, Ivy would have dropped to the floor right then and there. Instead, she clutched at the nearest support—which unfortunately was Saint—and allowed the shock of the moment to wash over her.

"Mrs. Maxwell?" Saint's dark gaze bore into hers. "The actress?"

Ivy nodded. Her throat was so tight. Would she be able to speak? "Priscilla."

He frowned. "You knew her?"

"She . . . came here often with her lover, Jacques Torrent. He's a painter." Pained, and yet horribly numb, she stared helplessly at him. She had wanted so much for him to be wrong.

"I owe you an apology, Mr. Saint. It seems the killer is linked to Maison Rouge after all. Only it's not just those who work here that he is after."

And Ivy knew from the way Saint looked at her, the way his eyes widened ever so slightly, that he now knew what she did.

That no woman connected with that house was safe—including Ivy herself.

Chapter 4

Underneath the sprawling city of London was a maze with walkways perfect for someone such as Saint to use for travel. Sewer lines, pipe lines, train lines. If one knew where they were going and what routes to use to get there, they could go almost anywhere in the city without ever going aboveground. This was how Saint managed to get from Chelsea to Drury Lane and then to Whitechapel later in the morning without turning himself into the vampire equivalent of fireworks.

Shortly after the news of Mrs. Maxwell's death, he had left Maison Rouge and headed for Drury Lane to find out what he could before the police and press destroyed what evidence there was left. Turning his back on Ivy and her distraught face had not been easy, not after holding her and giving what comfort he could. The realization that he simply wanted to hold her a little longer was what pushed him out the door.

Ivy Dearing, prickly little thing that she was, pulled at his heartstrings. She felt so deeply for those she cared about. A part of him wanted to care for someone again, even though he knew the pain it would bring would not be worth it.

Tennyson, the foolish git, hadn't known what he was talking about when he said it was better to have lost love than never had it at all.

Once at Drury Lane, Saint had found nothing to give him any clue to the killer's identity. There were already too many people there for him to pick up on a scent and the police weren't allowing anyone to get close enough for him to examine the body. Not that he had to examine it. One glance had been enough to give him all the information he needed to know the killer was one and the same.

The murder of Priscilla Maxwell was a mirror image of the brutality visited upon the Maison Rouge girls. Her throat had been slashed and her womb taken. She hadn't been beaten or raped as far as anyone could tell. Her clothes had been neatly arranged around her again and she'd been positioned like a sleeping child.

"Looks like the 'andy work of ole Saucy Jack," one onlooker remarked, drawing some astonished gasps and murmured agreements from others who had gathered just to catch a glimpse of the body.

It would only be a matter of time before the papers drew the same conclusion. In fact, it was nothing short of a miracle that they hadn't already. This murder garnered more attention than the others, after all, Priscilla Maxwell was famous.

Saint had a limited amount of time to gather all the information he could before people got caught up in the sensationalism. Part of the reason Jack the Ripper had never been caught was the lack of trustworthy evidence and changing statements. Whitechapel was a rough part of town and many who lived there were more than happy to supply information for a price. Unfortunately, much of that information was third-hand and distorted by drink, if not an outright lie.

The information from Drury Lane might not be any more dependable. And now people would want to toss in references to the Ripper case. Everyone would have something to say, hoping to see their name in the papers.

The police would never talk to him and that was just as well. There was one person who would know just as much if not more than Scotland Yard, and that was Ezekiel Cole. That was why Saint was in the tunnels below London, avoiding the killing rays of the morning sun.

He wasn't alone in the tunnels. Rats scurried by, as did the odd human. They looked at him with slightly feral eyes. A small band of ruffians approached, mistaking him for a rich toff whose purse could buy them food, drink and women for a week.

Had they any sense at all they would have realized that no proper gentleman would ever enter
these tunnels.

"'and it over, Gov," one of the men demanded cor-
dially, the light from his lantern shadowing his face
as he spoke. "And we'll leave ye to your business."

Had they not been as drunk as they were, or as
intent on the prize, they might have noticed that
Saint's eyes glowed in the dark, sharp and catlike.
They might have noticed that his teeth were long
and sharp.

They might have noticed that he wasn't human.

"Lads," Saint said, stepping forward, "be on
your way and you won't be harmed."

They chuckled at that—they always did. Six
hundred years of existence and this *still* happened.
There was always some foolish band who believed
they had strength in numbers, whose greed out-
weighed any common sense they might possess.

They rushed him. Saint sighed.

He didn't kill them and he certainly didn't feed
from them. There was no way in hell he was going to put his mouth on their grimy persons. But
the slight exertion it took to defeat them woke that
thing inside him that hungered for blood and he
knew he would have to feed soon.

He continued on and soon found the entrance
to his destination, coming up into the cellar of a
building near Baker's Row.

When he entered the back of the shop, the old man sitting at the counter jumped at the sight of him. "Dear God!"

Saint grinned. "Easy old man."

"Well I'll be buggered. Saint!" Jumping up from his stool he came forward with his lanky arms wide for a back-clapping embrace.

Ezekiel Cole had aged little in the past three years since Saint last saw him in Paris. He kept himself young on a steady diet of ale and younger women. He was crafty as a fox, but loyal to those whom he trusted. Saint knew he was one of those lucky few. He had known Ezekiel's father, and had proven his own loyalty on more than one occasion.

"What brings you to my little establishment?" Ezekiel asked, releasing his hold on him. "Do you have a little treasure for me?"

One of the best fences in all of England and France, Ezekiel had connections all over Europe. He and Saint had done business on many occasions.

"Today I need information, my friend."

The lines in the other man's brow deepened. "Of what sort?"

Saint picked up a gold pocket watch from the counter and toyed with it. Lucky that Ezekiel was his friend or he'd steal it. "Do you still know more about what happens in this city than the police?"

"I reckon so, and not a terribly difficult task neither."

He put the watch down and met the other man's gaze. "What do you know of these recent murders?"

Ezekiel didn't have much to offer, but it was something. Unfortunately, much of his information only seemed to support the suspicion that Jack the Ripper had indeed returned. The killer was believed to be left-handed. Their throats had been cut in the same manner and there was no sign of a struggle.

"Were the women drugged or intoxicated?" Saint asked. Ten years earlier most of the victims had been drunk at the time of their deaths. There had also been talk of the Ripper using grapes and drink to lure his victims into his clutches.

Ezekiel shook his head. "Not that I've heard. You know that Miss Madeline frowns upon such behavior at her *fine* establishment."

Saint ignored the mockery in the old man's tone. Ezekiel knew that Saint frequented Maison Rouge, but not that it was a safe house. No one knew that. "The women were in their right frame of mind then."

"Aye, so it would seem."

"And they went with him anyway." It all snapped into place. "They knew him."

It wasn't a great revelation, but at least it reduced the suspect list from every man in London to those who visited or had business with Maison Rouge on a regular or semiregular basis.

"Thank you, my friend. You've helped me a great deal."

Ezekiel shrugged. "Not sure what I did, but you're welcome all the same. By the way, last time he was in, Reign left something for you. It's in my desk."

Reign had left him something? It wasn't out of the ordinary. Unlike Reign, Saint didn't have a permanent lodging in London, so Ezekiel served as his post office. Saint checked in twice a month.

Stepping into the back room, Saint went to the desk and opened the top drawer. There was a small packet with his name on it. Inside was three hundred pounds and a note that simply read, *She's back. How did you know, you gypsy bastard?*

It took a moment to remember what his friend was referring to, but when he did Saint put the money and the note inside his coat pocket with a chuckle.

Thirty years ago, when Reign's wife left him, Saint had wagered three hundred pounds that she would be back—and when she returned Reign would want her back. Obviously, his premonition had come to fruition.

Still chuckling to himself, Saint returned to the outer section of the shop to find Ezekiel with a customer. His laughter died in his throat.

Ivy. As fresh as a warm spring day, she was the brightest thing in the entire shop. Fashionably dressed in a peach walking ensemble, she looked as regal and haughty as any aristocrat. Her father's blood was obviously showing.

She was standing on the opposite side of the counter from Ezekiel, a selection of jewelry laid out between them. Ezekiel held a sparkling brooch in his hand, but his gaze was fixed on Ivy, and his expression was unyielding.

"But it's worth at least twice that," Ivy insisted.

Ezekiel shook his head as he set the brooch with the other items. "Sorry, ma'am. That's my final offer."

Saint could smell her agitation. He'd know she was irked even if her face didn't give it away.

"Miss Dearing," he spoke, coming out into the shop. "What are you doing here?"

She looked as surprised to see him as he had been to see her. Her startled gaze raked him from head to toe and back again. "Mr. Saint. I'm . . . that is . . ." She sighed. "Obviously I'm trying to convince Mr. Cole that my jewelry is worth more than he's willing to give."

Saint approached slowly. "Are you in some kind of trouble?"

The look on her face told him how little she thought of that insinuation. "I'm trying to get money for the families of our murdered girls." She slid a sideways gaze toward Ezekiel. "I don't suppose that appeals to your generous nature, does it?"

The shopkeeper gave her a slight smile. "No. Being generous is bad for my business."

"Yes, I suppose it is."

Saint ignored their banter and came closer to take Ivy by the arm. He shot a meaningful glance at his friend, who immediately disappeared into the back room to give them privacy. It wasn't that Saint didn't trust Ezekiel, but the safety and secrecy of Maison Rouge was not something to ever be risked. That had been the agreement when Reign started the place.

"Reign will take care of the families," he murmured, once he was certain they were well out of earshot. "You needn't concern yourself."

Ivy pulled free of his grasp. "Reign isn't here," she reminded him tightly. "And if I don't concern myself, who will? You?"

He blinked. "Your mother—"

"Has enough to worry about," she interrupted, boldly staring him in the eye. "She keeps that house running for the five of you, just in case one of you decides to grace us with your presence. She believes you will save us, and even now waits anxiously for you to make an appearance. Should she dig into her own pockets as well?"

"Her pockets are deep enough," Saint remarked coolly. "She is well compensated for all she does— and appreciated."

Ivy snorted. "Oh, yes, you're so appreciative."

Anger practically shimmered around her. "Why do you despise me?"

She looked away, but not before he saw a glimmer of regret in her jadelike eyes. "I do not despise you. I just wish that you—or one of the others would step up and do what is best for Maison Rouge." She met his gaze once more. "Treat those girls as something more than a need fulfilled."

Her words struck a chord. Though he certainly cared about Maison Rouge and those who lived there, he was guilty of viewing them as being there for his benefit with little regard to the reverse.

"How much do the families need?" he asked.

She shrugged. "I don't know. How can you put a price—"

"What do you think is fair?"

She gave him a number. It was generous, but not foolishly so.

"Then they will have it." He could easily afford such an amount, and she was right—it was time he gave something back after years of taking.

Her eyes widened. "You'd do that?"

"You've shamed me," he replied softly. "I will personally insure that the families are looked after. You'll have the money by tomorrow evening."

Her face softened and in that moment he'd gladly bankrupt himself to enjoy the admiration in her eyes just a little longer. She offered him her little bundle of jewelry. "Take this."

Saint scowled at her as he stepped back. "I have no interest in your baubles, Miss Dearing. You've already impugned my honor, do not add further insult."

She was openly smiling at him now. "Thank you."

He grunted. He, who always had something to say. "By the way, you were wrong."

A tiny frown puckered her smooth brow. "When?"

He nodded at the bundle in her hands. "That brooch isn't worth twice what Ezekiel offered."

Her frown grew as she too looked down. "It isn't?"

"It's worth three times that much." Hand on her arm once more he gave her a little shove toward the front of the shop. "Now go the hell home before someone sees you for the easy mark you are."

She didn't seem the least bit offended by his words. In fact, she flashed him a smile as she paused at the door. "Thank you, Saint."

He nodded. The door chimed as it closed behind her and Ezekiel reappeared from the back room. "She played you, didn't she?"

Saint turned to his friend with a rueful grin. "Don't they always?"

And it was worth every penny.

Against Ivy's counsel, her mother let it be known that Maison Rouge would be reopening as of that evening. Her reasoning—or at least the reason she gave her clientele—was that she planned to celebrate life, not mourn the loss of it. So, that evening there would be a quiet salon with some of the most brilliant artistic minds in the city in attendance.

She hoped Saint knew what he was doing.

Already guests and clientele had arrived. Bodies lounged on the overstuffed russet-leather sofas, leaned against the heavy oak mantel and crossed the navy, gold and wine carpet to greet one another. These were regulars at Maison Rouge. There were stage actors and actresses, along with a few who were now working in the fledgling medium of cinema. There were writers and artists, politicians and celebrities of varying degrees of infamy. And among them were the girls of Maison Rouge. Tonight they would act as hostesses, astute listeners and intelligent companions. If they wished, they could entertain a guest in their rooms abovestairs, but Madeline had let it be known before the evening began that no one had to take part in the salon if they did not wish.

As for the guests themselves, most were there to express their sympathy to Madeline and to spend a quiet evening among friends.

But there was one there who was not a friend—at least, not in the same way that these people were. Saint had yet to make an appearance, but Ivy could feel his eventual arrival like the rumble of an oncoming train. Would he believe one of these people to be a murderer? No one who spent time at Maison Rouge on a regular basis could have possibly hurt Goldie or Clementine. But then what did she know? She hadn't thought Saint the kind of man to give money out his own pocket to help the families of dead whores.

"Ivy, don't you look ravishing this evening."

Smiling, her mind suddenly lifted of its awful thoughts, Ivy turned to greet her guest. Justin Fontaine was a dear friend and a most welcome distraction.

"Justin, how glad I am to see you!" She allowed him to take both her hands in his and pressed a warm kiss upon his freshly shaven cheek. Blessed with boyish good looks, Justin was fair and golden, athletic and intelligent. Only an awful sense of humor kept him from being too perfect. "When did you get back?"

"Just this morning," he replied, his blue gaze soft as it met hers. "I am so sorry I could not be here for you. Are you quite all right?"

His concern touched her and she gave his hands a gentle squeeze before letting him go. "I am, thank you."

"If there is anything I can do . . ."

Ivy spotted her mother sitting by a window, a glass of sherry in her hand. She was alone, her gaze distant. "You could go say hello to Mama. I know she will be happy to see you."

Justin followed her gaze. "I shall." He flashed her another smile and pressed a quick kiss on her cheek before taking his leave.

There. There was no way her mother could be maudlin in Justin's company.

Now if only Ivy could find such a remedy for her own depressed spirits.

Fate, with its amusing sense of irony, presented her with just such a diversion as she turned to take a glass of champagne from the footman passing by.

Somehow, Saint had managed to enter the room without her knowing. One minute he hadn't been there and now there he was, so relaxed and casual she might have wondered if he hadn't been there all along.

He wasn't the tallest man in the room at approximately six feet, but he certainly stood out as if he were. His lean frame was clad in black evening clothes, his tanned skin made all the more exotic by the snow white of his shirt and cravat. His thick wavy hair was brushed back from his face, leaving his features bare to Ivy's greedy gaze.

The golden glow of the lamps accentuated the high jut of his cheekbones, the strength of his jaw and the erotic pout of his mouth. The sensual canvas that was his face was marred by only one imperfection that Ivy could see and that was a scar that bisected his right eyebrow. Other than that he was a dark fantasy come to life. An angel thrust from heaven, reveling in his fall.

Unbidden and yet not of her own accord, she drew toward him. The heavy skirts of her silver and aubergine damask gown swayed about her legs. The gown was fashionably low across the neck and shoulders, but the depth of the purple fabric enabled her to feel as though she wore sufficient proof of her mourning without being obvious. The bodice was snug across her waist and hips and she smoothed the front of it with her gloved hands as she approached the vampire.

He was looking at a framed photograph upon the wall. "Do you like it, Mr. Saint?"

"Just Saint," he corrected automatically, not taking his gaze off the image. "And yes. I take it that from the length of hair in her hand she is supposed to represent Delilah?"

Ivy nodded, easing herself into a comfortable stance beside him. "She is."

"It is a lovely photograph. Ethereal and romantic— a vision of female power. I was so caught up in her expression and triumph that I did not even notice how scantily clad she is."

He summed up the work completely, and deep inside, Ivy thrilled at it. "That's because you see her as powerful. As a woman, not as a whore."

He glanced at her, as though intrigued by her insight. "I suppose so. Who is the model?"

"That is Goldie." Saying her friend's name brought a sharp pain right below her breast bone that was gone as soon as it came. "I took that photograph two weeks before she died."

This time his whole head turned. "You took this?"

His astonishment could have been offensive, but it amused her instead. "Are you surprised?"

"Honestly? Yes."

"Because I'm a woman?"

The look he gave her told her how little he thought of that remark. "Because it's a very sensual image."

She grinned. "You are wondering now if I prefer the company of women."

He shook his head, attention once more on her work. "No, I'm not. I know you prefer men."

"How do you know?" This should be interesting indeed. Such a brief acquaintance and already he believed to know something about her. But then, she had learned something about him as well.

"I can tell from the way you look at me."

"You are very arrogant."

"I'm very old." His lips tilted upward as that dark gaze flashed her way. "Old enough to know that while you might like the look of me, you aren't terribly enamored with the entire package. You used to like me well enough as a child."

No censure. No guilt. He was simply stating the

obvious, and it was obvious he had no idea just how much she had liked him in her youth. "Should I apologize?"

Another head shake, accompanied by a roguish grin as he finally turned his entire body toward her. Ivy's heart gave a little thump in response. That grin was what had snagged her heart years ago. "Don't. You'll like me again soon enough."

She laughed. "Now, *that* was arrogant."

He chuckled as well. "Indeed. It's part of my French charm, you see."

"I am beginning to, yes. Do you take anything seriously, Mr. Saint?"

He sobered. "My promise to you and your mother and to the girls of this house, I take very seriously."

There was more. In the depths of his obsidian gaze there was such regret and sorrow that Ivy's chest tightened at the sight of it. She didn't want to feel for him, but she couldn't help it. He had shown himself to not be the selfish creature she believed. In fact, he was beginning to show facets of the man that as a young girl she had wanted him to be.

"I would like to photograph you." It wasn't what she meant to say, but it was what came out.

He seemed as surprised by the announcement as she was, but he recovered a fair bit faster. "Why?"

"I've never photographed a man before."

"You of all people know full well I'm not a man."

"That should make it all the more interesting, should it not?"

He didn't smile at her attempt at humor. "I've never allowed anyone to capture my likeness before."

"Why not? Because years from now someone might see it and recognize you, unchanged as you are?"

"There is that," he agreed. "But mostly because the artist inevitably tries to make the subject into his own ideal, rather than portray the truth."

"I have no such illusions about you, Saint. I simply want to photograph you as you are." She didn't tell him that she wanted the chance to get to know him. Perhaps that would get him out of her system once and for all.

He stared at her for a moment before finally capitulating. "All right. You can photograph me."

It was all she could do not to jump up and down. "Wonderful. Perhaps we could start the day after tomorrow?"

He nodded. "Fine."

She might have controlled the urge to jump, but she couldn't fight the smile that parted her lips. "I promise I have no misconceptions of who you are."

Finally he smiled at her, but there was a mocking harshness to it. "My dear, you must have, else you never would have asked at all."

In the buzzing society of a St. James's Street coffeehouse, two men sat at a corner table, sipping cups of strong hot Turkish coffee. They looked for all the world like a student and mentor, or perhaps father and son. There was nothing about them that garnered attention.

"You are calling attention to yourself, my friend," Baron Hess, the elder of the two said casually. "You should be careful."

The younger shrugged as only the young and confident can. "The police have no clues. There is nothing to link me or the Order to the killings."

"Do you really believe you can do what no other has before you?"

"Yes."

"Your predecessor did not succeed."

A sneer curled the younger man's lips. "I am nothing like my predecessor. He chose common whores, hardly worthy of the honor bestowed upon them."

"The prophecy says nothing of the hierarchy of whores, dear boy. It says only that the women be of the oldest profession."

"They still have to be worthy."

The baron stared at his companion for a long while. The boy had a lot of fire in him, and much rested on his ability to correctly interpret the prophecy. "You said there were other things he did wrong as well."

"He took the wrong organs. The text clearly states that it should be the 'noble' organ. Most would assume it was the heart or something equally mundane, but a woman possesses something far more noble—that which nourishes life."

That would explain the specimen jars in the cellar of their meeting place. "Well, you have certainly proven yourself more reliable than he was."

The boy's smile was bitter. "And yet, they compare me to the Ripper all the same."

"What they call you does not matter. All that matters is that you succeed." The last to attempt this great task had failed miserably and had to be properly taken care of. They'd had to plant half a dozen red herrings to keep the police from discovering the truth.

The boy raised his cup. "I will succeed, of that you may be certain."

"And what of the final offering? Have you begun to earn her trust?"

"Yes. I spend quite a bit of time at Maison Rouge."

"And she is suitable?" So much death, but it would be worth it in the end.

"She is perfect in every way, just as the Order thought. The fallen child of a fallen woman. Her blood will bring the prophecy into being. But you already know that."

The baron did know. "Good." He didn't want anymore information about the girl. He didn't ask exactly what his companion had planned.

That was the one thing he didn't want to know.

Chapter 5

It was business as usual again at Maison Rouge and as much as Ivy hated to admit it, Saint had been right in having them reopen. Her mother's mood—and the spirits of the entire household—had increased dramatically over the last two days just by having something to take their minds off the horrible tragedies that had shaken them.

As for Ivy, she was only part of house business when her mother needed her, so she threw herself back into her photography to ease her grief.

She had a studio in what used to be a grounds-keepers cottage behind the house. It wasn't very large, but it had a separate room for developing and processing her work and it had a small toilet so she didn't have to run back to the main house every time nature demanded.

This was her private place. She could come here and leave the noise and bustle of the house behind.

She could escape the daily drama of the lives of the
girls at Maison Rouge and indulge in her art.

Usually she worked during the day—that was
when the girls were available to pose for her. This
sitting, however, was being conducted late at night,
after Maison Rouge closed its doors and all—or
rather most—of its occupants were asleep. Saint
wouldn't agree to pose for her until he could be
certain everyone in the house was accounted for
and safe.

Two nights had passed since the house reopened
without incident. No one reported any trouble from
any clients or outsiders. Still, Saint reigned over the
evening like some kind of guardian angel. He had
even gone so far as to hire extra footmen for the
club—men he knew could be trusted to protect the
girls and the guests.

Ivy appreciated his efforts, but he had yet to find
any information as to the identity of the killer. All
they knew was that the bastard was familiar with
the comings and goings of Maison Rouge.

But tonight wasn't about the killer. As much as
she wanted him found, she was obsessing on it and
it was affecting her sleep and her mood. Her mother
had faith that they—Saint, rather—would see justice done and so Ivy *tried* to share her conviction.

It was just so bloody difficult—trusting someone
else to do what she wanted so badly to see done.
Especially Saint, who in the past, had never pre-

sented himself as the trustworthy sort—charming yes, but as dependable as the wind.

She needed to distract herself, so instead of worrying over details of the crimes, this evening she would photograph Saint and find out exactly what kind of man he was.

A knock on the door announced his arrival, and her heart echoed the rhythm. Had he startled her, or was it anticipation that stirred her pulse?

"Come in," she called, arranging her camera so that it was balanced and steady on its stand.

He walked in like the night itself—dark, bright and unpredictable. Clad in his evening clothes, he had lost his cravat somewhere along the way. He seemed to lose his cravat quite often.

Ivy straightened as he closed the door, sealing them both inside the cottage. Her little studio shrank with him inside it. His presence filled every corner, wrapped around her like a warm, spicy velvet cloak. The bed in the corner that she hadn't given any thought to suddenly seemed too inviting—too obvious.

How was it possible that she could have such conflicting thoughts and feelings where he was concerned? Perhaps it was her old infatuation, or this new womanly desire, but she knew she'd like to take Saint to that bed and do things to him that would make the Rouge girls blush.

He looked around the cottage, his dark gaze

missing nothing from the brightly colored walls to the array of lights and mirrors she used to illuminate her subjects. Some photographers preferred to use "flashes" of light to brighten their work, but Ivy preferred a softer look. Fortunately, the dry plates she used in her work were more light sensitive so she could get a decent image with less glaring light.

"This is quite the enterprise you have here, Miss Dearing."

She preened. "Thank you."

He lazily sorted through a rack of costumes she kept on hand. "I think you must be very passionate about photography."

"I am." There was no question of that. She loved everything about the process—posing the subject, picking props and costumes, developing the image—all of it fascinated her.

Saint's dark gaze was bright as it met hers. "I am beginning to suspect you are passionate by nature."

She thrilled—just a little. "I am beginning to think you are a terrible flirt, Mr. Saint."

"How many times must I beg you to not call me 'mister'? It annoys me."

He sounded so put upon she couldn't help but chuckle. He had no objection to being called a flirt, only to being called mister.

"I beg your forgiveness, *Saint*. I suppose you

should call me Ivy then." If she was thinking about him sexually, Christian names were appropriate.

Cupid-kissed lips tilted. "Granted. Now, where do you want me? On the bed, perhaps? I'm told I have bedroom eyes." His tone was light, but the temptation to tell him yes was there all the same.

"I'm sure." She replied with a forced chuckle and pointed. "Right there is where I would like you."

She had a chair set aside for him. It was old and worn with the stuffing poking out of rips in the dark wine brocade. Two of the legs had snapped in half, so she'd had the remaining two filed down to match. Normally she covered it with lengths of fabric, but for him she would leave it as it was. There was something about its shabby elegance that suited him. A kind of poetry to pairing an age-less being with a piece of furniture that had out-lived its use.

He raised his eyebrows at it, but said nothing. Crossing the carpet, he sat down upon the dilapi-dated seat and looked up at her. "Now what?"

"Make yourself comfortable," she directed, moving to stand behind her camera. "What would you do if you were alone in your apartments?"

With a shrug, he stripped off his shoes and stock-ings. His waistcoat and jacket followed, tossed across the room, onto the bed. Just when the lump in Ivy's throat got to the point where she feared she might choke, he stopped.

"You do not like clothes, do you?" she asked, a sorry attempt to calm her own nerves.

Hanging his hands between his splayed knees, Saint gazed at her, a wide smile on his face. "No."

It was such a perfect pose, he was so relaxed and open. So natural. Before he could move, Ivy pressed the button that opened the aperture and captured him forever.

After a few more, she decided it was time to change things a bit.

"Would you mind changing into this black shirt? I think it will look interesting to have you so dark."

"I think you just want to see me half-naked," he teased as he rose to his feet. He caught the garment she tossed him with one hand and draped it over the back of the chair. Without modesty, he pulled his white lawn shirt over his head.

Ivy had seen seminude men before. She'd seen a few naked men as well. Even if she hadn't lost her virginity at eighteen to a rakish actor, she would still be terribly familiar with the male form, growing up as she had.

But she had never seen a man quite like Saint before.

The tan complexion of his face and arms continued onto his chest and stomach. Long, sinewy muscles rippled underneath his silky flesh. He had the build of a man who—when he had been human—used every muscle to lift himself, propel himself, defend himself.

He also had no modesty.

As he turned to retrieve the other shirt, the muscles along his ribs standing taut beneath his skin, Ivy's gaze settled on the shallow indent of the small of his back and slowly traveled upward.

He had a tattoo on the left side of his neck; a simplistic dragon like one might see etched on an old rune. And on the opposite shoulder, someone had branded him with the image of a cross. The two markings, coupled with his dark beauty robbed Ivy of breath.

"Why a dragon?" she asked as she set the camera for another use.

He paused, shirt in hand. "They like treasure," he replied with a slight smile.

"And the cross?"

His smile faded. "That one was given to me by the church in the hopes of driving out the devil inside me. As you can see, it didn't work."

Ivy didn't know what to say. Here was some true insight into who this man really was. What he had suffered—what he stood for. Someone had burned that cross into him, and since silver was the only thing that could leave a scar on a vampire, it must have hurt him terribly to have it done.

Fingers trembling, she waited for the right moment.

Saint's head came up and he glanced at her over his shoulder. The cast of his profile—the thick waves hanging around his face, the sharp tilt of his nose, the soft bow of his lips—completed the pose and Ivy seized the moment. The shutter clicked, capturing that amazing image for all time.

"Why did you do that?" he asked, his voice lower than usual, his brow pulled together.

"It was perfect," she replied honestly. "At that moment I felt as though I were seeing the real you."

"The real me?" His laughter scoffed at the notion as he pulled the black shirt over his head. "I don't remember him."

"I think you do." She didn't know where this was coming from, but every instinct she owned screamed that it was true. "I think you hide him away."

"I think you talk too much." It came out as a snarl, and she knew she had struck a nerve. "I warned you about making me into something I'm not."

"I didn't mean—"

He came at her so quickly he was little more than a blur. "Yes, you did."

"All right." She stood there, one hand on her camera, gaze locked with his. "I did. Why do you try to deny who you are?"

He stared at her—just a few inches away from

her now. "Good lord, woman, but you know how to plague a man."

She opened her mouth to respond, but the second her lips parted, Saint's were on them. He crushed her against his chest, his hands clasping her shoulders. His lips were warm and firm yet impossibly soft as they moved against hers. They demanded. They pleaded. And when his tongue slid into the recess of her mouth, she surrendered, matching each hot, wet stroke with her own.

They moved backward in a strangely graceful dance that he led, pushing her against the wall and pressing himself full against her. He held her hips tight as his own ground into them. She would have bruises later and she didn't care. His cock was hard, full with the promise of a night of undeniable pleasure. Her own sex ached and throbbed in anticipation of what this man could do to her body.

She wasn't a woman who gave herself indiscriminately. She hadn't many lovers in the past, and while they had all brought a varying degree of emotion out in her, none of them had inspired the same ferocity of desire as this vampire.

If only she could reach her skirts. She'd hike them up and wrap her legs around him and let him take her like a street whore in an alley. The image flooded her with sexual heat and she whimpered against his mouth.

It was Saint who broke the kiss. He rested his

forehead against hers. His breathing was almost as ragged as hers.

"I usually have much more finesse," he murmured with a rueful smile. "Forgive me."

"There is nothing to forgive."

"Oh, but there is," he corrected, rubbing the soft skin of his forehead against hers. "I want to take you until you are boneless. I want to drain you of strength. I want to fill you and take my fill of you. My dear, Ivy, I want to devour you. I want your juices on my tongue, flooding my mouth. I want your wetness on my face, your scent covering me. I want your blood in my veins."

Oh, God. He wasn't just talking about sex. What would it feel like to have his fangs pierce her flesh? To feel the sharp suction of his lips as he drank the life from her?

"What would it mean to you to have me in your mouth?" Her tongue slipped from between her lips, caressing the full bow of his lower lip. He tasted warm and sweet. "Am I dessert to you?"

"Life," came his hoarse reply, whispered against her mouth. "You are everything that is alive and beautiful."

Such pretty poetry had never affected her before, but his words, spoken in that raspy, honeyed tone melted her inside. His words alone had her hot and damp, aching to have him fill the emptiness inside.

"Take me." She leaned forward, brushing her lips against his cheek, breathing in the clean, night-smell of his hair. Oh, this was foolish and reckless and bound to bring regret, but the impulse would not be denied. "Take everything you want."

"Everything?"

She nodded, licking the velvety curve of his ear. "My body is yours. All I want in return is you."

"Is that all?" His tone, though still hoarse, was teasing.

"For now."

He lifted his head to gaze down at her, his body completely still. The heat of him soaked through her clothes. The tension in him coiled her insides like a clock wound too tight. If he didn't do something soon she was going to explode.

A tiny frown marred his brow. "No." And that one simple word was a splash of cold water. He released her, and stepped away as though he could no longer bear to be near her.

For Ivy the rejection was acute. "You've changed your mind about wanting to devour me, I assume?" She struggled to keep her voice level.

His dark gaze was shuttered and he turned his head away. He crossed the carpet, putting a distance between them that was more than just physical.

"No," he replied. "I want you, but I'm not going to take you."

"Why ever not? You needn't worry that I'm a virgin—I thought I made that clear before."

A chuckle, humorless and dry escaped him. "No, it is not that."

"Is it because of your friendship with my mother? Because—"

"Ivy." He turned fully to face her as he cut her off. "Stop. It has nothing to do with your virginity or lack of and it has nothing to do with your mother."

"Then what?" She hated sounding like some pleading, desperate woman. She'd heard her mother use that same tone with the man who was her father one too many times. She changed it immediately to one of confident command. "Explain to me why we are not naked on that bed right now."

"Good God, you'll be the end of me."

"I do not see the conflict here. It is not as though I will expect anything from you. I don't harbor romantic dreams. I won't want your love, I don't believe in it. I don't want anything but what you are willing to give." It wasn't a ploy, she meant it.

How sad he looked when he smiled. "Trust me, you don't want that. Neither of us do."

Dumbfounded, Ivy stared at him as he turned and walked out, leaving her standing there, feeling not as though she had been rejected, but that she had rejected him.

* * *

There wasn't enough whiskey in England to get Saint drunk. The one man strong enough to take him in a fight was God only knew where. There was really only one vice left and that was what had induced this foul state.

He should have just fucked her. Should have bent her over that chair and . . . He groaned at the thought of it.

He had been trembling with wanting her. Trembling with the need to have her and give her pleasure in return. Once again he was faced with proof of his own weakness—his own blatant stupidity when it came to women. He was no good against them, had no defenses. He didn't even try. Just a few days ago he had resolved to keep his distance from her and he had failed.

"For now" had stopped him, thank God. She'd want more than sex eventually—all women did. Hell, he would want more, and he wasn't opening himself up to that kind of pain again, especially since he might be in London long enough to actually become attached. His heart couldn't take it. It was the curse of immortality for a die-hard romantic.

It used to be that he enjoyed falling in love. He would enjoy the rush of emotion and the jubilant uncontained passion, and then leave. He never had to face the bitter consequences until Marta. Never had to face loss until her. He had watched her die knowing he couldn't save her.

Love—the lasting kind—was not something he would ever know, and after losing that wonderful woman, he hadn't the heart to settle for anything less.

He would have to stay away from Ivy, he knew that. No more flirting, no more late-night encounters. He had a task to do and he was going to see it done and leave London as soon as possible.

That was why he stood now, outside of Priscilla Maxwell's Kensington townhouse, looking for the best point of entry. Inside, among her personal effects, there might be a clue to the identity of her killer. It was a slim hope, but it was all he had.

He was behind the house, in an area that served as a small garden. It was dark enough that no one would see him, especially dressed all in black as he was. He was still wearing the shirt Ivy had put on him and the scent of her on it pricked at him like a needle under the skin.

One jump was all it took to put him on the balcony and to leave thoughts of Ivy behind.

He slipped a file between the edges of the French doors, easily popping the latch on the inside. The doors swung open and he stepped into what he supposed was Priscilla Maxwell's bedroom.

The police had been there already, but that didn't matter. Saint had purposefully waited to search the house, because he had no desire to run afoul of the authorities. They didn't know about the connection to Maison Rouge, and even if they thought of it, they wouldn't be looking for the same things as Saint.

Of course, he wasn't quite sure himself what he was looking for, but he would know it when he found it.

Priscilla's bedroom was a frilly, pink confection of a room. The wallpaper was handpainted with little pink flowers that matched the ones on the carpet and upholstery. The bed was large, a four poster draped with a sheer canopy. It was the room better suited for a young girl than a full-grown woman. Perhaps as an adult, the actress had given herself the bedroom she had always longed for as a child.

It was sad. Sad that she clung to such dreams and sad that she was no longer able to curl up in that bed with the satisfaction of having achieved them.

He searched under the mattress and found a diary hidden inside that he tucked into his jacket pocket. There was nothing in the jewelry box of any interest, although the thief in him saw several pieces that Ezekiel would pay a pretty penny for.

It wasn't until he turned his attention to the various paintings and photographs strewn about different surfaces around the room that his heart gave a curious twitch.

On the vanity was a framed photograph of Priscilla. She was nude save for strategically placed leaves, her long hair unbound and cascading around her like a pale waterfall. In one hand, palm up as in offering, she held a dark apple. The other arm had a slender snake wrapped around it, the head pointing toward Priscilla as though the reptile was whispering to her.

"Eve." His heart was more than just twitching now. He picked up the photo and stared at it in the faint moonlight. He didn't have to remove it from the frame to see who took it. Even if the style hadn't looked familiar, his instinct would have told him that Ivy had been the artist behind the camera.

Ivy had taken photographs of Goldie. Had she also photographed Clementine? And if so, had she portrayed the prostitute as another infamous woman?

It might be nothing, but it was too much of something to be ignored, especially if it meant that Ivy might be in danger—or rather, more danger. But he wouldn't think of that now.

He took the photograph as well, slipping it into a side pocket. Quickly, he moved about the room to make sure there was nothing else that might be important. Satisfied that there was nothing, he left the way he came. But instead of leaping down from the balcony, he leapt upward, taking to the sky.

He touched ground behind the Maison Rouge. The cottage still glowed with light within. Ivy was still there. Was she waiting for him? Had she stayed hoping that he would return? Or was she cursing his name as she worked off her sexual frustration?

How had she eased that frustration? And had she fantasized about him while she engaged in it?

He was half-hard when he entered the cottage. One would think him a boy of eighteen rather than a centuries-old man who should know better.

Ivy was sitting on the bed when he entered, tendrils of her honey-colored hair hanging around her face as she studied a stack of prints. He wanted to press his lips to the spot where her neck joined her back, run his hands down the gentle slopes of her shoulders, taking the neckline of her gown as he did. He wanted her breasts in his hands, in his mouth . . .

She looked up, her surprise blatant. "What do you want?"

Saint's desire died a quick death. Obviously he was the only one suffering from frustration. "I need to talk to you."

Her stubborn chin lifted as her full pink lips settled into a grim line. "If it's about what happened earlier I would rather not."

"It isn't."

She didn't bother trying to hide her surprise—or her disappointment. "Oh. What is it then?"

He took the photograph from his pocket and crossed the room to give it to her. She rose to her feet as he neared—a good thing, as he wasn't sure he could trust himself not to pounce on her and pin her to the mattress.

"This is your work, is it not?" he asked as he placed the frame in her hand.

Ivy stared at the portrait. "Yes." She looked up, green eyes filled with expectation and more than a little suspicion. "So?"

Saint gave his head a little shake at the defensiveness in her tone. "So, if my instinct is correct, I don't think Maison Rouge is the only connection between the murders."

She blinked. "What else is there?"

He couldn't keep the pity from his gaze. She wasn't stupid, she just didn't want to acknowledge what she already suspected.

"You."

Chapter 6

 ❦

How could Goldie, Clemmy and poor Priscilla have been killed because of her?

It was absurd. "I don't have any enemies, Saint. Not to the point where someone would kill to get to me."

"I doubt very much that anyone hates you badly enough to kill your friends. But I suspect that you might have photographed all three victims."

"I did." Oh, good lord, it was true. She sank to the bed once more.

"Even Clementine?" His voice was gentle, as though he feared this might be too much for her.

Her hand shook as she rubbed it over her face. "Yes. I've photographed practically every woman who has worked or visited Maison Rouge in the past two years."

"Who has seen them?"

"I couldn't begin to tell you. Mama held a show for me in the spring. For almost a full week my work was on display at the house. Anyone who came in could have seen them."

"Well, fuck." Then he looked abashed. "Forgive me."

She arched a brow. "You think I haven't heard that word before?"

"I was taught not to curse in front of ladies."

"I'm no more a lady than you are a gentleman." She flushed. "I'm sorry, I didn't mean . . ."

"Think nothing of it." He sounded sincere, but there was a flash of something in his dark eyes— hurt, perhaps?

Did she feel guilty? Yes. Would she give into it and try to apologize again? No. He was the one who rejected her. If he thought his feelings were hurt, he should think about what he had done to hers.

Unfortunately, his refusal of her just made him all the more appealing now. Perhaps she was a glutton for punishment, but she wanted him twice as much as she had hours earlier.

She should be ashamed of herself—thinking of her own desires when there was work to be done.

It was Saint who broke the growing uncomfortable silence. "I need to see all the photographs that you have. There has to be a connection somewhere."

"Of course." Quickly, Ivy crossed the carpet to the cupboard beside the fireplace. She kept all of her photographs in there. Despite the increased risk of having her work destroyed by fire, she found it was better to store them in a place less likely to be affected by England's often damp weather.

All the storage boxes were neatly stacked and labeled, with descriptions of the contents facing outward. She found the box marked MAISON ROUGE SHOWING, JUNE, 1899, and pulled it from the shelf. Surprisingly, even though it wasn't heavy, Saint was right there to take it from her.

"Eager?" she asked with a smile. "Or are you trying to be a gentleman again?"

"I'm not a gentleman, remember?" He didn't return her smile and shoved the box back at her. "You take it then."

Ivy staggered under the force of the gesture. "What is wrong with you?"

"When I first arrived here you berated me for acting like a scoundrel and now that I'm trying to be respectful you mock me. Please pick one opinion of me and stand by it." He grabbed the box from her again and strode over to the table against the far wall, leaving her staring after him, dumbfounded.

"*Me* pick an opinion?" She followed after him, rigid with growing ire. "When you first arrived here you spoke to me as though you couldn't wait to get me into bed, and then when I offer myself to you, you reject me. Perhaps *you* are the one who should pick one opinion and stand by it!"

The box slammed down onto the surface of the table with so much force that one corner of it literally sagged. "Perhaps you are right."

Ivy stared at him, wide-eyed as he removed the lid and started removing photographs. That was it? That was all he was going to say? And devil take it, was he not going to tell her what that opinion was?

"So you were never serious?" Her pride shrank as she made herself ask. "It was all just a game?"

He shot her a look that would have incinerated most men. In Ivy's case however, it simply made her heart thump. "Now you're being ridiculous."

"What?"

"Of course it wasn't a game. It isn't a game. I've wanted you since the first moment I saw you. Are you pleased now that I've admitted it?"

She was astounded. "Then why did you refuse me?"

"Because . . ." He blinked. "I can't concentrate on finding a killer if I'm preoccupied with you."

She choked on bitter laughter. "Was that supposed to be a compliment?"

He looked down at the battered box. "This conversation is finished."

Like hell it was. "You've had girls at the house. Why not me?"

"You are not one of the 'girls.'" He shot her a tired glance. "Besides, I promised your mother I

would find this killer and I'm not going to let anything or anyone—including your delectable little
self—stand in my way."

She couldn't argue it, so she didn't. He was right.
Knowing that he wanted her lessened the sting.

"I respect that," she replied as somberly as she
could. Respect it, yes. Abide by it? Perhaps not.
Their number-one priority would be to find this
killer, but it also meant working very closely together.

Very closely. And while Ivy would never do
anything to jeopardize finding the monster that
killed her friends, there was no reason why she
couldn't indulge in a little seduction after hours,
so to speak. She'd be risking complete humiliation,
but it was a risk she had to take. She had wanted
him for so long, she didn't want to regret not trying. Not when it was so painfully obvious just how
short life could be.

Saint's dark eyes were narrow, the fringe of his
lashes like the softest velvet as he regarded her
warily from across the room. "No more talk of it?"

Ivy shook her head, biting her lip to keep from
smiling. This was the first joy, the first spark of life
she had felt since Clemmy and Goldie had been
killed. "No more talk."

There would be nothing but action from here on.

"Good." His expression was a mix of relief and
disappointment—a fact that warmed Ivy's heart.

"I need the guest list for the week of your show. I assume your mother still keeps track of the comings and goings of the clientele?"

Ivy nodded. "It's written in code, though. I don't understand it."

"That's all right. I will."

"You will?"

He grinned—a sudden and unexpected gesture that made parts of her body tighten in the most exquisite manner. "Who do you think taught it to her?"

She might have returned his smile, had she been able to. But at that moment, Ivy was flooded with a most peculiar emotion. It was as though someone flicked a switch inside her that made her angry and hurt and sad all at the same time. It was jealousy.

She was jealous of her own mother. And suddenly she found herself wondering, just how "close" her mother and Saint really were.

The gramophone in the corner of the parlor played a lively selection of "ragtime." It had been sent to Madeline from a friend in America where the lively piano music was growing in popularity.

The recordings weren't so clear that one might believe there was a real band hidden in the room, but Saint was still amazed that someone had managed to capture music inside tiny grooves on a flat disc. He stood in a corner, drink in hand, tapping his foot to the rhythm as several of the Maison Rouge girls danced with clients.

He had been asked to partake in the dancing, but he refused—not because he feared he might look queer or because he thought it wouldn't be amusing, but because he needed to stand back from the groups and watch. He needed to discern if there was a killer among them.

What he didn't need was to watch Ivy flirt with the young man who so clearly adored her.

"His name is Justin Fontaine," came Madeline's voice near his ear. "He's a gentleman painter. Would you like to meet him?"

Saint spared the briefest of glances for the woman next to him before turning his attention back to Ivy and her lover. "Of course. I want to meet all the potential suspects."

"Suspect? Justin?" He might have smiled at the astonishment in her voice were he not so hopeful that this blond Adonis of a boy was guilty of something.

"Everyone's a suspect, Strawberry." He took a sip of his whiskey. It was smooth and faintly smoky, just the way he liked it.

"Saint. I cannot believe—"

"I know." He smiled ever so lightly as he cut her off. "That is why I'm the one trying to find the killer. Not you."

"Surely you do not suspect the girls."

"Our culprit is most likely a man, given the strength needed to commit the crimes."

"Of course it's a man. A woman would never be capable of such hate."

He laughed—loudly and openly—causing more than a few intrigued glances to flash in their direction. "You know as well as I what a lie that is."

Madeline smiled at him and for the second time he noticed the lines around her eyes. She was growing older, and the knowledge weighed heavy on his heart. Someday he would come to Maison Rouge and she would no longer be there. Perhaps Ivy would be the madam and he would notice that time had worked its villainy on her as well.

As if pulled by the mere thought of her—the desire to make certain she was still young and ripe—Saint found himself seeking her out in the crowd. It didn't take long; she was staring at him and her mother with eyes so narrow and suspicious he blinked.

That was jealousy in her gaze. Jealous of her own mother? With him? The very thought was laughable.

Who was she to be jealous when she was practically screwing that young buck right under his nose? He'd never liked big, athletic blond pretty boys, as they always seemed to get what they wanted. He didn't trust them—except for Chapel, of course.

"Good heavens," Madeline turned more toward him. "What did you do to make Ivy look at you like that?"

"I refused to bed her," he replied before he could think. "And it's not *me* she's looking at that way, it's us. You."

Saint had never seen horror so delicately expressed. "Tell me you are joking."

"My darling friend, you know I haven't a sense of humor." He took a drink from his glass.

"But why would she be jealous of us?"

He spared her a glance. "Obviously she's wondering just how intimate we are with each other."

"Oh, good lord." Gingery brows drew together. This conversation was bringing out the Irish in Madeline. "Did you plant that notion in her head?"

"It is entirely of her own planting." He knew better than to try to make a woman jealous. It never turned out well.

"If you refused to sleep with her, why are you looking at Justin as though you'd like to rip his throat out?"

Intimate enough with the family so that they called him by his Christian name, eh? Bastard. "You're being overly dramatic." And did it not bother her in the least that her daughter had tried to seduce him?

Obviously not. "Am I?" she demanded. "Or are

you as jealous of him as my daughter seems to be of me?"

"I haven't known Ivy long enough to form any such attachment."

"She certainly formed one to you."

Saint's head whipped around so that he could see if she was jesting as he hoped she was. "You lie."

"I most certainly do not," she replied with little indignation. "She cried for days the last time you left here. Though I didn't notice, but a mother always knows these things. You slept with every girl here and ignored her."

She made it sound as though it had been wrong of him to keep his hands off her daughter. "Ivy is safe from me, Maddie." It came out almost like a sigh. "You needn't worry."

She was still frowning, but less now. "It's not Ivy I'm worried about."

"Never say that you are concerned for my well-being?" There was a time when he could have carried off such a statement with foppish flare, but now it came out sounding defensive—even to himself.

"When was the last time you allowed yourself to experience real love?"

"We are not going to have this discussion." He took another drink. Would that he could get drunk. Just this once.

"It was Marta, wasn't it?"

Saint shook his head. The pain that came at the mention of her name was so dull now he was ashamed. "It doesn't matter."

"You haven't been with any of the girls since your arrival."

"I did not think it would be right, given the circumstances." That and because not one of them had turned his head.

"'Right' has never stopped you before."

"Fine, I'll fuck your daughter." In trying to keep his voice low, it came out as a growl. "Is that what you want?"

"Do not try to shock me, Saint." Her smile was so femininely superior. "It will not work."

"What I want is for you to shut up. Is that at all possible?"

"Saint—"

"For Christ's sake, woman!" He closed his eyes, regaining some semblance of control. "Introduce me to some of these people so I can figure out if one of them is a killer and get the hell out of this house and this city."

Wisely she said no more on the subject and obligingly took him around the room. It wasn't until Madeline began telling people that he was a talented musician friend from Paris that Saint began to wish he had never crossed verbal swords with her at all.

Of course her ruse made these artistic types all the more eager to accept him, but it also meant that they were equally as enthusiastic about having him entertain them.

"I hate you," he murmured as they left the last group. He had met painters and writers, politicians and aristocrats. Of course, there were those patrons who did not visit the salon, who took their pleasure with one of the girls, paid a fortune for the privilege and then left, but those were not the clients who concerned him. Whoever killed the girls was someone who had seen Ivy's work. He was certain of it.

Madeline grinned at him—a cat with the taste of canary in her mouth. "You love me," she corrected.

Of course, as luck would have it, just as the words left her mouth, Ivy appeared by her mother's side. She was wearing a lower-necked gown this evening and Saint didn't need keen eyesight to see the flush that rushed upward from her chest to crest in her smooth cheeks. But the scent of all that heated blood, the warmth simmering beneath her ivory flesh, flooding his senses with the delicate bouquet of her—the pleasure of that was his alone.

"Ivy." Madeline smiled as though nothing was amiss, brilliant actress that she was. "How fortunate that you happen upon us just now. Mr. Fontaine, you are the last I believe to meet my good friend, Mr. Saint."

The little minx actually had the audacity to put an emphasis on the word "friend." Perhaps Mr. Fontaine's skull was as thick as his bicep and he missed it, but Ivy certainly didn't, if the tightening around her mouth was any indication.

Jealous. Over him. What a terrifying revelation. He didn't want her jealousy. He didn't want her to feel anything for him. He didn't want to feel anything for her. Desire he couldn't help, she was just the sort of woman who inspired the urge for a tumble, but anything else would be a disaster on his part.

Ivy cleared her throat. "Allow me. Mr. Saint, may I present Mr. Justin Fontaine. Justin is a painter."

More Christian-name intimacy. Had she already slept with Fontaine, or was he simply another on her list of potential conquests? No, she hadn't slept with him yet—the look on Fontaine's handsome face was far too hungry as he watched her.

The young man's right hand was in Ivy's—a fact made less annoying by the glimmer of silver on his ring finger. Not having to shake hands meant Saint didn't have to worry about the burn that would follow from contact with that ring. "A pleasure, Mr. Fontaine."

"Saint is a musician," Madeline added, her bright smile resting on her daughter.

Ivy's dubious expression said what her mouth did not. "How lovely."

"Are you going to play for us, Mr. Saint?" Fontaine asked with all the enthusiasm of youth. "You'll find this crowd very appreciative of live music."

Putting on his most humble yet charming smile, Saint bowed his head. "Since I am a great admirer of appreciation, I will play indeed—if, of course, Madam Madeline commands?"

His old friend looked at him as though she wasn't quite certain what he was up to, but she was willing to find out. "Of course. Everyone," she turned around to face the room, clapping her hands, "Saint is going to entertain us."

The music on the gramophone came to a stop as Saint crossed the carpet to the grand piano standing in the corner. Everyone watched him as he walked; he could feel their gazes upon him, and he imagined Ivy's to be the hottest of them all.

He stepped in between the piano and the bench and flicked out the tails of his coat so that he might sit.

He didn't need the music book open before him. He didn't even need to look at the keys. Six centuries had given him plenty of time to hone his skills in many venues other than thievery, and piano was one of them. It kept his fingers nimble—a useful skill no matter what one's occupation.

The room buzzed with soft chatter as he placed his fingers upon the keys. The melody that came was one of his own creation, written years before—after Marta's death. It was moody and romantic and was sure to bring a tear to more than one eye. He could play it now without weeping himself. In fact, he could play it now without his heart feeling as though it was being ripped out of his chest.

What did that say about him? He had adored Marta. Loved her with every inch of his being. How could that simply fade?

If he had learned one lesson over the course of his long, long life, it was that love was a gift and he was like a spoiled child, caring more about the thrill of tearing open the wrapping than about what lay inside.

He closed his eyes as he played, not wanting to see the faces of those watching him. Music took him to another place, a place that was his alone. There, in the darkness behind his eyes, he could be alone with his thoughts, and face the truth without fear of condemnation.

His fingers drifted over the keys, cajoling just the right amount of tone. He loved the piano for its sensitivity to touch. A light stroke brought a soft, almost breathy sound. He could evoke so much emotion from the force of his finger tips. The same notes could just as easily represent anger as they could joy.

When the last note faded, Saint opened his eyes and looked up. The entire salon stared back at him, applauding madly. All except for Ivy. She stood between her mother and young Fontaine—both of whom were clapping—silent and still. One hand was held over her breast bone, obscuring some of the flush that colored the soft flesh there. Her full lower lip trembled and her eyes were wet with unshed tears.

She knew. She knew what that music had once meant to him, and she felt it. She watched him as though seeing him for the first time. He had revealed too much of himself without even knowing it.

Saint stood and moved from behind the instrument—a little faster than a normal man should have been able to. It didn't matter that all eyes were on him as applause and cheers of "bravo!" clamored around him. He cared only about Ivy.

He stood before her, his gaze locked with the bright green of hers. At that moment, she was the most beautiful woman he had ever seen in his entire life and he'd have given his immortality to ensure that she never cried again.

Madeline's hand on his arm was the only thing that kept him from reaching out and taking Ivy in his arms and kissing her right there in front of all these people. In front of Justin Fontaine. "That was beautiful."

Saint tore his gaze away from Ivy, breaking the spell he was under.

He smiled his thanks, and graciously accepted the praise that began to pour in from the others who closed in around him. When finally the crowd cleared, he turned back to where Ivy had been standing, only to find her gone.

And so was Justin Fontaine.

"Ivy, are you quite all right?"

Coming to a stop in the middle of the foyer, Ivy wiped at her eyes with the back of her hand. She had to get out of the salon before she embarrassed herself by openly weeping over Saint's performance—or by grabbing him and kissing him as she wanted.

Of course he would have to be talented. Was there anything the man couldn't do? Any persona he couldn't slide into like a hand into a well-worn glove?

She had been so arrogant, thinking he had shown his real self to her that night in her studio. The real Saint could not be seen with one look. It would take detailed study to peel away all the layers and find the truth beneath.

Turning, she plastered a smile on her lips. "I'm fine, Justin. Thank you for your concern."

A frown marred his otherwise perfect face. "I've never seen you distraught before. That Mr. Saint, did he do something to offend you?"

Yes, he wounded my pride by refusing to sleep

with me. But she couldn't very well admit that out loud to a man who made it clear on more than one occasion that he thought her all that was virtuous and good.

"Because if he did," Justin continued. "I would have little choice but to confront him on it."

In any normal situation Justin might be the victor of such a confrontation, as he was definitely the larger and more athletic of the pair. But Saint could rip him apart—literally—with his bare hands. And even if Saint weren't immortal, he was a wily, sly sort of man who no doubt knew a hundred different ways to fight dirty.

"No," she replied. "I was simply overcome by the emotion of the piece he played. Was it not beautiful?" Admitting to a sense of sentimentality was far preferable to the alternatives.

Justin shrugged. "I preferred what was on the gramophone."

Of course he did, and Ivy had the sore toes to prove it. She smiled somewhat self-consciously. "I suppose I must seem like a silly, overly sensitive woman to you."

"You? Never. You are practical and forthright and everything that a woman should be."

At one time she would have taken that for the compliment she recognized it as, but that was before Saint told her that he wanted to devour her.

"You are a good man, Justin." A very good man. Why could she not want him the same way she wanted Saint? It was pathetic to lust after a man who would still look young and beautiful long after she had turned to dust.

"Would you care to go for a drive?" he asked, a strange brightness lighting his gaze. "We could take the carriage around the city."

Alone with Justin in a closed carriage. Ivy didn't have to be a genius to understand what he was suggesting. Did she want to go with him? Did she want him to kiss her and try to make her feel all the wonderful, desperate things Saint did?

Yes. At this point she wanted nothing more than to know that this desire could be felt for someone else, that it wasn't only Saint who demanded such longing.

"Yes." The admission was thick in her throat, as though the words themselves didn't want to come. "I would like that very much." There would be no coming back from this. If she found that Justin didn't inspire the same feelings as Saint, what then?

"I just have to fetch my coat."

"Are you going somewhere, Miss Ivy?"

Ivy closed her eyes as the low velvet of Saint's voice washed over her. She hadn't even heard his approach. Bloody vampires must walk like cats.

Opening her eyes, she turned to face him. "Yes. I

am going for a drive with Justin." She purposefully used the other man's Christian name. She wanted Saint to know that she wasn't about to sit around and watch him flirt with her mother.

"Not alone, I hope." He didn't even try to be subtle, the bastard.

"That is none of your business," she informed him, hands on her hips.

"Oh, but it is. There's a killer on the loose."

Justin joined the conversation—if it could be called that. "Ivy will be safe with me, Mr. Saint. I can assure you."

Saint's expression was nothing if not cordial. "I'm certain you will do your best, Mr. Fontaine, but as a friend to Madam Madeline and Maison Rouge I cannot in good conscious allow Miss Ivy to go out unchaperoned."

"I am not a little girl," she ground out between clenched teeth. "Nor am I some silly aristocrat who knows nothing of the world."

His face was void of emotion as he looked at her, but his gaze burned and she knew he was doing this for the same reason she had agreed to go in the first place. Spite. "I never claimed that you were."

"I am perfectly capable of looking after myself. And Justin will be able to protect me should I need it."

"Indeed you are and indeed he is."

"So there is no need to bother one of the footmen." They were needed there, watching over the girls. Watching over the house.

He smiled, all ease and affability. "No need at all."

She eyed him carefully. "So you agree that I can go."

"Of course. By all means, Miss Ivy, go for your drive."

"Thank you."

Saint's smile grew, as did the fire in his gaze. "But I'm coming with you."

Chapter 7

If only she knew how to kill a vampire.

Exactly two minutes after she bade Justin good night—which was approximately five minutes after he withdrew his offer of a drive—Ivy went in search of Saint.

She found him on the back terrace, slouched on the balustrade, smoking a thin cigar.

"Why did you do that?" she asked as soon as the French doors closed behind her.

He shot her a tired, lazy look. "Do what, darling?"

"Treat me as though I am a child—and I am not your darling." Oh, but she would like to be. How amazingly bizarre was that? This man drove her to distraction with his glib tongue and seemingly careless attitude and yet all he would have to do is crook his finger and she'd come running.

"Compared to me you *are* a child."

She ignored that. "You acted as though Justin can't be trusted."

He shrugged. "I don't know that he can."

She could have hit him at that moment. Too bad it wouldn't hurt him. "Or perhaps you're jealous of Justin and didn't want me going off with him."

Saint tilted his head, but he didn't hesitate to answer. "All right."

Idiot that she was, the idea of his jealousy warmed her in ways Justin never had. "You're not going to deny it?"

"Would you believe me if I did?"

"No." Lying had never been a talent she could claim. She much preferred honesty—blunt as it might be—to subterfuge.

Another shrug before taking a long inhale off the cigar. The tip flared bright red in the darkness. Ivy simply watched him; a dark shadow in the even darker night.

He exhaled a fine stream of smoke. "When I'm gone you can do whatever the hell you want, but until this killer is caught, you *will* do what I think is best." There was no threat in his voice, just the simple conviction of a man who knew how to get his own way.

"And if you want to screw Fontaine," he continued, rising to his full height. "I've no way of stopping you, but screw him here, not someplace where I can't protect you."

She stared at him, an unwelcome heat rushing her cheeks. "I do not want to 'screw' Justin."

"No?" The hand holding his cigar hovered near his face. "You might want to tell him that then."

He had the audacity to inquire into her personal life, then she would do the same. "Are you sleeping with my mother?"

He gave his head a little shake. "I beg your pardon?"

"You heard me." She squared her shoulders, prepared for whatever the answer might be. "Are you sleeping with my mother?"

The look on his face shamed her. "You are unbelievable. Your mother is my friend."

Relief, sharp and tangy, washed over her. That was a no, then. There was no way his disgust was false. She was so relieved she didn't even care that it was aimed at her. "And Justin is mine."

He tossed the finished cigar to the stone floor beneath his feet and crushed it beneath his heel. "It is obvious Mr. Fontaine wants more from you than friendship."

He was right, of course. Ivy knew it. She looked away rather than allow him to see that knowledge in her eyes, and see it he would with that damn catlike gaze of his.

He sighed and came toward her. "Ivy, your life is your own. I have no right to tell you how to live it or who to live it with. I only want you to be careful."

Her gaze snapped back to his. "I do not understand you."

There was the flash of teeth in the darkness. "That makes two of us."

"You confound me at every turn. You are jealous of Justin but you say you do not care if I take him for a lover. Is this true, or do you spin lies just to confuse me?"

He studied her for a bit, but ignored her question. "I'm going out for a bit. You'll be safe here in the house with the men I've hired. When you wake tomorrow I would like to look at all of your photographs. I would also like to go through the client list—especially those who might have had a connection with Goldie and Clementine as well as Mrs. Maxwell."

Of course he was able to go out without a chaperone. He was nigh on indestructible. He could even rise during the day provided he avoided the direct light of day. "Why can't we do that tonight?"

"Because I need to check a few things."

She stared at him, waiting for a better answer.

He sighed. "I need to feed."

"Why not do that here?"

"It would be wrong, given all that has happened."

Even though she respected and appreciated the sentiment, she didn't want him to leave. "But that is part of the reason this place is here—to provide blood for you."

He massaged the back of his neck with one

hand. "Be that as it may, no one here is my private cattle and I refuse to treat them as such."

"Hmm."

Thick black brows rose, but he kept his expression one of disinterest. "What?"

"That is very selfless of you."

His head tilted back as he gazed down at her, as though he was trying to get a better view. "And that surprises you?"

"Honestly? Yes. You are proving yourself to be much more considerate than I ever would have thought."

He surprised her further by chuckling. "I do not know whether to be annoyed or amused by your bluntness."

"You are laughing. I'd say that's amusement."

A smile lingered on his mouth. It changed his face so much, that slight tilt of his lips. "I suppose so."

"I do not mean to annoy." Swallowing she looked down. She might prefer honesty, but that didn't mean she liked directing it at herself. "I do not mean to be cruel."

"Honesty is only cruel when combined with malice." He smiled once more, his gaze soft as she reluctantly brought hers to meet it. "You care too much about people to be intentionally malicious."

That was quite possibly the nicest thing anyone had ever said to her, and she had the pain in her chest to prove it. Perhaps that was what prompted her to approach him, much like a child approaches a strange dog—with such openness but equally wary.

"You do not have to go out to feed," she told him.

He nodded. "Yes, I do." And she knew he referred to not wanting to bother the girls.

"No," she said firmly, coming to stand directly in front of him. "You don't." There was a lantern above his head and it bathed him in a warm, golden glow that made his eyes seem like smoldering embers.

The brightness within that dark gaze brightened as he began to understand.

"You can have my blood."

Saint stared at her, the sweet bow of his mouth parting. "You don't know what you're offering."

"Yes, I do. I'm offering you sustenance so you do not have to leave us here—unprotected." She couldn't help but smile when she said it, it was such a blatant ploy.

"Do you mean to torment me or tempt me?"

"A little of both."

He chuckled—coarsely. "I thank you for your generous offer, but I cannot take your blood."

Another rejection. "Why the hell not? It's as good as any other."

His gaze burned now, flames dancing within the

ebony depths. "I dare say." His voice was hoarse and rough.

"Then please explain to me why it is that you refuse everything I offer?" Her frustration rose to new heights. "It is not as though I'm offering you my heart."

There was something in his expression that gave Ivy pause. Perhaps those words hadn't been the best to use, but she wanted to assure him that she wasn't asking anything in return from him. All she wanted was the experience he could offer.

"Because, my foolish little girl, I would have you inside me." He took a step closer so that there was nothing between them but a sliver of night. Whenever she drew breath, her chest brushed against his. Could he feel the increasing tempo of her heart?

"I would have your taste on my tongue," he continued, lowering his head so that his breath was hot against her temple. "I could empty myself inside that delicious body of yours until I was empty inside, feast on you until I was glutted and you would beg me to continue. I could do that and so much more, until you crave me as much as I crave you."

Ivy swallowed, but there was no moisture left in her mouth. Warm fingers brushed the side of her face, down her throat to rest ever so lightly on the pulse that hammered at the base. "If you're trying to scare me, it's not working. Quite the opposite."

There was an unyielding harshness in his expression. "You are too dangerous a distraction for me and I am too much like death for you to play with, no matter how tempted either of us might be."

Probably she should be frightened now, but still she wasn't. "Is that why you didn't bed me? Because you're afraid of becoming . . . enamored of the taste of me?"

His fingers came up to her chin, lifting her face so that she had no choice but to meet the frankness and unabashed desire in his gaze. "Of becoming obsessed with possessing you. I'm afraid you are exactly the kind of woman to inspire such insanity."

She smiled, but it was shaky. For the first time since his arrival she felt a frisson of fear toward him. "Was that a compliment?"

His lips twitched. "I suppose it could be taken as such, but as tempting as you are my dear, I intend to resist."

He had released her chin so Ivy was able to nod in supplication. "Then I have no choice but to accept that."

Saint's shoulders seemed to loosen, as though a great weight had been lifted off them, and Ivy almost felt foolish for thoughts running through her head. Almost.

Perhaps intimacy with a vampire was a dangerous thing, and perhaps she was insane to want to bring such danger upon herself, but want it she did. All he did by telling her it was a bad thing was make her want it more.

Oh, she hadn't been lying when she told him she'd accept why he didn't want her. She had meant it. But she hadn't said she wouldn't try to change his mind.

Saint returned to the house well before dawn, fed but not satisfied. Satisfaction was asleep in her bedroom upstairs, but he knew better than to think upon it.

In the darkness of his room he undressed and crawled into bed, setting the little clock on the table to chime in a few hours. Of all the inventions he had seen over the years, this had to be one of his least favorite, but also one of the most convenient. He wasn't one who required a lot of sleep, but he liked to enjoy it whenever he took to rest. However, waking a slumbering vampire was potentially dangerous to the person doing the waking, even if the vampire was well fed, and so he wanted to be alert and awake before Ivy showed up with her photographs.

He meant what he'd told her the night before. It was dangerous for him to engage in any kind of intimacy with her; and the peril wasn't only to his own heart. Vampires were sensual creatures and one taste of her would not satisfy his appetite, not when he was also avoiding drinking from the girls. Hers would be the only scent in the house that drew him and such attachments could be dangerous to the human's very life. Trying to turn them into vampires wasn't an easy solution either—something he unfortunately knew firsthand.

No, it was simply better to fight the attraction. The girl—woman—annoyed him, amused him. Got under his skin until he itched and yet he found himself looking for her whenever she wasn't near.

In fact, her face was the last thing he saw in his mind before he fell asleep. He didn't dream—he rarely did—he simply drifted off into deep and comforting darkness until the clock beside his bed rang. He destroyed it trying to turn it off, but it did its job all the same.

As was his habit upon rising, he made for the bathing chamber off his bedroom and attended to his daily toilet, which included a shave and shower. He loved showerbaths. It was so invigorating to stand beneath a rush of warm water and scrub the grime of daily life away.

Afterward, with a towel wrapped around his hips, he stood before the mirror to shave. It was one of the few human rituals he maintained, as vampire hair grew just as human did—perhaps even faster. Vampires weren't the cold undead things Bram Stoker made them out to be; they had hearts that beat, lungs that drew breath—though not as often as mortals. His old friend Dreux had thought them demons. Perhaps that was why Dreux rose one morning and walked out into the dawn.

Saint didn't care if he was a demon. He didn't care that the face reflected in the mirror didn't look *exactly* as it should. It wasn't as though he remembered what he used to look like. He was what he was and he had no problem with it. In fact, until lately he had always enjoyed being exactly what he was.

Only lately—the last fifty years or so—had he begun to wish for something more.

A knock at his door interrupted his thoughts before they could become too maudlin. "Come in."

He wiped the last traces of water and shaving soap from his face with a soft towel and walked into the main room to greet his visitor.

It was Ivy, of course. She entered the room like a breath of summer—warm and sweet, earth and sky. Her honey-colored hair was up in a loose twist on the back of her head, casting a golden halo around her face. Her ripe figure tucked into a pale blue gown that reminded him of jasmine petals in the moonlight. Like the girls of the house, she opted for looser stays that didn't pinch her waist as much as fashion dictated, but allowed for more freedom of movement.

What else did she have in common with the girls? Growing up at Maison Rouge, had she learned how to pleasure a man by listening, perhaps observing? Madeline would never have allowed her to work there, of that Saint was certain. She would have wanted more for her daughter.

But Ivy Dearing did exactly what she pleased, was used to having things go exactly as she wanted.

That did not bode well for his determination to resist her.

"Good morning, Ivy."

She looked up as the door closed behind her. The expression on her face as she took in his state of undress would have been laughable, were it not so damn flattering.

"Good morning." She raked the length of him with an appreciative gaze. "I'm sorry. I hadn't realized you might not be . . . dressed."

Saint grinned. She was a shameless flirt. "A situation that is easily remedied." It was wrong, but he was filled with the sudden desire to torture her as she had been torturing him by offering her body and her blood. He moved toward the wardrobe, casting a glance over his shoulder as he opened the door. "Do you mind?"

Challenge lit her jade gaze. "Go ahead."

With a shrug, Saint dropped his towel.

Her breath was a soft gasp that he never would have heard were it not for his sensitive hearing. Saint selected clothing from the wardrobe, trying to be as casual as he could be with her gaze

burning over him. Dare him, would she? Imper-
tinent chit.

Out of the corner of his eye he watched her
watching him. Her greedy gaze openly roamed
over his nakedness, taking in every sinew, every
hollow. He almost groaned as she licked her lips.
They could be dry, he supposed, or she could be
sizing him up for a bite of her own.

Familiar tightness began to fill his groin as blood
surged into his cock. Did she notice?

Quickly, before his attempt to tease her bit his
own ass anymore, he practically jumped into a pair
of trousers and pulled a shirt over his head. He
didn't tuck the shirt in, leaving it to conceal his
unfortunate condition as he turned to face her.

At least he could take some satisfaction in the
fact that she looked completely discomposed.

He gestured to the somewhat battered box in
her arms. "You brought the photographs?"

She stared at him for a second before nodding.
"Yes." She held the box out to him.

Saint took it and went to the table to open it. She
followed after him.

"You have a very nice behind," she told him.

Hands braced on the table, Saint's head fell forward as laughter erupted from him. Raising his
gaze to hers, he grinned. Of course she knew what
he had been trying to do. "Thank you."

Ivy returned the grin as she came to stand beside

him. "Perhaps next time you won't rush to cover it quite so quickly."

"There won't be a next time," he informed her firmly, but with a smile, as he removed the lid from the box.

"Pity." Then she turned her attention to the photographs. "These are all the images I've taken of women. I thought they were the most important since all the victims thus far have been female."

Saint nodded, impressed with how easily she switched from flirtation to gravity. "I don't expect there to be any male victims. Unfortunately, crimes like this are generally directed toward one sex only."

"Why is that, do you think?"

He tilted his head. "I do not know. Perhaps because men who commit these crimes have a need to feel powerful and they find women easier to overtake."

Her lovely face was hard and cold. "Bastards."

"Just so."

"You've killed before, haven't you?"

She must already know the answer to that. "Yes, but never simply for the pleasure of having done it. I think our killer likes to do what he does."

"Because it makes him feel powerful."

"Yes."

"But you do not have that same need." This seemed to be an important point to her.

Saint looked at her, a little stung by the implication that she seemed to think him without conscience. "I know I'm powerful. I do not need blood on my hands to prove it."

"I've offended you."

"Not yet, but I think you're headed in that direction."

She flushed. "Forgive me. I don't mean to compare you to this monster. I'm just trying to understand why."

"Don't. You never will." That was all he intended to say on the subject for now. If he could make it so, Ivy would live in a lovely world where nothing like this ever happened. She would not know the pain of loss. She would not know that her friends had died for the sake of slaking a madman's lust.

But then Ivy would not be Ivy and that would truly be a tragedy. In a country of demure roses and forgotten weeds, she was an orchid.

And apparently, he was on his way to becoming a damn poet.

They sorted through the photographs together. Ivy had grouped them according to subject. There were several of Mrs. Maxwell, Clementine and Goldie. There were many other women as well, some of whom worked at Maison Rouge and some of whom did not.

Saint couldn't find a single thing to link the dead ones other than they had posed for Ivy. All of the women were photographed in a variety of settings and costumes that ranged from classical to modern, sedate to scandalous.

"Who is this?" he asked. "She looks like you."

Ivy glanced at the photograph in his hand. A soft smile curved her lips that filled Saint with a feeling of warmth. "That's my sister, Rose. I photographed her last year when our father was out of town and she was able to sneak away."

"Do you see her often?"

"Not often enough." Then her face closed down and Saint knew there would be no more conversation. He moved on.

"I like this one." He held up an image of Clementine, shadowed and dark, her face heavily painted.

"Jezebel," she replied. "That's one of my favorites as well."

"I like your use of light and shadow. It's very evocative."

"Many people think my work is masculine," she remarked. "What do you think?"

He knew from her tone what she wanted to hear, but he wasn't going to spare her feelings. He would tell her the truth.

"At first glance, it does appear the work of a man." He gestured to one photograph of a scantily clad, reclining woman. "You've made her so sensual—a fantasy figure for men to desire. But, once you look past that and see the vulnerability in her gaze, notice that she is not presented as an ideal but rather a realistic example, then you begin to realize that a man could not have possibly been behind the camera."

"Why not?"

"Because a man cannot embrace a woman's faults until he loves her. A woman embraces the faults and then falls in love. That is the beauty of what you do."

He was startled to see tears well up in her eyes. "Ivy, my darling, I meant no offense."

"I'm not offended, I'm touched." She dabbed at her eyes with the tips of her fingers. "Forgive me. I'm not usually so missish."

Saint smiled. "You are forgiven."

"You seem to know a lot about women."

"I've known a lot of women. I've been around for a long time, remember."

"Yes. And were you lovers with all of them?"

Jealous again, was she? "Most. I was a bit of a lothario in my younger years."

"That would be the first three centuries of your life?"

He chuckled at her droll tone. "Four."

"And now?"

He shrugged. This conversation was far more serious, more intimate than he liked. "After a while, sex for the sake of sex becomes boring. Meaningless." And he would know. For years following

Marta's death he screwed any woman willing. And there had been many.

"I suppose there are only so many positions."

She was trying to make light and he appreciated that. "It is difficult for vampires to have relationships with human women."

"You said before that it was dangerous."

"It is. There is often so much loss, so much pain."

Her eyes narrowed as she lay a hand upon one of his. "Who was she?"

"There have been many." He didn't want to tell her about Marta. "Love was an emotion I embraced like some men embrace the thrill of hunting or making money. I wanted to fall in love and I relished every opportunity."

"But?"

"But human women grow old. They get sick. They die."

"You have the power to stop that, do you not? To make your lover a vampire?"

"In theory that is an easy solution, but some people do not take to immortality and they go mad. Sometimes the blood exchange goes bad. Sometimes the human simply does not wish to become a vampire—there are some less than savory aspects to the affliction, you know."

"I can imagine."

He looked down. "The last one was Marta. She

was a Romanian noblewoman I met quite a few years ago. She was unhappy in her marriage and I was smitten by her wit and her beauty. I didn't care that she carried her husband's child, I simply wanted to be with her."

"What happened?"

He looked away, his mind peering through the years until he found the image he sought. It was like looking at one of her photographs he felt so removed from it now. "She died giving birth. I tried to change her, but it was too late. She had wanted to wait until after the baby came because we didn't know what the change would do to it."

"Did the child live?"

Saint shook his head. "The baby died as well." The old pain came back to him, but more as memory than an actual feeling. That wound was healing, as they all did, but the scar remained.

"Do you still believe in love?"

"Of course." He damn well didn't believe in much else. "Don't you?"

Ivy surprised him by shaking her head. "I believe love is simply a lust-induced euphoria. Once the lust has been satisfied, all the good feelings that came with it fade away."

"That is a very bitter view for one so young."

"I grew up in a whorehouse, Saint. I heard men proclaim their love while in bed with one of the girls, only to treat her like dirt when he was done.

I saw what the notion of love did to my mother. My father professed a deep and abiding affection for her until she told him she was pregnant. Then he tossed her out into the street. She had been his mistress, you know."

He nodded, suddenly very sad for this poor little girl. "I know."

"Of course you do. You found her. You brought her here."

"I did."

"Thank you."

He didn't reply. He didn't want any responsibility for her life.

She continued, "Love isn't real. Friendship is real. Lust is real. But the idea of not being able to live without another person—that's just foolishness." Her gaze met his. "Don't look at me like that."

"Like what?"

"As though you pity me. Trust me, I'm much better off this way."

Saint only arched a brow in response. Someday, someone would come along and teach Ivy exactly what it was to fall in love. And his heart filled with dread at the thought, because he would like to be that man.

Chapter 8

◦──◦◦──◦

"**D**o you believe in love?" From her well-padded perch in a lovely open carriage, Ivy pulled her gaze away from the fluffy clouds high above her head to the man beside her.

Justin's eyes were almost the exact color as the sky itself. "Of course. Don't you?"

She was beginning to think maybe there was something wrong with her. "I'm not sure." Then honesty took over. "No, I don't. Not really."

Laughing, Justin reined the matched blacks, pulling them over onto the shoulder of the path. They were driving through Hyde Park, enjoying a beautiful late summer day.

Enjoying it as much as they could with two of Saint's men following behind them at a discreet distance on horseback.

With the carriage at a stop, Justin angled his body toward hers on the seat. His arm stretched across the back, his broad, tanned fingers almost brushing the shoulder of her pelisse. She could lean in, scoot across the smooth leather and invite his embrace, but she didn't.

All she could think about was Saint's fingers—how long and strong they were. The small tattoo on the back of his left hand that he told her was the Chinese symbol for luck—a thief's best friend.

And then she felt guilty for thinking about anything other than finding the monster who killed her friends. She had no business being out with a handsome man, thinking about another while Clementine, Goldie and Priscilla went unavenged.

"You don't believe in love at all?" Justin sounded astonished.

"I believe in the love a mother has for her child. I believe in the deep-seated affection one family member can have for another, or that which exists between friends. But the kind of love that the poets go on about? No, I do not believe it is real at all."

"That is only because you have yet to experience it." His tone was a little too smug for her liking.

"I'm neither a child nor an idiot, Justin. You needn't patronize me."

He laughed. "I was merely stating a fact. How could you believe when you've never seen it? No offense, my dear, but a brothel is hardly the place to learn about true love."

"I saw what *love* did to my mother."

"You saw what being in love with the wrong man did to your mother."

Ivy scowled. "You're beginning to sound like Saint." The second the words left her mouth she realized it had been a mistake to mention him.

The blasted man couldn't leave her alone—not even for an hour's enjoyment.

"Ahh, the mysterious Mr. Saint." Justin's well-shaped lips formed a smile. "How did you manage to get away without him threatening to sit between us in the carriage?"

The image that conjured up made Ivy snicker. "Good fortune." The kind of fortune that came with the sun being high in the sky.

"He has an interest in you, you know."

"You're wrong."

Justin pinned her with his bright gaze—as blue as the sky above. "He doesn't like you being with me."

"He told me he didn't care if we went to bed together, just so long as we did it at Maison Rouge so he could protect me. Does that sound like a jealous man to you?" She probably shouldn't have shared that with him, but she was accustomed to being totally open with Justin.

He bent his elbow and set his jaw against his palm as he regarded her. "Do you want to?"

"Want to what?"

"Go to bed with me." He didn't look the least

bit shy or uncertain, merely . . . curious. Very curious.

Oh, God. "Justin, we're friends."

A rueful smile curved his wide lips as he straightened on the seat. "Have you never thought of being something more?"

"I . . . yes, I've thought of it, but . . ." Bloody hell. She hadn't expected this.

He spared her any more humiliation by putting a hand upon her shoulder, silencing her stammering. "It's all right, Ivy. I understand."

"I don't think you do." She frowned. How could she possibly make him understand? "I like you, Justin."

His gaze met hers evenly. "Just not enough."

No, and she hadn't realized it until just this moment. "You deserve someone who believes in love and all that."

"Perhaps you could try?"

Ivy couldn't help but grin. What woman wouldn't when confronted with such golden charm? "I could do that, yes." Perhaps it would happen, perhaps it wouldn't. Once the murderer was caught and Saint was gone . . .

Lord, why did it always have to come back to *him*?

A few brief days and he saw more in her work than her own mother had. A man who was drawn to her because she was human—because to him she was the forbidden fruit in the garden. Was that why she was drawn to him? Because he was dangerous? Because she knew he would leave her as her father had left her mother?

Men left. She wouldn't know what to do with one who stayed, let alone one who stayed forever.

She didn't know what made her look up at that moment, what pulled her gaze to a passing carriage, but her breath caught in her throat as she met the gaze of the man inside it.

It was her father, Baron Hess. Decked out in all the finery a titled gentleman should wear—although not the height of fashion. With him was his wife and daughter—Ivy's heart pinched at the sight of the sister that she couldn't publicly acknowledge without causing Rose embarrassment.

Ivy inclined her head at her father, her gaze cold. His wife's face flushed a deep red as she looked at Ivy. Of course the woman knew who she was. Rose flashed her a secret smile.

She had met Rose a long time ago when she foolishly went to visit her father. They stole moments whenever they could, secret meetings when there was little chance of being seen. They never spoke in public, but they always shared a smile. It wasn't much of a relationship to have with a sister, but it had to do.

She watched them as they drove past and continued to watch them long after it was polite to do so. Her sister, she noticed, was the only one who watched back.

Ivy raised her hand slightly and waved. Rose waved back—until her mother snatched her hand.

"Are you all right?" Justin's voice was wrought with concern. Of course he knew who the family was and what they were to Ivy. Everyone in London probably knew.

"I'd like to go home now, Justin." It wasn't that seeing her father had ruined her day, but it made her want to be near her mother.

It made her want to be near Saint, if that made any sense.

"Of course."

On the drive back to Maison Rouge, Justin asked her if there were any new developments in the search for the killer. In this case, Ivy realized, honesty was perhaps not the best option. If she told Justin that she had photographed all three of the victims he might very well take it into his head that she needed protection—and really, did she need more than Saint and his underlings?

"The police do not know what they are doing," she told him instead.

"And the press will report whatever sells papers," he added. "What do you think of speculation that Jack the Ripper has returned?"

"I hope it is nothing more than that—speculation."

He shrugged. "Thankfully, the papers haven't given much support to that particular theory."

"Only because Mrs. Maxwell wasn't a prostitute."

A sardonic smile curved his lips. "There are those who feel the title of actress is merely a synonym for whore."

"Still? I would have thought society beyond that now." She watched the city roll by. "And Justin, I truly despise that word. There are many less honest ways to earn a living than willingly selling a commodity one has to offer."

"Point taken. My apologies."

The rest of the ride passed in relative silence. Once in a while one of them would speak and the other respond. A short conversation might even result, but neither of them felt pressured to talk and the long stretches of silence were not uncomfortable.

What proved uncomfortable was Ivy's arrival home. After seeing her to the door, Justin took her in his arms and kissed her. He was solid and strong and smelled of apples. His mouth was firm and warm and felt lovely on her own, but his kiss did not inspire her to thoughts of total abandonment, although she would be lying if she claimed to feel nothing at all. With a little more effort, Justin just might persuade her to think of him as more than merely a friend. After Saint was gone.

He left her with a smile and the promise to call again soon, and Ivy entered the house wondering how she felt.

The house was quiet save for the staff going about their business and the odd girl flitting about like an exotic butterfly. They would all be getting ready for dinner and after that, the evening's entertainment.

Ivy climbed the broad, winding staircase to her own room with every intention of napping before dinner. She wanted to work on finding the killer with Saint that evening. They had nothing substantial to go on and every moment they failed to uncover a clue was another moment the killer eluded them.

She opened the door to her room and walked in to complete darkness. All the drapes were drawn over her windows, blocking out any trace of the late afternoon sun.

They had been open when she left. But despite this, she closed the door, enclosing the room in almost total blackness.

"Did you enjoy your outing?" came a low, silky voice from the darkness.

The most delicious shiver ran down Ivy's spine as she turned toward the sound.

Saint lay on her bed, a shadow against the white pillows and quilt. She didn't have to see his face to know he was watching her. It wasn't fair that he could see her so much clearer than she could see him. She would rather like to enjoy the sight of him on her bed.

"Yes," she replied, tossing her bonnet on the stool of her vanity. "I did." The vanity hosted a small lamp. She turned it on.

The bed creaked faintly as he rose, slipping through the darkness into the light as he came toward her. It wasn't until he was mere feet away from her that she could truly see his features.

He did not look pleased.

He drew a deep breath, lifting his face as he did so, like a cat sniffing the air. "You've been with Fontaine." His tone was as dark as the room itself.

"Yes." Instinctively, she crossed her arms over herself, only to uncross them again. "You needn't worry, I took two of your men with me."

"He touched you."

Is that what all this drama was about? "Not that it is any of your business, but he kissed me, yes."

Any sane woman would fear the strange glow that leapt into his eyes, especially given the lack of light in the room, but Ivy never laid any claim to sanity. Her heart tripped against her ribs at the sight of him, seething with jealousy.

"I cannot stand his stink on you." The words came out as a growl—hardly human at all.

"I think he smells rather nice. Like applesauce." She was baiting him, fool that she was.

Saint lunged at her, silent and swift. His fingers slid into her hair, his thumbs pressing on her skull just below her ears—not hard enough to hurt, but with enough pressure so that she couldn't have pulled away even had she wanted to.

His mouth slanted over hers, hot and gently insistent, not at all the punishing, bruising assault she expected. His lips molded against hers, urging them apart so that he could taste her with his tongue.

Ivy's hands came up under his arms to grasp his shoulders, clinging to him as she melted inside. *This* was what a kiss should be between lovers. This was what had been missing when Justin kissed her. It had nothing to do with technique and everything to do with the emotions inspired by the simple act of mating mouths and tongues.

It was this man—this vampire—who made all the difference. She wanted him, and in more ways than she wanted to admit, even to herself. She didn't understand it, but it was true. She didn't even know if he would prove himself to be the man she wanted him to be and find the killer. She knew only that her life would be forever changed for having him in it.

He released her as suddenly as he had grabbed her, thrusting himself away as though her lips burned him.

"Now," he said roughly. "You smell of me."

And just like that, he turned and strode from her room, leaving her standing alone. Perhaps she should have felt rejected once more, but she didn't. In fact she felt just the opposite.

Saint had put his scent on her. He had marked her.

As his own.

Before Maison Rouge opened its doors for the evening, Saint went out to hunt. He wasn't hungry, he simply needed to burn off some restless energy. And he needed to be away from Ivy for a little while.

He had to find this killer and find him soon. The faster he left London the better off they would all be. Ivy would turn to Fontaine and everything would work out as it should.

Except, that Saint didn't want Fontaine to have Ivy. He wanted her for his own.

He had known her all her life. Now, after barely a week in her company he was possessive. That had to be a record, even for him.

He tried to push thoughts of her aside as he traveled the catacombs below the street. When he was far enough away from the house, he rose to the surface through a train tunnel, found a dark alley and scaled the side of a building to reach the roof. From there he flew the rest of the way to his destination.

He didn't know why he could fly, but ever since he and his companions had become vampires almost six centuries earlier, flight had been one of his abilities. In fact, he didn't know much about his kind and their history. He knew what he was and accepted it. That was good enough for him. He knew his weaknesses and he knew his strengths. What more did he need?

Ezekiel was out front, closing for the day. This time, Saint made noise to warn of his approach.

The old man bolted the main door and turned with a smile. "I was hoping you would come."

Saint raised his brows. "Were you?"

"I have some information. It isn't much, but it might prove useful."

"How much do you want for it?"

Ezekiel made a face. "Don't insult me, boy, you and I are beyond that."

Saint had to laugh. He remembered a time when he had called Ezekiel "boy." "All right, old man."

A bright flush colored the fence's cheeks. "Christ, sometimes I forget."

Grinning, Saint clapped him on the shoulder. "Don't get your knickers in a knot. What is this information you have for me?"

"Yesterday I had one of my regular customers in here—a fancy gent with a bit of a gambling deficiency. Sometimes I take information as payment from him."

So Ezekiel had branched into moneylending. Interesting. "And?"

"It seems he had been in this fancy coffee shop over on St. James's and he chanced to overhear two other gents talking. About those two unfortunates who got themselves killed."

Saint didn't bother to correct him that the girls hadn't "got" themselves anything. He was too impatient to hear the rest. "Go on."

"One of them told the other that he had proved himself more reliable than his predecessor. And then the other griped that the press was still comparing him to Saucy Jack all the same."

Anticipation raced through Saint's veins. "Did he get a good look at the men?"

Ezekiel shook his head, looking for all the world like a dejected terrier. "That's where he got fuzzy. He said he weren't payin' much attention—he just overheard that little bit. He didn't even think much of it till later."

"Damn." He was no further ahead then he had been—except for confirmation that the killer at least presented himself like a decent gentleman.

"He did say that the other toff—the one doing the congratulating—was older. Said he looked like aristocracy."

And there was only what? A few hundred of them in all of England. Jesus.

"And he said that the younger one made men-

tion of something he referred to as the 'Order.'
Said there was nothing to link him to it, or rather
them."

Instead of answering any of his questions, this
information simply raised more. Gentlemen who
belonged to some kind of secret organization? Was
that where his killer came from? If that were the
case it was going to be even more difficult to find
the bastard. Groups like that—such as the Freema-
sons—were a close-knit bunch and they took care
of their own. There had been rumors that Jack the
Ripper belonged to just such a society.

And the Ripper had never been identified.

He did not relish having to share this information with Ivy. Perhaps Madeline might know something. Men were notoriously loose-lipped when a
woman had them by the cock. The killer might
have said something about this "Order" to one of
the girls during a visit.

"Thank you, my friend." He shook Ezekiel's
hand, mindful of the rheumatism that distorted
the old man's knuckles. "I'm in your debt."

Ezekiel rubbed his jaw, a mischievous glint in
his eyes. "You could sell me that brooch you stole
from me at a discounted price."

Saint laughed. "Not a chance."

He didn't stay much longer talking to Ezekiel,
but he asked the old man to contact him at Maison Rouge if he heard anything else. Then, he left

Whitechapel and quickly made his way back to Maison Rouge.

As soon as he entered the house through the underground entrance in his room, he smelled it.

And it stopped his heart cold.

He ran out into the cellar and up the stairs to the ground floor. Emily, the housekeeper was walking by the stairs as he burst through the secret door into the corridor.

"Mr. Saint?" She paled when she looked at him. "What is it?"

He ignored her, having no idea what to tell her. He attracted the attention of several of the girls and the few clients who were just arriving.

Vaguely he was aware of Ivy's presence. Out of the corner of his eye he caught sight of her standing just inside the parlor with Fontaine.

"Saint?"

He ignored her too, and bounded up the stairs, taking them two at a time and faster than he should have in front of so many humans.

Ivy was quick behind him, followed by Fontaine and others. Saint increased his pace just enough to make certain he found the mess before the rest of them saw it.

The house girls had their rooms in a certain section of the first floor which was linked by a staircase to the second, where the remainder of the bedrooms were. It was up that staircase that Saint ran.

He ran down the corridor to the second to the last door on the right. It looked no different than any of the others, but he knew without a doubt that this was the one he sought.

His fingers trembled slightly as he gripped the doorknob and turned. The door swung open, and a draft of warm, thick air rushed at him, filling his mouth and nostrils with the damp, heavy scent of fresh blood. So much blood. And so much more than that.

She was on the bed, peaceful as a fallen angel in a black lace peignoir, a silk scarf around her neck. She didn't look dead. She didn't look as though her killer had sliced her open, but that's what had happened. He knew that beneath the blood-soaked scarf her throat would be cut, and that beneath the saturated black lace her womb would be missing.

He should have been there. He could have stopped it. He could have caught the bastard.

But he hadn't been there. Had the killer waited until a moment when he knew Saint would be gone?

How the hell could he have known? Saint hadn't left by normal means. The killer could have known only if he'd inquired about Saint upon his arrival, or if one of the girls had volunteered the information.

Either way, there was also the disturbing revelation that the killer was familiar enough with the house that no one would be the least bit suspicious of seeing him come up here.

He didn't dare entertain the hope that anyone

had seen the bastard. He would be too careful for that. He was flaunting his work in Saint's face.

The smell of blood obliterated any other scent that might otherwise have been left behind. He couldn't even track the son of a bitch.

Footsteps—several sets—rapidly approached the door. Quickly, he ducked out into the corridor and shut the door behind him, just in time to intercept all who had followed—which were most of the occupants of the house.

"What is it?" Ivy demanded, her face ashen as she gasped for breath. "Is Daisy all right?"

Saint met her gaze directly. "Send for the police," he instructed. When Ivy tried to push her way inside, he stopped her.

"You are not going in there," he told her, and he meant it. He'd literally knock her out himself if he had to. He looked up as Fontaine approached. "Neither are you."

Tears welled up in Ivy's bright blue eyes. "Tell me she's not dead."

Not caring that Fontaine was there, or that there was an audience, Saint took her in his arms and held her close. "I'm so sorry, Ivy."

Her sobs tore at his heart, ate at his soul. This was all his fault. Somehow the killer had known he was gone, had known when to strike. And now he was laughing at Saint's ineptitude.

He was laughing at them all.

Chapter 9

It was just after one o'clock in the morning when the police were finally summoned to Maison Rouge. Prior to that, Saint had his own men stationed at every exit as he conducted his own investigation.

A few of the "gentlemen" present were upset at being treated like common criminals, but they did not try to leave. Better to be questioned by Saint and allowed to go than to be discovered by the police and have their names in tomorrow's papers.

Saint examined the room first. He shut himself inside Daisy's room and went over it as thoroughly as he could. He stood a better chance than the police of finding any physical evidence, but the only thing he found was a faint impression in the dead girl's cheek, near her mouth.

It looked like a tiny chalice. There was no explanation for it—no connection that Saint could reach at that moment, but it was the only clue he had.

Crouched by the bed, he gently turned Daisy's head back where it had been. "Poor thing. You deserved a longer life than this."

Her flesh was not completely cold, so she hadn't been dead that long. Someone who had been there that night had done this. It might be a guest, it might be a member of the staff. The knowledge was a dark stain spreading across his mind as he rose to his feet and left the room to rejoin the others downstairs where he had put them.

Ivy was standing just inside the parlor door when he walked in. "Well?" she demanded. "Did you find anything?"

Anyone else he would have ignored. Instead, he reached out and gave her hand a squeeze. She was colder than the girl upstairs.

One by one, he met the gazes of those present. Some were red, swollen from tears. Some were openly hostile, while others were scared and confused. "I need to speak to each of you privately," he told them. "I promise to take as little of your time as possible."

Of course the killer would be a good liar, and Saint wasn't expecting a confession. What he hoped, however, was to watch for any signs of untruth, or perhaps sniff out the scent of blood on clothing.

Because there was no way—no way in hell—that the killer hadn't gotten at least a speck on him, not having done what he did.

He began with Lord Brennan who was belligerent, but obviously upset by the evening's tragedy.

"Daisy has always been a great favorite of mine," he explained.

"Were you with her tonight?"

"No. I was with Agatha. I like variety." His eyes grew large. "What if I had been with Daisy tonight? Why, I might have been murdered right along with her."

Saint cocked a brow. More than likely Brennan's presence would have saved Daisy's life rather than brought on his own demise. "A narrow escape indeed."

Next followed Lady Victor and her lover, Mr. Atwater, both of whom came to Maison Rouge as voyeurs and both of whom were visibly shaken. And they were followed by a Mr. Foster, a Mrs. Clift, twin brothers Albert and Edward Barnes, who liked to share one girl between them. Then came the vicar from Kensington—Barrie was his name, a painter named Gerard and his friend M. Revierre who was in London on holiday, an actress named Mrs. Grace and finally Justin Fontaine.

None of them showed any distress outside of what could be expected. None of them smelled of blood or had visible signs of it on their persons. And several, such as the Barnes brothers and M. Revierre, all had witnesses to corroborate that they'd been occupied all evening.

Fontaine had arrived just a few moments before Saint himself and hadn't left Ivy's side except to relieve himself.

Saint was at a loss. Had the killer somehow managed to sneak in and sneak back out without anyone noticing? He had his men check around all the windows and outside entries just to be sure. Daisy's room smelled only of blood, and the house smelled of so many people that no one scent stood out. He also seized the evening's guest book to check for anyone who might have left early. A quick glance told him there had been only one—Jacques Torrent, Priscilla Maxwell's lover.

His jaw tightened. Had Torrent managed to fool Ivy and Madeline as to his true character? Had he killed the girls from Maison Rouge as well as his own lover?

Madeline was so distraught he couldn't even discuss the possibility with her, so he sent her to bed with a spoonful of laudanum and the promise that he would make everything all right. It was a lie and they both knew it, but she went anyway.

"You should go as well," he told Ivy. At that moment he truly felt his age—every useless year of it. "I will handle the authorities."

She was white as a sheet and her eyes were as pink as a rabbit's, but her back was straight and her expression was one of quiet resolve. "Thank you, but I would like to be here during their investigation."

He nodded, and then his gaze went to Fontaine's. The boy had been Ivy's shadow for the past few hours, never straying very far, following her every move.

"I trust you will stay with her?" he asked, rubbing the back of his neck.

The young man nodded, much of his normal vigor subdued. "Of course."

"Good. I hope you will do a better job than I have." With that, he gave them a slight bow and turned to leave. Footsteps followed after him, angry little pitter-patters that almost made him smile despite the weight on his heart.

"Saint, stop."

Oddly enough, he did. All she had to do was ask—nay, command—and he did whatever she wanted. He pivoted on his heel to face her.

"Yes?"

A frown knit her fair brow. She looked so fragile he wanted nothing more than to take her in his arms and take her somewhere else—anywhere but here.

"What did you mean by that last remark?"

"Exactly what I said. This never would have happened if I hadn't told your mother to reopen the house. If I had only stayed here rather than go out tonight."

"Yes," Ivy agreed. "And it might never have happened if I hadn't photographed each woman.

Do not indulge in martydom, Saint. It doesn't suit you."

"A girl was murdered here tonight."

Her eyes filled with tears. "I *know*. That bastard came into my house and killed my friend. Into *my house*." Her finger stabbed the air as she made her point. "I want him dead, do you hear me? Dead. And you are the only person I know who can give me that. You are the only person I *trust* to give me that."

He gaped at her. Why was it that words seemed to abandon him in the presence of this woman?

"You made a mistake." She wiped at her eyes with the back of her hand. He didn't even have a handkerchief to give her. "How do we know that Daisy was killed while you were out? It could have happened while you were here—under our very noses."

He shook his head. "No. I would have heard something." Above all the music and the laughter and conversation, wouldn't he have heard cries for help? Or would he have simply brushed them aside as cries of passion?

Or had Daisy even been given a chance to cry out? If she had known her attacker, she might not have had time to make a sound at all.

"Nobody here blames you." He hated the compassion in her gaze as she spoke. Wanted to close his eyes against it. "Please do not blame yourself.

Just find this monster and give these girls the justice they deserve."

And then she walked away, back to Justin, who put an arm around her stiff shoulders and led her to a sofa. The blond man sat beside her and tried to comfort her.

Ivy didn't want comfort—of that Saint was certain. She said she wanted justice. And what's more, she wanted *him* to give it to her.

And by God he was going to.

The next day the papers proclaimed that Jack the Ripper had returned. It had taken them a while to make the connection, but when they did they ran wild with it for the next week. The house phone rang often enough that Saint was about to rip it out of the wall, but Ivy called the operator and asked her not to connect anymore calls. She also instructed Emily to turn away any callers who were not intimate friends.

Without the constant ringing and knocking, the house was quiet, almost too much so. Saint spent his nights—and even some days—looking for things he might have missed in Daisy's room. He read the girl's diary—also Priscilla Maxwell's—and went through her possessions. He pored through the client list and made note of every man—or woman—who had ever requested Daisy's services and cross-referenced it with similar lists for Clementine and

Goldie. There were several names that popped up on all three.

"Who?" Ivy demanded when he told her what he had found. Why had he told her? Partly because he thought she should know, but mostly because he simply wanted to talk to her. Most of her time in the past few days had been spent caring for her mother, who was very emotionally fragile. She also took care of everyone else at Maison Rouge—which was of course, closed once more.

"One of them is Jacques Torrent," he informed her, as they sat across the desk from each other in her mother's office. It was late and they were alone. "The second is Lord Brennan."

"Neither is that surprising. Jacques was a tomcat and Lord Brennan liked to think of himself as a rake, but he is more of a . . ."

"Shovel?" he suggested with a faint smile, as he took a sip of wine.

To his delight, Ivy actually chuckled at his joke, erasing so much of the exhaustion and tension from her lovely face. "A rusty one at that. But seriously, I cannot imagine either of them being capable of murder."

"Everyone is capable of murder given the right circumstances."

She rolled her pale green eyes. "Of course they are, oh, jaded one. You think the worst of everyone."

"That's a bit like one dog calling another a bitch, isn't it?" He tilted his head. "You aren't exactly the first one to think the best of someone either."

He had her there and she knew it. Wisely, she didn't argue. "Fine, both men could have done it. Who is the third person?"

"Priscilla Maxwell."

Ivy's jaw dropped. "You have to be joking."

"She had appointments with Goldie, Clementine and Daisy over the past six months. Did you know that she liked women?"

"No. Of course, I've heard about girls entertaining Priscilla and Jacques together, but I always assumed that was purely for Jacques's pleasure."

Saint's lip twisted into a parody of a smile. "You make that sound as though only a man could enjoy such an encounter."

She shrugged. "I cannot imagine it."

"You do not have much of an imagination at all, it seems."

"I can imagine pouring this glass of wine down your pants."

"Ah," he leaned across the desk, locking her gaze with his own. "But then I'd have to take my trousers off."

And just like that, the lightness of the exchange was ruined and charged with something deeper, more . . . electric.

They looked away at the same time, and Saint

was very much aware of how inappropriate his re-mark had been.

"Is it possible," he began, in an effort to break the uncomfortable silence, "that Torrent killed the women out of some kind of jealous revenge?"

"That seems a little far-fetched given that he joined in as often as he did, don't you think?"

She was right, but it was all he had. Except for the mysterious imprint on Daisy's cheek. A chal-ice. Saint failed to see the relevance—except for his own past. It had been a cursed chalice that turned him and his companions into vampires, but there was no way there was any connection between himself, his friends and these murders. Neither Reign nor he had been in town for the first two.

"Perhaps you should search Jacques's apart-ments just to be sure," she suggested.

"I did. Last night. I found portraits of Priscilla and a few other women, but nothing that would indicate any violent feelings."

Ivy nodded. "Several of the girls here posed for Jacques. I did."

"You?"

"Yes. A few months ago."

"Did you have an affair with him?"

She laughed—no doubt finding the jealous edge to his voice amusing. "No. I just posed. Given all that you've uncovered, I think we've ascertained that Jacques liked his women a little more sexually free than myself."

"I cannot imagine it," he quipped, throwing her own words back at her.

A slow smile curved the lush bow of her lips. "I can prove it. There's a showing tomorrow night and Jacques is going to be one of the featured artists. I hadn't planned on attending, but perhaps, given your suspicions, it might be advantageous for the two of us to go. What do you say?"

His first instinct was to say no. He hadn't left the house since Daisy's death and he didn't want to put anyone's life at risk again. However, with the house closed and everyone in mourning, there weren't many people coming and going—and no one came or went without escorts. And no one went to bed without Saint personally checking the locks on all windows and doors.

The killer was not stupid—arrogant, yes. He would not risk getting caught when traffic through the house was at such a lull.

This "showing" Ivy mentioned was a chance to find evidence that might incriminate Torrent, or prove his innocence. Or maybe they would learn nothing, but after one fatal mistake, Saint couldn't bear to make another.

His gaze locked with Ivy's. "What time should I be ready?"

* * *

The next evening, Ivy dressed for seduction.

"You look beautiful," Emily told her, as proud as a mother. "Like a lady."

Ivy didn't tell the older woman that few respectable ladies would wear such a gown. Instead, she embraced her, strangely warmed by the praise. "If I am beautiful it is because you made me so."

Emily smiled, the faint lines around her eyes and mouth deepening. "Mr. Saint won't know what to do with himself."

Oh, but Ivy had a few ideas of what to do with him.

To some, it might seem in poor taste for her to have such thoughts given the circumstances, but the last few weeks had taught her just how fragile life was and she resolved to stop waiting and go after what she wanted.

And she wanted Saint.

Her desire for him had only grown since Daisy's murder. Seeing the regret in his black gaze had tugged at her heart. The effort with which he threw himself back into trying to find the killer rather than giving up, gave her new respect for him.

She would admit, if only to herself, that she needed some of his resolve. She needed his strength. She might seem stable and sturdy to those around her, but inside she was trembling—a little girl hiding in the corner.

She needed something—anything—to bring

some rightness back to the world. She needed to not be afraid, if only for a little while.

That was why she hadn't told him the nature of the art they were going to view that evening. And it was why she was wearing a dangerously low-cut silk gown in such a dark shade of violet it was almost black. It was dark enough for mourning and daring enough for temptation, leaving most of her shoulders and upper chest bare. Her corset pushed her breasts upward, and together, giving the illusion of a more than bountiful bosom. She dabbed a little perfume in the valley there.

She was downstairs, adjusting one of her dangling, diamond earrings when Saint finally joined her.

She watched him approach, her heart pounding in her throat. He was beautiful. Dressed entirely in his usual black, the only color on him was the gold and red Oriental embroidery on his waistcoat. His thick, wavy hair was brushed back from his face, allowing her to drink her fill.

He seemed to have grown even more handsome since his arrival at Maison Rouge. That was impossible, of course, but the sight of him definitely set her heart to pounding.

His gaze roamed over her, settling for a brief moment on the swell of her breasts, before rising to meet hers. "You look very *impressive* this evening."

Ivy grinned. "So do you."

He took the soft black shawl from her hand and draped it over her shoulders. His breath brushed the back of her neck, tickling the fine hair there. She shivered just a little, imagining him closing his eyes as he breathed in her perfume.

"Shall we?" Her voice was husky as she turned to face him.

Thick black lashes lifted, revealing a hot gaze that made her want to say to hell with going out and pounce on him right there.

"Of course," he murmured, taking her hand in his own. The warm roughness of his palm against hers was both alarming and comforting. As foolish as it was—as romantic as it sounded—it was almost as though their hands were made to entwine this way.

Her mother's carriage waited in front of the house for them as they exited the house together.

"It would be faster to fly," he remarked, eyeing the conveyance warily.

"But then I would have to tell you where we are going and I want it to be a surprise."

When he didn't say anything, she cast a sideways glance at him. "Is there something wrong?"

"It's so small."

"It's not a terribly long drive and there's more than enough room for you to stretch your legs."

"I don't like to be in tight spaces."

That made her stop in her tracks. "You're afraid of a carriage?"

He turned to face her with a scowl. "I'm not afraid. I just don't like it. It makes me feel trapped."

She might have chuckled were it anyone else, but there was something in the way he said the world "trapped" that made her want to comfort rather than ridicule him. The fact that he felt comfortable sharing it with her touched her deep inside.

"We'll fly, then. It doesn't matter."

Saint's shoulders stiffened. "Yes, it does. You planned this and I'll be damned if I'll ruin it."

Ivy watched in bemusement as he strode purposefully toward the carriage. The footman opened the door and Saint stopped, gazing back at her. "Coming?"

The expression on his face told her not to speak of it any further, so Ivy climbed into the carriage without a word. Saint followed, seating himself on the opposite side, his head against the padded backing.

Ivy watched him for the entire drive. He sat so still at times she thought he might be dead, his eyes closed. He was pale, his face taut, but he never complained, never made a peep the whole way into London.

It was his silence that told her just how much the carriage ride bothered him. Odd, he didn't seem to mind it in the cellar of the house, or those tunnels he used to get around the city. But both of those were much larger than this carriage.

It wasn't until the carriage finally came to a stop that he opened his eyes and looked at her. "Are we here?"

She smiled, trying not to look too sympathetic. "We are."

Saint left the carriage first. A visible change overtook him once he was outside. His color returned to normal, his posture relaxed. The Saint she knew was back again, and offering his hand to help her to the ground.

He looked up at the sign just above the door of the building in front of which they stood. "Eden?"

"It used to be a social club seventy years ago. Now it's a place that can be leased to hold private functions, such as parties."

"And art shows?"

She smiled. "Those too."

His gaze bore into her. "What aren't you telling me about this showing?"

"I told you, it's a surprise." She looped her arm around his. "Shall we go in?"

He stared at her a few seconds longer before giving in. Ivy gave their invitation to the doorman who allowed them inside.

Eden was the epitome of grace and elegance. In its day it had been "the" place to go for fine dining and entertainment. The interior shone with polished marble. Chandeliers sparkled above, accentuated by discreetly placed electric lights, as to not destroy the elegance of days long past. Thick, velvet drapes hung in every window.

"I think I might have been here once before many years ago," Saint remarked as they walked toward the ballroom. "Did the Earl of Angelwood use to run this place? With his wife?"

Ivy nodded, impressed with his memory. "Their family still owns it. I believe there's a portrait of the earl and the countess somewhere upstairs."

"They're dead now." He said it not as a question, but as though he had to remind himself of how much time had passed.

Ivy squeezed his arm with her own. "Yes." She wasn't going to tell him that the earl and countess had both been dead for almost thirty years.

Two footmen opened the huge oak doors for them, giving them entrance into the enormous room where the photographs, sketches, sculptures and paintings were on view.

It only took Saint one quick glance around before turning to her with an accusatory glare. "What the hell?"

She grinned up at him. "What's the matter, Saint? Don't you like erotic art?"

Chapter 10

~~~
◦◦◦◦◦◦
~~~

"**I**vy Dearing and the vampire are here," Baron Hess said, in way of greeting.

The younger man bowed his head ever so slightly to acknowledge the baron, who had kept him waiting a good ten minutes. His gaze remained focused on all of the photographs in front of him. "That makes sense. She has work on display here."

"Does she?"

He almost smiled at the interest in the older man's voice. "You're looking at them. What do you think of her work?"

The baron ignored his question. "Will they be surprised to see you here?"

"I've nothing to hide."

"Haven't you?" The baron's eyes narrowed at the photograph before him. "Is that who I think it is?"

"The vampire himself. That's quite a nasty scar on his shoulder, isn't it? Catholic bastards."

A moment's silence followed as the other man took his time studying the image, his mouth twisted in a faint sneer. "Are they romantically involved?"

"I don't think so."

"You should know. We cannot afford to underestimate him."

This time he spared the older man more than a glance. "I don't."

"Do you not?" His companion moved to another framed image. "That was a dangerous thing you did the other night."

Casually, the younger man followed. He owed this man some respect because of his position within the Order, but as a person he didn't think much of Baron Hess at all. "He was gone. It was safe. No one heard or saw a thing."

"But they could have."

"They *didn't*. Now, do you have anything useful to tell me or are you here simply to waste my time?"

"Watch how you speak to me, boy." A sharp, clear gaze pinned him. "You haven't earned the right."

"Haven't I? Which one of us has almost completed all the steps for the ritual?"

"You were picked for the task because of your expendability. You'd do well to remember that."

"Just as you were picked for your task so many years ago? Perhaps that is the great difference between us. I have no intention of washing my hands of what is expected of me."

"Oh, there are greater differences than that." The pompous, mocking tone was like a thorn in the younger man's side. "You won't have earned any respect until you're successful."

"I will be."

The older man shrugged. "Not if the vampire catches you."

"Why aren't *we* catching the vampire?" He dared another glance at his companion, even though it was important that their conversation seem nothing more than two slight acquaintances discussing art. "He is ripe for the taking."

"Everything is falling into place. We do not want to ruin it by being impatient. We can use the one we have to lure the others."

"There is such a thing as being *too* patient. We should move while we can."

The other man took a step closer, so that their shoulders were almost touching. "If you ruin this by doing something impulsive," he began, his tone deadly soft, "I'll kill you myself, and send your bones home to your mother, do you understand?"

The younger man smiled. "Of course." But he didn't mean it. Soon he would be a favorite of the Order and the baron would answer to him. That's what kept him patient.

"Good. Now get out of here. I don't want the vampire—or my daughter—to see us together."

"No," the young man agreed, turning away. "We wouldn't want that."

"These are Torrent's paintings?" Saint gazed around at the brightly colored canvases adorning the wall of the small salon. Torrent was one of the few artists displaying work at Eden that had a room dedicated solely to their work.

Ivy nodded as she stood beside him, her body turned toward his. "They are. What do you think?"

He thought that Jacques Torrent had perhaps too much enthusiasm for bondage and *ménage à trois*, but other than that, the man was very talented.

"He has good use of color," he remarked, his gaze falling on a painting depicting a lush-figured woman lying nude on a bed, her wrists and ankles bound to the posters with airy-looking scarves. Not one inch of her splayed form was hidden from view and Torrent had captured every detail—so much so that Saint almost believed that if he were to touch his finger to the woman's sex it would come away damp.

"I find his work very sensual," Ivy said when he didn't offer any further criticism. "It's almost as though you can smell the subject's perfume, the musk of sex. See how her belly is flushed?" She pointed to another painting in which the woman was pleasuring herself with an ivory phallus. "He never misses a detail. I can feel her arousal."

Saint did not need to know that. "I certainly like his work better than the drawings of the woman with a candle up her arse."

Ivy laughed, her jadelike eyes sparkling as her gaze met his. "So do I."

Saint looked away. One glance at her and his thoughts went where they shouldn't go.

His gaze fell upon a very graphic but somehow beautiful representation of a half-naked young woman sitting in a chair with a man kneeling between her spread thighs. He had his mouth on her, his tongue buried deep in the auburn curls. From the flush on the girl's cheeks, the way she clutched at the man's hair, Saint would have to surmise she liked it.

He would like to make Ivy flush like that. Taste her on his lips, lick her sweet slit—the tiny little button inside—until she shuddered and came all over his face.

Thank God he was wearing a long enough coat to hide his crotch. Many more thoughts like that— and they'd been occurring to him with increasing frequency all evening—and he'd be walking like a hunchback.

"I see nothing in these paintings that would indicate that Torrent is the man we're looking for—

nothing to convince me that he isn't either." He turned to her with a carefully neutral expression. "And since the man himself isn't even here, I think it is time we took our leave."

"One moment." She clutched his hand in hers. "There is one more display I want you to see."

Dear Christ, he wasn't going to survive it. He was beginning to suspect that she had brought him there, not just to see Torrent's work, but to torture him with a thousand sexual images. Yet, despite that misgiving, he followed where she led. She could be leading him into a room full of people ready to stab at him with silver daggers and he'd follow. A lapdog with fangs, that's what he was becoming.

Instead of a dagger room, she led him into another small salon set up much like the one that housed Torrent's work, only this one displayed photographs.

Beautiful, erotic photographs.

There was nothing as obvious as some of the other work he'd viewed there that evening. Nothing quite so blatant and colorful as Torrent's work. These images were subtle shades of black and white—delicate, tantalizing grays accentuated with soft highlights and seductive shadows.

Bodies entwined under gossamer fabric, revealing the hazy outline of a nipple, the soft curve of buttocks. In another a nude breast was just barely covered by a strong, dark male hand. Faces were shadowed, eyes closed in sublime pleasure.

Saint swallowed. These photographs were taken by someone who understood seduction. This artist knew the difference between revealing too much and revealing just enough. With a close image of a woman's face, lips parted in rapture, the photographer captured the essence of climax without any overt images.

And then he saw it. Among some individual portraits—mostly ethereal nudes—was a photograph of a lone male. He was shirtless, his trousers hanging low on his lean hips. His back was to the camera, profile turned ever so slightly. Saint recognized the tattoo—and the scar on the man's back.

"Do you like it?" Ivy asked, her voice a hot breath against his ear.

Did he? He wasn't certain. He wasn't sure he liked being on display and yet . . . was that how she saw him? Was that how he looked in her presence?

He nodded—a stiff jerk of his head. "Yes. I like it. I like all of it."

She smiled happily. "I have some that are naughtier but I wanted to display what I find erotic—not what I think other people might judge as such."

His brows rose. "You did a fine job."

She pointed at one in the center of the wall. A woman draped in a fine lawn, the outline of her breasts visible. Her aureoles were a faint shadow, nipples, tight little pebbles. And lower, the shadow of her pubic mound was little more than a hint—the tease of something there but not quite defined.

"That's me," she told him.

He groaned—actually groaned. "Fuck."

Startled, Ivy stared at him. "What? I think it's lovely."

Turning so that they faced each other, barely an inch between them, Saint gazed down at her, his blood racing. They were alone in this little room, though people passed by the door. He took one of her hands in his and guided it between his legs, to where he was hot and heavy and hard for her. "It is lovely. Feel how lovely I think it is."

Green eyes brightened. Pink lips parted. "Oh. *That's* lovely." She rubbed the aching length of him with her palm. He knew then that she had planned this evening.

"That's it," he announced, throbbing under her touch. "We're leaving." If she wanted him so badly, who was he to deny her? He wanted her just as much.

Ivy didn't argue. He didn't expect her to. In fact, he rather expected that she was silently crowing in victory. He didn't care. He'd fought his attraction to her since day one. He wanted her. He was going to have her, damn it.

They didn't say good-bye to anyone, didn't stop

to chat at all. They paused long enough to collect their outer garments and then he pulled her from the building and down the steps to where their carriage was among the many waiting.

Inside, Saint pounded on the roof so hard his fist left a dent. The carriage jerked into motion and the second it did, he pounced on Ivy. His hatred of enclosed spaces didn't even register he was so desperate to have her—even just a taste.

He ravished her mouth, sucked her tongue, bit that full lower lip. She tasted of warmth and champagne and her soft little tongue rubbed against his. His hands tugged at the neckline of her gown. He tried to be gentle, but even so the delicate fabric tore under his enthusiasm.

Saint tore his mouth away from hers. "I'm sorry."

Ivy gazed at him, eyes heavy lidded and bright with desire. "You are forgiven, but only if you do not stop."

He had no intention of stopping. He lifted one of her breasts from the confines of her corset, studying the puckered, delicate pink nipple before lowering his head to it. It was hard and sweet against his tongue. He licked it, sucked it—drawing moans of pleasure from the seductress clutching at his shoulders.

With his mouth securing her breast, he slid his hands beneath her skirts, lifting the layers to seize the fine linen drawers beneath.

And ripped them down the center. She gasped, but didn't protest. The scraps fell from her legs, leaving her lower body bare to his touch. His fingers brushed the velvet curves of her buttocks, teased the cleft between before gliding around to the humid valley between her thighs. Her pubic hair was damp, the lips of her sex slick. He stroked her, searching out the tiny terrace that readily swelled beneath his touch. Ivy writhed against his hand, gasping. Still teasing her nipple, he lowered himself to his knees before her, his free hand pushing yet again at the damnable skirts of her gown.

He wanted this woman so badly he was willing to sacrifice all finesse to have her. He'd take his time with her later, but for now—perhaps for this entire night—he was going to take her and give himself to her with all the romance of a drunken sailor. As long as she came with him—as long as he heard her cries of ecstasy, that was all that mattered.

His mouth released her breast as he eased his hand from that succulent valley. Wrapping his fingers around her thighs, he pulled her forward on the bench and then lowered his head beneath her skirts.

Her hips jumped when his tongue touched her, and a soft moan escaped her lips. Saint paused long enough to breathe her in. He knew of men who didn't like the smell of "cunny." He wasn't one of them. What man—what lover of women—

wouldn't enjoy the clean salt musk of his lover's sex when she was ready for him?

Holding her open with one hand, he licked her, tasted her. Slowly, he eased two fingers of his other hand inside her tight wetness, slowly thrusting in tandem with every motion of his tongue.

Her breathing was ragged. Her hands clutched at the leather seat. "I want to touch you," she rasped.

Pushing back her skirts, Saint raised his gaze to hers, so that she could see what he was doing to her. His only response was to lazily drag his tongue along the swollen cleft. Ivy shuddered but she did not climax.

"Lie down," she commanded, lifting herself away from his mouth.

He did as she bid, settling his back against the floor of the carriage. It was cramped and he had to place a boot on either seat to get comfortable, but it was worth it when he saw Ivy descending upon him. He was too out of his head with wanting her to mind the close quarters or to feel trapped.

She straddled him, her thighs warm and trembling on either side of his head. Her skirts spilled all around him, encasing him in a sweet, soft prison. Slowly, she lowered herself over him, until her sex was within mouth's reach. He reached for her, wrapping his arms around her perfect round thighs, and drawing her down so he could feast upon her once more.

Ivy's hands were busy at the front of his trousers. Deftly, she unfastened them, pulling the front open and releasing the eager length of his cock. And when her soft, wet lips closed around the head, Saint groaned into her fragrant, damp flesh.

She licked him, sucked on him, worked him until he was groaning between her legs. His own tongue picked up speed, thrumming against her hooded button until he felt her start to shiver. She moved against him as he thrust his hips upward. She engulfed the entire length of his cock, and held it there, stroking him with her tongue, gripping him with her lips and mouth like a hot, wet vise. Her little cries hummed against his aching flesh and just when he thought he couldn't hold out any longer, she came in his mouth, convulsing and keening as his own climax tore through him. Sparks and light exploded behind his eyes as release rocked his body.

Afterward, Ivy eased herself off him and back onto the bench. As he refastened his trousers, Saint watched her. She watched him back. Even though he knew he had given her pleasure, there was still hunger in her eyes, stark and terribly arousing.

"Please tell me you are not done with me." Her voice—so husky and low—sent a tremor down his spine. What was it about her that made him react in such a way. She made him a creature of instinct, of pure base emotion.

He sat up, placed a hand on either side of her and lifted himself to his knees, so that their faces were only inches apart. Her juices clung to his mouth and he was hungry for more.

"My dear Ivy, I won't be done with you for a *very* long time."

The carriage stopped in front of Maison Rouge, but neither Saint nor Ivy entered the house. Instead, they ran like children toward her cottage, laughing and tripping over their own feet in their enthusiasm for each other as the heavens opened above them.

Ivy carried her ruined underwear in her hand.

Inside the cottage she tossed her cloak on the bed. Then she seated herself in the same chair he had sat in while she photographed him and watched while he lit a fire. Within seconds Saint had flames casting a warm glow throughout the room.

He rose to his feet, tossed his coat on top of her cloak and started toward her. Goose bumps dotted her flesh as she thought about all the things he might do to her—all the things she might do to him—before dawn came.

She watched him approach. There was no sound except for rain tapping on the roof, the fire crackling in the hearth and the roaring of her own breath in her ears.

He moved like a lazy tomcat, all ease and languid grace, coming toward her with a purpose that would not be denied and therefore no need to rush.

It seemed her plan for seduction—consummated seduction—was about to come to fruition, but who was the seducer here and who the seduced? He had her quivering like a virgin again even though she had yet to recover from what he had done to her in the carriage.

Slowly, he sank to his knees before her, the chair so low that they were eye to eye. The soft black worsted of his trousers brushed against her skirts. His dark gaze—ebony and glowing with the flames from the fire—never left hers as he raised his right hand and trailed the backs of his fingers down her cheek. His flesh was warm—so warm and smooth. The gold band on his middle finger brushed a cool kiss upon the corner of her mouth. He was so surprisingly gentle, as though she were made of some fine porcelain rather than flesh and bone. Ivy's heart caught in her chest. This was how she had always dreamed he would be.

The firelight cast his features into fierce relief, accentuating the already ridiculously sharp angle of his cheekbones, the soft hollow beneath his full lower lip. He was a dark angel, at home in darkness and flame, waiting to consume her with his own fire.

Ivy opened her mouth to speak—to utter some

sound that might ease the tension gathering between them, but he turned his hand, pressing the tip of one finger against her lips. "Sssh."

She closed her mouth, kissing his finger as she did so. With agonizing slowness, that finger trailed down the curve of her chin to her throat, and lower to the torn neckline of her gown. He could tear her clothing to shreds and she wouldn't care. His hand was long, his fingers nimble and strong. Perfectly formed, they might have been delicate but for the faint scars that decorated them and the tendons that strained to control his incredible strength.

He trailed his fingers over the rise of her breast. Beneath her corset her nipples tightened at the slight contact—at the promise of more. Down, down his hand slid, across her abdomen, down the length of her lap, cupping her knee as it slid even farther. It wasn't until he reached her ankle that she realized his other hand had joined in and both were under her skirts.

His touch was gentle, yet firm, as his hands caressed her calves and the tops of her knees. Her skirts climbed upward, draped delicately over his forearms as Saint nudged her legs apart, easing himself between her splayed thighs as he slid her skirts up over her garters with agonizing slowness.

How dark his skin was against the soft pink of her delicate stockings. Shivers of anticipation raced through her as he urged her closer to the edge of the chair, easing himself deeper into the valley of her thighs.

He was so close she could feel his heat. The fabric of his trousers rubbed against the delicate flesh on the inside of her legs and underneath her muscles twitched. He had yet to kiss her or fondle her in anyway and already she was damp again with her body's readiness for him. Her heart thumped triumphantly in her chest, and every pulse point in her body throbbed in response.

She ached for him.

Raising her gaze, she caught him watching her with heavy-lidded his eyes. His lips were slightly parted, curving into a smile that took her breath, as he pushed one hand farther up her thigh, and between, to that heated place that ached for his touch, touching the curls of her sex with a delicate reverence that made her gasp.

He sat back a bit, his gaze never leaving her face as his fingers stroked the slick cleft, finding the plumpness between that shivered and tensed at his slightest touch. Another gasp as he teased that tight peak. Every stroke stoked the fire within her, had her gripping the arms of the chair so tightly her knuckles were white.

"Don't fight it," he whispered, breaking the silence. "This time, I want to hear your cries."

A shudder wracked her as his words, spoken

in that honeyed velvet voice, coupled with the exquisite torture of his fingers, wound the tightness within her. She moaned.

"That's it." His thumb continued to stroke the firm hood of her sex as he eased one long finger into the tight, wetness below. Ivy's body seized the welcome intrusion and squeezed. Her head fell back against the soft padding of the chair, her brow tightening as a moan of sheer pleasure escaped her lips. His finger thrust once, twice, and was gone. Then there were two inside her, curving upward, stroking with an intensity that filled her with the most amazing sensations. It was almost too much, too incredible. And then she came in a flood of pleasure that actually made her head spin.

Before she could recover, or even lift her head Saint had unfastened his trousers and guided his long, hard cock to the entrance of her body. Their gazes locked as he grasped the top of the chair above her shoulder with one hand and pulled. One thrust and he was buried inside her, his chest pressed against hers, his breath hot on her temple.

Gasping, Ivy wrapped her legs around him, lifting her hips off the edge of the seat to better accommodate him.

"Oh." His voice was soft and low and so full of wonder that her heart twisted at the sound. Saint was still, his cheek against her temple.

Her body took him so readily, so easily it was as

though they had been made to fit together. Inside, Ivy quivered and convulsed in delicate staccato as he slowly began to move.

"That's it," she whispered, urging him on with the answering surge of her hips.

His free hand came up and cupped her chin, tilting her head back so that his lips could brush hers, as soft as a butterfly's wing. That soft caress moved across her cheek, the tip of her nose, even along her forehead before coming to rest on her mouth once more. He held her face as though he were afraid she might turn her head. She would have told him there was no chance of that, had she been capable of coherent speech.

He filled her, eased out of her and filled her again. Liquid heat eased the friction between their bodies, heightened the ache in her sweet spot. The angle of his body above hers had his pelvis grinding into hers with every thrust, deepening that delicious ache, building the tension toward its desired conclusion.

He licked her lips, tasted her mouth, their breath mingling together in shallow gasps and jagged moans. Ivy held him, pulled him in with her legs as the tempo of his thrusts increased. Still gripping one arm of the chair she arched upward, pushing herself against him. Her other hand found the back of his head and fisted in the thick waves there. She pulled his hair as she returned his kiss with all the ardor she felt, working her hips until climax washed over her in ripples and tremors that shook her entire body.

Before her own cries of pleasure could subside, Saint began thrusting in earnest, pushing himself deep inside her so hard the front legs of the chair lifted off the carpet and the back of the heavy oak frame groaned and cracked beneath the strength of his fingers.

He shuddered, groaning his release into Ivy's mouth as his body came inside her.

When he lifted his head it was to regard her with heavy-lidded eyes. Having him this close, still inside her where she could feel his enduring warmth, brought Ivy to the brink of tears. He was going to think her an idiot, becoming so girlish now.

"You are so beautiful," he whispered, rubbing his cheek along hers. "So beautiful and soft and wet. Ahh, Ivy. I wish I could stay inside you forever."

"We have all night," she murmured, smoothing the thick waves of his hair back from his face.

A slow smile curved his perfect lips. "Then that will have to do. For now."

Chapter 11

$\sim\!\!\infty\!\!\sim$

"**W**hy haven't you bitten me?" Ivy ran her fingers along the line of muscle running the length of Saint's abdomen. They were in his bed, in the quiet cavern of his apartments below Maison Rouge, and he had his arm around her shoulders, holding her against his naked warmth.

"I've told you why. It's dangerous."

"I know that was the excuse you gave me. Now I want the truth."

Saint frowned, shooting her a suspicious glance. "You said you would never be 'on the menu,' remember?"

The man had a memory like a swatch of velvet—everything stuck to it. She flushed with the reminder. "It's a woman's prerogative to change her mind."

He shook his head, obviously not finding the quip as amusing as she had hoped. "I'm not going to bite you because it will complicate our relationship."

"Sex hasn't already done that?"

He sighed. "If I bite you, that makes you mine. You become a part of me."

"So?" It was obvious from her shrug that she didn't understand. "You bite the people you feed from."

"Only once. The more blood you take from a person the more they become a part of you."

"And?"

"It is a very intimate thing."

She watched him, wide-eyed and expectant.

"I don't want to take a part of you with me when I go," he said softly.

"Oh." That much honesty was surprising even to her. She didn't quite understand, but she caught the gist of what he meant. He didn't want to get attached. "Saint, I . . ."

"I'm sorry." He flashed a rueful smile. "I shouldn't have said anything."

Maybe not, but Ivy wanted to say something. She wanted to tell him not to go. She wouldn't try to stop him, though. She would let him go because she would not be like her mother, lamenting and pining for a man who tired of her and tossed her aside. There was no future for them, she knew that. He was a vampire and she was human.

She could become a vampire. Saint could take her blood and give her his and they could be together forever. The very notion made her mentally shake her head. She didn't believe in forever. They'd have a few years at best before one of them lost interest. That was the way these things went. And then she'd be immortal and alone.

All she had to do was think of watching her mother die—of watching everyone she loved die—and she understood just how lonely his life might be.

But the idea of watching the world change with Saint at her side? Of waking up forever with him? Maybe it was just the afterglow of delicious love-making talking, but she could easily imagine giving up sunlight for that.

"Do you like the taste of blood?" She asked because that was the only dark spot in her little fantasy about running off into the night with him.

"Yes."

She wrinkled her nose. "But, it tastes like licking a penny."

He laughed at that. "Blood doesn't taste like that to me."

"How does it taste, then?" She could tell he didn't want to talk about it. In fact, he looked very much as he had whenever she had tried to get him to touch her or kiss her before finally wooing him into her bed.

"What is the most delicious thing you've ever had to eat?"

She flashed a coy smile, her fingers twirling lazy circles on his hard, flat belly. "Besides you?"

Was that a blush in his cheeks? "Be serious."

"Chocolate. Are you saying that blood tastes like chocolate to you?" No wonder he liked being a vampire.

He shook his head. "Yes and no. Every person has a unique smell—the smell of their blood. I can smell it. It's almost as though my tongue doesn't work as a human tongue anymore. I taste a person's essence. So if they eat a lot of spicy foods, then they taste spicy to me. Or if they are a truly good person they might taste faintly sweet. Nothing like licking a penny at all."

"You said you can smell how they will taste?"

"Yes."

"Is that how you hunt?"

"Sometimes. Sometimes you don't have that luxury and you just have to eat what you can find."

It was still difficult to remember that he was talking about people when he talked about eating. It was vaguely disconcerting when she thought about it. "How do I smell?"

He stilled. His gaze faltered, but he managed to hold hers regardless. "Like spices drenched in wild honey and vanilla."

"Oh." That sounded good.

"I would like very much to taste you," he murmured, his hand sliding down to cup her tightening breast. "I want you on my fingers and running down my chin. Once would not be enough. Even now the scent of you tempts me. Do you understand the danger now?"

Hot and shivering, Ivy did understand. Finally, she knew that being with this man would mean being consumed by him, literally as well as figuratively.

But if she were a vampire then she could consume him as well. If she was a vampire she could know what he tasted like.

She needed to change the subject, before impulse drove her to do something she might later regret.

"Have you found out anything about that strange symbol you found on Daisy's cheek?"

He released her breast and slid his hand down to her ribs, the air between them cooling to pleasantly warm rather than steaming. "Ezekiel thinks it sounds familiar, but there was nothing distinguishable about it to make it easily identifiable. It could be anything."

She raised her gaze to his as she lazily traced the crude dragon on his neck. "Surely you must have some idea?"

He arched a brow at her, obviously amused. "Must I?"

"Yes." She sounded so resolute he almost smiled.

"It may be a ring. It's the only thing I can think of that might have been on the killer and come in contact with Daisy's cheek."

"He hit her." Bastard.

"Or the ring was turned around and he pressed it into her cheek when he silenced her."

Monster.

"Poor Daisy." For the first time in the three days since the murder, Ivy allowed the tears to come. "She wasn't even twenty. Her birthday is . . . was next month."

Saint was silent.

Guilt came then, as hot and swift as her tears. "If I hadn't photographed her, she would still be alive."

"I told you not to think that way."

"How can I not?"

"Because it will drive you insane."

She wiped at her eyes. "Are you speaking from experience?"

"No. I try very hard not to think at all. My friend Dreux thought too much—felt too much. One morning he got up and walked out into the sun and exploded like fireworks."

Ivy stared at him, the gruesome image emblazoned in her brain. "And you saw it?"

He shrugged. "It was a long time ago."

From the tone of his voice, the subtle shift in his expression she knew he didn't want to talk about it anymore and she couldn't blame him. It must have been awful.

"Is it possible that the killer wasn't someone on the list the night Daisy was murdered? Could someone have accessed the house through the tunnel you use?"

"No. Not without my knowing. No one could come through this room without leaving a scent behind."

She sighed. There went that theory. "Do you still suspect Jacques?" she asked.

"He is the most obvious choice, but I'm not convinced of his guilt. Tying women up is not the same as cutting them open."

Ivy's stomach gave a little lurch, and Saint noticed. "I'm sorry, darling."

She nodded. "You know I have a difficult time believing Jacques could do such a thing, but if not him, then who? We are right back where we started—with nothing."

"Not quite nothing. We have the symbol the killer left behind on Daisy and we know that you photographed the victims."

Ivy smiled. "I wanted to photograph Daisy as a mermaid but she insisted on being Cleopatra. She wanted to be remembered as one of the greatest seductresses of all time."

Saint stiffened beside her and Ivy looked up. "What is it?"

"That's it. Christ, I can't believe I didn't think of it sooner. How can I be so old and still so stupid?"

Ivy gaped at him as he raved. "What are you talking about?"

"The girls. You photographed them as Eve and Delilah, Jezebel and Cleopatra. Great seductresses. Fallen women. For some reason the killer targeted those women not because you photographed them, but for what you photographed them *as*."

Were it possible to feel both elated and terrified at the same time, Ivy felt just that.

"If you're right, then any girls who I've photographed as fallen women are still in danger."

"How many more are there?"

She counted them off mentally. "Three. Eliza, Mary and Beatrice."

"Are they still here?"

"Mary is. Usually the girls only go out on their nights off, but since we're closed again, and because everyone is so upset, a few of the girls have been spending more time with their families. I believe Eliza went home yesterday to be with her mother and Beatrice was spending the night with her sister."

Throwing back the covers, Saint released her and slipped out of bed. "We have to find them and bring them back. They're not safe out there."

"They were escorted by your men and both were told to send word when they wished to return to the house."

"Ivy, he already killed one girl inside this house. He can get to them anywhere."

In his dark gaze Ivy saw a reflection of the

guilt she felt, and in the paleness of his cheeks she saw the fear she also shared. She would not lose any more friends to this monster. She would not.

She jumped out of bed as well, reaching for her discarded underthings. "You go get Eliza. I'll get Beatrice."

He yanked on his trousers. "You're not going anywhere."

"Saint, you cannot get both of them before dawn." Quickly, she pulled on her chemise. "We need to act quickly. We have to save them both."

"Fine, but you'll take at least two men with you. Robert and George, they're the best."

Hauling her gown over her head, she turned her back to him so he could button the back. "What about Mary?"

His fingers raced up her spine. "I'll put guards on her room—inside and out."

Ivy faced him. "Promise me you'll be careful?"

Saint's palms came down on her shoulders, warm and strong. "I will. Take a pistol with you. And if there is trouble, I want you to use it."

Ivy nodded. She wasn't a killer, but if she had the chance to shoot the son of a bitch who had butchered her girls, she was going to take it.

He kissed her then. It was short and urgent, but it filled Ivy with a strength she never knew she possessed.

"We'll save them." His black gaze bore into hers. "I promise."

And she believed him.

Saint tried not to think about Ivy being out on her own—even if she was with armed guards—as he soared through the night sky to the East End neighborhood where Eliza Newton spent most of her life prior to coming to Maison Rouge.

His relationship with Ivy wasn't important when compared to the need to find this killer, so Saint put all thoughts of her to the back of his mind where they should be as he landed on top of a roof. It was crooked and missing some shingles, but it was sturdy enough to support his weight and that was all that mattered. Carefully, he moved down one steep side to peer down at the street below. Eliza's mother's house was just across the street.

It wasn't a fine house, which would have been out of place in this part of the city, but it was by no means a hovel. From what Saint could see it boasted more than one room and was cozy and warm inside.

Through an open window he spied Eliza and her mother sitting at the worn table, having a cup of tea and sharing a plate of bread and cheese. They were early risers, the pair of them. Her mother was laughing at something Eliza had said and the girl was watching her with a loving smile on her lips. It was a homey little scene that made his heart ache.

It would be nice to have a home and someone to share it with.

With a quick glance to make certain he wouldn't be seen, he jumped from the building into a shadowed section of the street. He tugged his coat into place and smoothed a hand over his hair as he crossed to the other side. Eliza's mother would be more likely to allow her daughter to leave with someone reasonably respectable-looking, rather than someone who looked as though he had literally just fallen out of the sky.

A coach pulled up beside him—this part of London rarely if ever saw automobile traffic. Saint turned, on guard should Jacques Torrent or anyone else he recognized from the house climb out.

"Evenin' Mr. Saint."

"Jackson?" It was Madeline's own coachman. "What are you doing here?"

"Miss Ivy sent me. She thought Miss Eliza might want a drive home."

"That was very thoughtful of her." Instead he was wondering if Ivy had sent the man because she was thinking of Eliza's comfort or if she simply didn't want him holding the girl in his arms as he flew back to Maison Rouge with her. Arrogantly he allowed himself to think the latter. Everyone at Maison Rouge knew he was a vampire. Being all right with offering up blood was just one of the duties of being a Rouge girl.

Ivy was simply possessive. He liked that.

He was still smiling when he knocked on the door. Eliza answered it and when her pretty round face went white at the sight of him, Saint's good mood faded.

"My apologies for interrupting your evening, Eliza."

"Mr. Saint. Has something happened? Is everyone at the house all right?"

He held out a hand to stop her questions before she got herself worked into a state. "Everyone is fine, but if you have had enough of a visit with your family, I think you should return to Maison Rouge with me tonight."

She regarded him with narrow blue eyes. She was a sweet little thing with dark brown hair and pink cheeks. "Why?"

He wasn't going to lie to her. "Because I think you might be in danger."

"Danger?" Casting a furtive glance over her shoulder, she gestured for him to step back and when he did she joined him on the front step, closing the door behind her. "Do you mean from the killer?"

"Yes." Saint stepped down onto the walk and gestured to Jackson and the carriage. "Gather your things and I'll take you back to Maison Rouge."

Blue eyes watched him with suspicion. "How do I know you are not the killer?"

"Because you'd be dead by now if I were."

She seemed to accept that explanation. "I can't leave my mother. She needs me here. She sent for me."

"Bring her with you, then."

That idea she didn't seem so enamored with. "I cannot."

"You have no choice, my dear. You are coming with me, so if your mother needs you so badly then she must come as well."

Was it his imagination or did she swear under her breath? She looked yet again over her shoulder, which was draped with a brightly colored shawl— the only hint that she was not the simple lower-class girl that she now appeared to be.

"Into the alley," she directed him and then walked into the darkness herself not waiting to see if he complied.

Saint followed. He was very close behind her just in case. So close, that when she whirled around to face him, she almost collided with his chest.

"Oh, Mr. Saint!" she cried, clutching at his arms with her little fingers. "I feel so awful."

He looked at her hands and she removed them, so he placed his own on her shoulder. He wasn't terribly comfortable with being clutched at. "About what, Eliza?"

"I lied to you." She appeared the very picture of youthful guilt. "I was told to go to my mother's. I was told to go and wait for you."

Shite. This could not be good. "By who?"

"My brother."

He frowned. "Do I know your brother?"

"I don't think so, sir. He said he was told by another man. This man, he paid my brother a lot of money, sir. Even more than I make in a month at Maison Rouge. My mother, she was able to buy new shoes for my younger sister—and a new shawl for herself."

Saint wasn't angry. How could he be at either Eliza or her brother? He was nothing to them, but their family was everything. He would have done the same thing in their position.

"So, you were supposed to lure me here. Why?" He hadn't been in London in years and other than trying to find the Maison Rouge murderer, he hadn't ruffled any feathers that he knew of.

"I don't know, sir. Oh, I really am so terribly sorry!" Her face crumpled. "Ivy's going to hate me!"

"Is it a trap, Eliza? Or was it all just to get me out of Maison Rouge?"

She shook her head, swiping at her wet eyes with the back of her hand. "Really, Mr. Saint, I don't know! I took the letter the man gave my brother." She handed him a folded slip of paper that she took from the pocket of her skirt.

Saint opened it. The note was short. It offered Eliza's brother Jack the sum of one thousand pounds to do all that Eliza had already told him. It was signed, however, not with a signature but with a sigil. A hand, palm up with a chalice sitting on it.

He gave the letter back to Eliza. "Listen to me, the person or persons who gave this to your brother are the same who killed Clementine, Goldie and Daisy."

Eliza's face lost all color as agony and grief filled her eyes. "No."

"Yes. You tell that to your brother and warn him to stay away from them. Now, I want you to get into the carriage Ivy sent for you—" A scuffling in the alley behind them caught his attention.

So it was a trap, then. If his hearing didn't deceive him—and it never did—they were starting to close in from all sides. But was the trap for him or for Eliza? Or both?

"Get in the carriage and go," he commanded, pushing the girl out into the street.

He didn't have to say it twice. Eliza scrambled into the carriage and Saint yelled at the driver to go, just as three men stepped into the alley from the street. They paid no attention to the carriage as it careened away from them.

"Evening, gents," he remarked with forced joviality as the men moved closer. Four more came out of the shadows flanking him. At least three more moved in from behind.

"Be quiet, vampire," one of them commanded as he aimed a small crossbow at Saint's chest. The spear was tipped in silver.

They were all armed, and Saint intuitively knew that every weapon either had silver on it or in it. Vampire hunters, they had to be. How else would they know what he was and what to use against him? And what could they possibly gain from committing these murders?

"I don't suppose," he began, turning around in a small circle to face all of the men moving in on him, "that one of you blokes is the man they've been comparing to Saucy Jack?"

One of the men laughed while the others grinned. Saint turned to the one laughing. "Did I say something funny?"

The man stopped laughing, but his amusement never faded. "As if we'd tell you."

Saint shrugged. "I could always beat it out of you, I suppose." And with that, he sprang into action.

Saint seized the man with the crossbow, took the weapon from him and then shot him with it, right through the heart. He died instantly, before his companions could even think to react.

The others panicked and immediately attacked. One rushed him. Saint grabbed him by the head and broke his neck with little more than a flick of his wrist. Another came at him as his comrade fell to the dirt. Saint sent him flying into the side of the neighboring building. He fell and didn't get up. When the fourth attacker had his ribs crushed by a single blow, the remaining men seemed reluctant to come at him.

"It's been fun," he told them, "But if you'll excuse me . . . ?" Eliza's carriage was well on its way now and he needed to get back to the house to check on Ivy. He hadn't the time to fight with fragile humans who didn't know how to use the weapons they had against him.

He crouched to spring into the sky. His feet had just barely left the ground when the remaining men started screaming, "Drop it!" He didn't know what they meant at that moment, but as he lifted in the air, he found out.

Men positioned on the two buildings that made the alley held some kind of net, which they dropped on him.

As soon as it touched his skin he felt the silver burning into him. The fine mesh dropped him to the ground so hard that the cobblestones beneath him cracked with the impact. Saint lay there, his face averted from the netting, covering his head with his arms. The silver could only burn his bare flesh, but it weakened him enough that even if he could touch it, prolonged exposure would burn him beyond recovery.

So he curled into a ball to protect himself and

remained silent as his joyous captures kicked him. It hurt more than it normally would have, but he would not move. He would not try to fight back. He was already in too much danger as it was.

One of the men spat on him. "That's from the Silver Palm, you filthy vermin."

Another man cuffed the one who had spat. "Shut up, you fool!" He cast a nervous glance at Saint. They obviously weren't supposed to tell him who they were.

The Silver Palm. They were an old arm of the Knights Templar shunned for practicing dark arts. They were also the original possessors of the cup that turned Saint vampire. Was it possible that these killings really were about him and the others? It was almost too fantastic, and yet all the evidence was there.

They picked him up, the netting burning him as it shifted against the flesh he couldn't protect. He refused to cry out. He was loaded into a coach, with silver bars in the blackened windows.

His last thought as they drove away was of Ivy. With him gone, who was going to look after her? No one.

And with that thought burning in his mind, Saint resolved to fight for his freedom.

Fight and win.

Chapter 12

"**W**ho the hell are you?"

It was obvious that Beatrice's sister was not impressed with someone pounding on her door an hour before dawn.

"My name is Ivy Dearing. I'm looking for Beatrice. Is she here?"

"Maybe." The woman raked her with an insolent gaze. "What do you want with her?"

"I want to take her back to Maison Rouge. We're concerned for her safety."

"Given the fact that a girl was killed there a few nights ago, I think she's safer where she is." She pushed the door. Only Ivy's boot kept the thin wood from closing in her face.

"Do you honestly believe you can protect Beatrice?" Ivy demanded through the opening, her jaw clenching at the pain in her foot. Beatrice's sister was putting all her weight on the door and

Ivy's boot—not to mention her foot—wasn't thick enough to withstand the pressure.

"Do you?" the other woman countered, still pushing.

Before Ivy could answer, one of the men with her reached out a burly arm and shoved against the door. Hard. It flew open, and Beatrice's sister flew with it.

The man, whose name was George, if she remembered correctly, stepped inside the little room and glared down his broad nose at the woman. "I can protect her. Now, where's Bea?"

The door on the opposite side of the room opened and a very sleepy-looking Beatrice walked out in a demure flannel nightgown. "George? Ivy? What are you two doing here?"

George's face lit up and he stomped across the apartment, the floorboards sagging under his massive bulk. "We've come to take you home, Bea. Where you're safe."

To Ivy's surprise the girl smiled at George as though he had ridden in on a white charger, banners blazing. "All right. I'll get dressed and be ready in just a moment." Then she turned on her toes and skipped back into the bedroom.

Ivy cast a glance at Beatrice's scowling sister, whose nightgown was a bit threadbare. The roots of her hair were dark from where the henna had grown out, the rest of it a dark red. She'd bet money that this woman was envious of her sister's life, obviously being a woman who had to apply her trade on the street. Ivy might have suggested she visit Maison Rouge for an interview, but the woman was too hard-looking now, the street having taken its toll on her. She wouldn't fit in at the house, and it would be rare that any wealthy client with a sense of personal hygiene would want her.

It was difficult not to feel sorry for her all the same. Perhaps she was right. Perhaps Beatrice wasn't safe at Maison Rouge, but if Ivy didn't trust in Saint's abilities then she had no hope whatsoever of seeing this murderer brought to justice.

"We'll wait in the carriage," Ivy announced, unable to stand the woman's scowl any longer. "Come, George."

The big man hesitated, but only for a moment, before following her.

"I apologize for waking you," Ivy said to the woman as they walked past. "Thank you for your time."

The woman stopped her. "I'm not giving back the money."

Ivy flinched at the blast of whiskey-stale breath. "I don't know what you're talking about."

Hands on her hips, the strapping woman straightened her shoulders, in a manner that was clearly challenging. "The money I was paid to have Beatrice come stay with me."

Had Beatrice been forced to pay her own sister for a visit? Ivy couldn't imagine ever charging her own sister for the pleasure of her company—in fact she would gladly pay for a few hours with Rose.

"Keep it," she said disdainfully. If Beatrice had paid herself, Ivy would personally recoup her loss.

It didn't take long for Beatrice to join them in the carriage and within minutes of closing the door they were on their way back to Maison Rouge, with the gentle giant George going out of his way to ensure Beatrice's comfort. The whole process had been fairly quick and free of obstacle. Hopefully, Saint's retrieval of Eliza had gone just as smoothly.

When they arrived at Maison Rouge, George took Beatrice to her room while Ivy waited for Saint in the parlor.

She didn't have to wait long. But it wasn't her vampire who burst through the door.

"It's Mr. Saint!" Eliza gasped, her face as white as a sheet.

Ivy's heart stopped dead. "What about him?"

"They've taken him." The girl's pretty face contorted with tears. "Oh, Ivy! I think they're going to kill him!"

If his mobile prison arrived at its destination, Saint knew he wouldn't live to see another sunset. He wasn't like Chapel or even Bishop who would rather play a situation out and see where it ended. Saint however, had a tendency to suspect that every situation was going to culminate in his death.

That was why he was lying face down on the coach floor, trying not to panic like a little girl as he wriggled himself into position. His hair and clothing gave some protection from the silver's burning effects, but it weakened his strength. Only two things could help a vampire overcome silver and that was bloodlust or sheer fury.

He was working on fury. His hatred of enclosed spaces helped. He used that fear to fuel the rage inside him.

He thought of the night Marta died. The memory, two and one-half decades old, stirred a little heat within his blood, but it brought more regret than anything else. He thought about the animal killing Ivy's friends and the heat intensified.

He thought about Ivy being left at the mercy of just such an animal should he give up and die and the heat burst into an inferno. He would not desert her. He would not leave her to die, or worse leave her alive knowing he had failed her.

With whatever strength he could muster, he drew back his fist, feeling the sting of silver as he did so. Then he ploughed his hand through the floorboards of the carriage—once. Twice.

He moved quickly, unsure if his captors had heard the crash. The hole was big enough for his shoulders to fit through, but the effort brought the netting around his upper body, pressing the fine threads to an exposed section of his forehead and the upper section of his left cheek. His flesh stung and then began to burn.

As he reached through the hole, pushing himself as far as he could, Saint smelled his skin as it was being singed, the sickly sweet odor turned his stomach as the pain seared his skull. Still, he reached outward, the fire beneath his skin extending now to the hand reaching between the netting for the carriage wheel.

He endured the pain, pushed past the weakness. His only thought was of Ivy as he finally wrapped his burning fingers around a spoke of the front right wheel. It took all of his strength, but the carriage staggered as the wheel stopped. Sweat ran down his forehead, rivulets of blood dripping into his eyes as he pulled, jaw clenched, body on fire.

The wheel snapped.

And then the entire carriage flipped and Saint knew nothing but darkness and fire.

There was no way anyone could "kill" Saint. The man was invincible. Wasn't he?

Ivy didn't know and that not knowing, that fear of discovery is what drove her to race around the house, shouting for any and all available men—and women—to come with her to save her vampire.

Because a world without Saint was not an option. And after all he had done for her and for this house, she was not going to abandon him. She was not going to let the bastard who took her friends take her lover as well.

It took perhaps a quarter of an hour to gather everyone, but those few minutes brought dawn that much closer. If they were going to find Saint and bring him home, it would have to be before the sun rose—unless they were lucky enough to be near one of his tunnels, and provided they were lucky enough that he was able to give directions.

She took all she could with her. George and three more of Saint's men were armed and by her side, as were half a dozen of the girls, including Beatrice and Eliza.

Poor Eliza, she felt so guilty. There was a small part of Ivy that thought the girl *should* feel guilty, but that didn't stop her from giving the girl a reassuring squeeze before they headed out. After all, Eliza had willingly given them the whereabouts of her brother, who would hopefully know where the bastards had taken Saint.

Had Beatrice been similarly duped? Someone had paid her sister to keep her, just as Eliza's brother had been paid. Ivy kicked herself for not asking Beatrice's sister more questions—not that the awful woman would have answered her honestly.

"We don't have long," Ivy told them all as they prepared to leave. She sat on the back of Anna-belle, the horse her mother had bought her for her twenty-second birthday, astride and not caring if her legs showed. "The sun will rise soon. As soon as we find Saint we get him into the carriage, wrap him in blankets and get him back here as quickly as possible. Understood?"

Every head nodded in the predawn gloom.

"We do not know what sort of state he'll be in." She nearly choked on the words. "So stay away from him unless you are getting him into the car-riage. I'll stay with him."

"Pardon me, Miss Ivy, but I don't think that is a good idea."

Ivy met George's gaze evenly. "I appreciate that, George. However, that is the way it's going to hap-pen. Now, let's go. We're wasting time."

They tore out of the yard with Ivy in the lead, George, Eliza and one carriage bringing up the rear. Jackson stayed behind with the other in case he was needed.

Hunched over the neck of her mare, Ivy spurred the animal toward the city, to the tavern where Eliza's brother spent his evenings serving ale.

They didn't make it to the tavern. A quarter mile from their destination there was an accident in the street, blocking traffic.

A black coach with blacked-out windows lay

on its side on the cobblestones, a huge hole ripped in its floor. The horses had been unhitched and seemed unscathed but skittish, held by a man who was speaking to them in a low voice.

The rear doors of the coach were open and in front of them, on the damp street lay a dark shape wrapped in something that looked like silver netting. Three men were hauling on it, dragging it across the rough stone toward another conveyance—one similar in style to the one lying on the road.

The bundle snarled as one of the men kicked it. Then, it stiffened and shifted. In the streetlight Ivy saw a face through the mesh, and it turned toward her.

Her heart leaped into her throat. *Saint*. Blood shone in the light, the smell of burnt flesh drifted on the air and she knew the sparkling, delicate net was made of silver. What else could do such damage?

A quick jab of her heels and Annabelle burst forward, racing toward the men who were now lifting Saint into the second coach as though he was little more than a piece of old furniture.

She stopped a foot from one of them and pulled a pistol from her pocket. She aimed it at the man's head. "Put him down."

The man laughed, but some of his amusement died when he saw that she had reinforcements with her. "Sorry, lady. We've got our orders."

Ivy pulled the trigger. The bullet didn't hit him in the skull—she had changed targets—but it found a home in the meaty front of the ruffian's thigh instead. He dropped to the street with a scream.

Ivy didn't have time to feel the satisfaction of having dropped the bastard. She was yanked from her mount as soon as the man fell. Two of his companions seized her and one of them punched her—hard—in the stomach. Gasping, eyes burning with tears as the breath was ripped from her lungs, she fell forward. A brutish hand on her arm was the only thing that kept her from hitting the cobblestones herself.

Saint snarled again. The smell of burning intensified and Ivy looked up to see the net extending as Saint reached out. His fingers through the mesh were bloody and raw as he grabbed the man who had punched her. He slammed the man into the side of the coach with enough force to render him unconscious. Ivy didn't want to think of what the result might have been had Saint used his full strength.

The man holding her released her when set upon by George and another. The remaining men scattered when faced with six angry, rifle-wielding prostitutes.

Hunched like an old woman, her entire body aching from the blow it had suffered, Ivy clung to the coach door.

"Are you all right?" Saint's voice was hoarse, but it brought tears of relief to her eyes all the same.

"Am I all right?" She sniffed. "I'm fine. Did they hurt you?"

"I'll heal."

Her fingers pulled at the silver that imprisoned him. The thin strands of metal bent but didn't break, cutting into her hands like miniature blades.

Saint shook his head at her. "Ivy, stop."

Tears were running down her face now as she continued to struggle. "It won't come loose!"

"Ivy!"

She stilled then, her gaze meeting his. The tenderness in his eyes surprised her. There was blood on his face and it was impossible for her to tell how extensive his injuries were.

"The net will have to be cut," he told her softly. "Get me back to Maison Rouge. Dawn is coming."

She looked up and saw the familiar orange seeping across the sky. Her gaze dropped back to Saint's face and she saw the pain there. Even though the sun was just peeking above the horizon, it was already starting to burn him with its light.

"Help me!" she cried over her shoulder. Reason slipped away from her. She knew only that she had to save Saint—that he was most important, above all others.

Suddenly she was being moved aside by strong

hands, pushed out of the way by burly bodies. Her vision was blocked as the men worked to get Saint into the coach without harming him any further. Two of the girls took hold of Ivy and led her back to the carriage.

"Don't worry," Beatrice told her with a squeeze. "He'll be all right. Your man will be all right."

Her man. Was Saint hers?

"I'd put a bullet in anyone who tried to hurt my George too," the girl was saying as she helped Ivy into the carriage and tucked a blanket around her. Ivy was very cold all of a sudden.

"I shot a man." Her voice was distant in her ears. Peering outside, Ivy saw him still lying there on the street. "What will they do with him?"

"Keep him alive till Mr. Saint can talk to him, I imagine." Beatrice's smile was grim but victorious nevertheless. "Then the rest is up to him."

Yes. Of course. Beatrice shut the carriage door just as the coach carrying Saint rolled by. Thank God for the blackened windows, but he would have to stay imprisoned in the silver until they could cut him out. What kind of lasting damage would it do? Could it kill him?

"Take me home," she commanded quietly. "I want to be with him."

Beatrice nodded. "I'll get George."

The remaining men put the injured man up on the bench of the carriage and tied him there and then George lifted his bulk into the driver's side. Eliza, pale-faced and trembling climbed in beside Ivy. Annabelle, tethered to the back of the carriage, followed behind.

"Oh, Ivy, I'm so sorry."

Lifting up her blanket, Ivy patted the seat next to her. "Dearest, this is not your fault. Do not blame yourself." She meant it. She was too tired, too afraid to feel otherwise.

Eliza slipped under the blanket to sit beside her and the two of them held each other all the way home.

It seemed to Saint that it took hours to get him out of his silver prison when in reality it didn't even take one. Ivy wanted to be there, but he told her no. He didn't want her witnessing his disgrace, his weakness. It was bad enough that she had come charging to his rescue as she had, risking her own life to save his own worthless one.

Foolish, beautiful little twit.

In the end it was just him and George in his apartments below Maison Rouge. George, a former pickpocket whose big hands belied a nimble grace. He carefully snipped through the netting as quickly as he could, all the while protecting Saint from as much further injury as possible.

When the opening was big enough and the netting lay all around Saint like a sparkling, deadly bed, George reached down and offered his hand. Saint took it and rose to his feet on legs that were so weak they shook.

Rather than cling to the big man, Saint instead braced himself against the side of his bed. Some of his strength had returned just from having the net removed, but it would be a little while yet before he was totally himself again.

"Thank you." He locked gazes with the big man as he offered his hand. "I owe you my life."

"You owe Miss Ivy your life. I've never seen a woman so driven in my whole life." Chuckling he shook his head. "You are one lucky bastard to have a woman want you that bad. Did you see her shoot that little prick?"

Saint had seen it. It had terrified him and filled him with pride at the same time. "She's quite the woman."

George knew it was a lame response as sure as Saint did, his expression gave that away easily. He gathered up the remains of the net. "Do you need anything else?"

Ivy safe. Ivy as far away from these crazy bastards as humanly possible. But he knew he wasn't going to get that. "Blood," he replied.

George nodded. "I'll get you some." He moved toward the door, his arms full of glittering silver.

"George."

The big man turned, his rough face blank.

"One of them mentioned the Silver Palm."

Fair eyebrows rose on a wide, ruddy brow. "I didn't think they existed anymore."

"Seems they do. Find out what Ezekiel knows, will you?"

Another nod and then Saint was alone. Sagging, he rested his forehead against the heavy mahogany bed frame and closed his eyes.

The Silver Palm. He'd heard stories of them, long ago after he had turned his back on the church and embraced a life of blood and thievery. An ancient order—a splinter cell of the Templars that was as different from those knights as Saint and his brethren were from "normal" vampires. He hadn't heard of them in centuries.

What in God's name did they want with him? Better yet, how were they involved in the killing of these poor, innocent girls? They had to be the "Order" that Ezekiel's informant mentioned, and if so then it wasn't a mere coincidence. These killings weren't just about the victims, but about him and the rest of his brotherhood. But if they wanted to kill him, why hadn't they done that in the alley? If they wanted to hurt Maison Rouge, why not just burn it to the ground?

His mind refused to form any reasonable explanations, so he stopped pushing and resolved to think about it later, once he knew what Ezekiel had heard.

Instead of thinking he ran a hot bath and sprinkled some healing herbs and oils in the water before stripping off his soiled clothes and easing his aching self into the tub. The exertion left him feeling as weak as a child, but the bath felt so good he didn't care.

When the door opened, he assumed it was George bringing him blood, but one sniff was all it took to ascertain the identity of his guest. He had smelled her before he saw her when she came to his rescue in the street and he knew her without looking now as well.

Opening his eyes, he watched her approach. With her hair down, clad in a thin gown and wrapper she looked so sweet and angelic—so much like an angel he could weep at the sight of her.

And he must look like he'd been dragged to the very bowels of hell and back.

He smiled weakly. "Vanity compels me to tell you that I had hoped to improve my appearance before seeing you."

Ivy didn't smile at all as she came to stand beside the tub. In fact, the poor thing looked as though she might burst into tears at any moment.

"I'm just happy to see you." Her voice was huskier than normal. "I don't care how you look."

Saint's smile faded. "Thank you." His throat was too tight to say anything else.

He remained silent as she removed her clothes,

watching her smooth, pale skin as each flimsy garment fell to the floor. He didn't say anything as she climbed into the tub to straddle him. He simply breathed her in and ignored the hunger that gnawed at him.

"I was so frightened," she confessed as she dipped a cloth in the water. "So scared I would never see you again."

The cloth was hot as it touched his battered face, the water igniting the burns there. He ground his teeth and lay back. It had to be done and having Ivy be the one to do it made it easier.

"I'm not that easy to be rid of." He tried to keep his tone light and teasing.

A hot drop landed on his lips. He licked it away and tasted salt, not soap. Horrified, he raised his gaze to see the tears coursing down her cheeks.

"Your poor hands." She made a hiccupping noise. "Your face."

She meant the burns from the silver, of course, and the various other wounds his attackers had inflicted upon him.

"They'll fade." Sliding his arms around her, he pulled her flush against him, regardless of the stinging cuts and abrasions. "Ivy, love, they'll fade."

Her cheek rested on the top of his head. Her arms circled his neck and her fingers stroked the damp ends of his hair. "You'll have scars."

"Some." The netting had burned part of his

temple and upper cheek bad enough to leave permanent scars. They would be faint, but noticeable all the same. His hands had gotten the worst of it. Right now he was raw between the fingers and blisters were forming below his knuckles.

"Blood will help," he murmured against the delicate flesh just above her breasts. Christ, she smelled good. "And sleep. I'll be as healed as I'm going to be by sunset. You'll see."

She moved back and offered him her neck. "Take my blood."

"Ivy . . ."

"Don't argue with me!" She was on the verge of tears again. "You need it. Take it. I want you to take it."

He should refuse. He knew that on some level, taking her blood was a point of no return for both of them. At that moment, though, he didn't care. At that moment, he knew that she wanted this as badly as he did.

There was a tingling in his gums—a kind of tightening as the muscles there pushed his fangs into full extension. He sat up, tightening his grip on her and drawing her closer once more, so that she was locked against him, trembling in his arms.

"Don't be afraid," he whispered.

She glanced down at him as she swept her long, honey-colored hair to one side. "I'm not."

And then he realized that it wasn't fear that

made her tremble, but desire. And that caused a stirring in other areas as well.

Her hand went between them as he pulled her hips downward, guiding the head of his cock to the entrance of her body. She was ready for him and he slid fast and deep into the hot, silken wetness. When he was buried as far as he could go, he pierced her neck with his fangs, just above the curve of her shoulder, shuddering as she filled his mouth with sweet spice.

Ivy shuddered as well, her nipples hard and tight against his chest as she gasped and cooed. Her sex gripped him tightly as she moved her hips against him.

Saint drank, his strength returning tenfold with every swallow—his desire increasing with every thrust. He forgot the pain, forgot the fatigue in his soul. There was nothing but Ivy. Ivy in him, Ivy around him. Every sense was filled with her— overwhelmed by her—until he could no longer distinguish where she began and he ended.

He drank only what he needed from her, even though he could have gone on, glutting himself on her intoxicating essence. He licked the small wounds made by his fangs closed and lifted his face to watch her as she rode him.

Her bright eyes were heavy lidded as her gaze met his. Slowly, she lowered her head, and when her lips touched his, he moaned. When her tongue slid into his mouth, his entire body jerked in surprise. She was tasting herself on his tongue and it pushed him over the edge.

He came in a violent spasm, his entire body gripped by the intensity of emotion and sensation. He clung to her, afraid that if he let go he would be swept away forever and never find her again.

Ivy wrapped around him like her namesake, wringing his body with her own as she cried her own release into the air before collapsing on top of him.

They stayed that way for quite sometime. Silent and entwined as the water cooled around them. Once they moved the spell would be broken and he would delay that for as long as he could.

And *that*, he thought a little dismally, was the first step in exactly what he had been trying to avoid. The reason why he had fought so hard to not take Ivy's blood.

Biting her changed everything. She was inside him now, a part of him. She had given herself to him freely, body and blood. She belonged to him now.

And he was going to do everything in his power to keep her.

Chapter 13

❦❦❦

"**D**on't ever put yourself in jeopardy for me again."

Those were the last words Saint said to her before going to sleep later that morning. He made the command after seeing the bruising that had appeared on her belly.

"I won't," she promised, but it was a lie. She would gladly do it all again to bring him back. She would risk her very life for him.

It was an unsettling thought.

Ivy would have stayed in bed with Saint for the remainder of the day were it not for the growling in her tender stomach and the fact that Millie was supposed to be joining her and her mother for luncheon that day.

And as tempting as it was to cry off, this would be the first time her mother had gotten out of bed since Daisy's murder. Ivy intended to make sure her mother did indeed rise and have a normal meal.

Leaving Saint alone was one of the most difficult things she had ever done. Even though he was far from vulnerable, he looked so battered and scarred as he slumbered among the white linens.

The burns on his face and hands had lessened as he had promised they would, but he would scar, that was for certain. And while it broke her heart to know that he would forever bear reminders of this horrible day, she knew it could have been much, much worse.

She pushed the thought away as tears prickled the back of her eyes. She had done enough crying of late. She refused to do any more. Saint was alive and that was all that mattered.

She had told him about what Beatrice's sister had said to her about money and he agreed that it must have come from the same source as that paid to Eliza's brother. The whole situation boggled Ivy's mind. Surely the girls hadn't been killed to get to Saint—not when he hadn't been in town when this horrible madness began. Were the killers trying to get him out of their way? How had they known that he was a vampire?

Had someone at Maison Rouge betrayed Saint? That was impossible. None of the girls would do that, and she refused to think otherwise.

She ran upstairs to her room to change, choosing a high-necked blouse to hide the fading red marks on her neck. If she hadn't felt the fullness of his fangs piercing her flesh she might have thought it all a dream.

An incredible, arousing, soul-shaking dream. One she did not want to wake from even though it scared her to the depths of her very being.

There was a lot of guilt attached to the satisfaction she felt whenever she was with Saint. Guilt because they had yet to find the killer. Weeks had passed since Saint's arrival and the killer was the one with the upper hand. They would find the bastard. And then Maison Rouge could rest knowing that its girls had been given justice.

Her mother was already in the front parlor where a small table had been set up for luncheon. She was fussing over the silverware placement and adjusting the ivory lace tablecloth even though Emily had already set the table with an efficiency Buckingham Palace would envy.

Ivy went to her mother and kissed her smooth cheek. "I am happy to see you up and about."

Her mother looked more frail than Ivy had ever seen her, but there was surprising strength in the hand that patted her own. "As am I. Thank you for giving me no choice."

Ivy smiled. "We'll get through this."

Madeline drew a shaky breath and nodded. "I know, but I feel so guilty for not being able to protect them. Those girls . . ." Her eyes brimmed with tears. "They were almost as dear to me as you are."

Ivy drew her mother close and held her for a moment, until the older woman withdrew from her embrace, composed and tearless once more. "I must concentrate on better things."

"Saint will find the man who did this, Mama. We must have faith in that."

Her mother eyed her suspiciously. "I remember a time when you were not so certain of his abilities. What has changed?"

Ivy shrugged. "He has proven himself dedicated to the cause. Are the injuries he sustained not proof enough for you?"

Madeline held up a hand as if to ward off attack. "My dear girl, I never needed proof."

No, she hadn't. Ivy turned away, embarrassed and confused. Her thoughts on Saint had changed so much. Her feelings had changed so much. She had gone from not trusting him to risking her life to save him so very quickly. How had this happened? It was more than infatuation. A girlhood crush didn't inspire such loyalty.

"Are you in love with him?" Her mother's question was like a blow to her already battered stomach.

"Are you?" She fired back, suddenly angry. Her mother should know better than to ask *her* that.

Her mother laughed as though the notion was so thoroughly foolish. "Dear God, child. No."

At that moment Ivy would have rather eaten

glass than admit to having feelings for Saint and risk her mother's ridicule, or worse, her pity.

She was saved from continuing the conversation by the arrival of Millie. Ivy had never been more relieved to see her former nurse, but her mother's question kept ringing in her head.

In love with Saint. Impossible nonsense. What she felt for him didn't feel like she thought the illusion of love would. And yet, she had already admitted that she would trade her life for his. That she would do anything to protect him and keep her with him.

That sounded like the terrible obsession her mother once fostered for her father. When Saint walked away, would she throw herself into a pit of despair as her mother had? Or would she beg him to take her with him when he left?

Either course of action made her feel sick. Fortunately, the feeling didn't last long in Millie's buoyant presence.

"How are the two of you?" Millie asked, bussing them both on the cheek.

"As well as can be expected," Ivy replied, giving her friend a smile. "You have certainly brightened our day."

"Yes," Madeline agreed, gesturing for them both to sit. "Other than those nasty people from the papers, you're the only company we've had."

Millie made a moue of distaste. "Has it been that awful?"

Ivy shot her an arch look. "They're saying Jack the Ripper is back and that he's a client here."

The older woman's dark eyes widened. "Oh, how awful!"

That, in Ivy's opinion, was an understatement, but she knew Millie was aware of the gravity of the situation and meant no offense.

Millie turned her attention to Madeline as Emily entered the room with a cart bearing their meal. "Will you have to close the house, do you think?"

"We're already closed because of mourning," Madeline replied as she assisted Emily in unloading the cart. "Once the killer is caught we will reopen."

Ivy didn't miss the reassuring smile her mother flashed Emily. There was something not quite right about it.

Apparently Millie shared the same thought because she waited until Emily had left the room before speaking again. "Are you entertaining not reopening?"

Madeline shook her head, spearing a bite of fish with her fork. "We have to. Some of these girls have no other place to go. But if the killer isn't caught I fear many of our regular clients will be afraid to come back."

"Afraid for their lives?" Millie's eyes were even wider now.

"Afraid for their reputations," Ivy replied dryly. "Being at the center of a murder investigation isn't good for discretion."

"The house will reopen," Madeline insisted, gazing down at her plate. "But under new management."

Ivy dropped her fork. "Excuse me?"

Her mother raised her gaze. It was clear and resolved—a look Ivy had seen many times in the past that meant her mother had come to a decision and would not be swayed.

"I'm retiring," Madeline announced. "The two of you are the first I've told. As soon as I can find a suitable replacement I will sign over management of the house—upon Reign's approval, of course."

Millie said something, drawing her mother's attention, but Ivy wasn't listening. She just sat there, dumb and astonished with her mouth gaping open. Why had her mother never said anything to her before this?

And then her mother turned to her, her expression a mixture of contrition and resolution. "Ivy, dearest. Reign has already approved you. Before I offer Maison Rouge to anyone else, I want to offer it to you."

To some women, the offer of a madamship and the running of a whorehouse might be insulting or at the very least, astonishing. To Ivy, however, who as a young child had played at running a brothel when other little girls held tea parties, the offer was only mildly surprising.

"I—"

Her mother placed her hand over Ivy's. "You don't have to say anything now. Think about it. You have a trust from your father to keep you for many years. You do not have to work."

Oh, yes, and Ivy intended to use that money well. At one time she had entertained giving it back, but spite made her keep it.

"But," her mother continued, "the girls here know you and trust you. The change would be easier for them to accept and if anyone can bring Maison Rouge out of this nightmare, I know it is you." And then her mother smiled as sweetly as only a loving mother could and lightly touched her fingers to Ivy's cheek.

"But Ivy might want to marry some day," Millie interjected. "There aren't many men who would accept his wife owning a brothel."

The words weren't said with any kind of malice, only simple common sense and honesty. Ivy smiled in response. "Then I will simply have to find one who can accept it."

Oddly enough two of them came to mind. Justin and Saint. Justin would stand beside her and help her run the business and not even blink. Justin, who always accepted her, always gave in to her wishes and who never told her what to do.

Justin, who never demanded that she not try to protect him as he would her. Justin, who never claimed to want her heart or her love—who never asked for anything at all.

And yet, it wasn't Justin she wanted to run to at the moment. It wasn't Justin she wanted beside her for the rest of her life.

It wasn't Justin at all.

When Saint awoke later that day he rose, dressed and left Maison Rouge via the tunnel entrance from his apartments. He did this for the simple reason that he didn't want Ivy to know he had gone out. She would only worry.

He had vowed that morning, somewhere between the bathtub and his bed, that he would put all he had into winning Ivy's heart. Old promises be damned. Love was the only thing that made immortality bearable. That meant convincing Ivy that love wasn't the awful affliction she thought it was. It also meant making himself more vulnerable than he had in two decades.

Vulnerability wasn't something he could afford until after this damnable killer was caught.

So he took the coward's way out of the house at sundown and ran through the tunnels that lay beneath the city until he found a good spot to surface, just blocks from his destination.

New darkness covered the city—that shade of

blue gray that didn't seem dark enough for street-
lights one moment and impossible to see in without them the next.

It was the kind of neighborhood where those
who belonged felt comfortable enough to sit outside on their steps, or stand on the street and be
social. Two women swapped stories over a shared
cigarette and yelled at their children to get out of
the street. A young couple—who didn't belong
there—brushed past him as they hurried to a waiting carriage. They didn't want to be there when
night finally took the city full against her bosom.

As for Saint, he felt full alive once the sun was
gone. The wounds from that morning had healed.
Only the netting scars remained, pink and delicate
on part of his forehead and cheek. His hands had
the worst of it, but he could flex his fingers without
much stiffness. By the next evening they would be
as healed as they were going to get for some time.
It would take years for the scars to fade and even
then they would never go away entirely. The cross
on his back was proof of that.

Good thing personal vanity had never been one
of his vices.

George had given him directions to the empty
warehouse where their prisoner was being held.
Even if Saint hadn't known the direction, he would
have known the site. He could smell the man's blood
from the street. Smell his anger and his fear.

Someday, he would catch the scent of the man who had hit Ivy, and then he would end that bastard's existence. But right now, he would be satisfied with this.

He entered the warehouse through a door in the back. George and the others were waiting inside, in a large empty room that was dark except for the light from the lamps outside. A bright ribbon of yellow fell across the dirty floor, onto the man tied to a rickety chair in the center of the room. His thigh had been bandaged and blood soaked the white linen.

Saint looked at George.

"We took the bullet out," the big man explained. "And cleaned the wound. He'll live—if you want him to."

The remark was not lost on the man, who might very well have shouted out were it not for the gag in his mouth.

"Has he said anything?" Saint asked, watching the man carefully.

George shook his head. "We've had the gag on him the whole time, waiting for you."

"Very well." Closing the scant distance, Saint moved to stand before his prisoner and yanked the rag from the man's mouth.

"What's your name?"

The man spat at his feet.

A humorless chuckle whispered from Saint's

throat. Leaning forward, he flicked his forefinger against the prisoner's forehead. For most it would have been a harmless gesture, but the man's head snapped backward under the force of the blow and hit the back of the chair.

"Seeing a few stars, aren't you?" Saint taunted as he smiled grimly. "Now, what's your fucking name?"

"Beatty. John Beatty."

"That's better. Now, Mr. Beatty, what is your association with the Silver Palm?"

Ezekiel hadn't much information for them, only that he'd heard reports of the Order of the Silver Palm making a resurgence of late—whispers of the society were popping up all over Europe. No one seemed to know what they were up to, which was hardly surprising given the secretive nature of the group.

No doubt feeling the sting of the welt sprouting between his eyebrows, Beatty didn't try to play tough this time. "I've been hired by them twice. That is, the boys I run with were hired by 'em."

"To do what?"

"Once to make certain some mucky muck got to the train on time and then to be in that alley this morning. They gave us the weapons and the net."

So the Silver Palm knew about vampires and they knew Saint was one. They obviously suspected he might show up.

"Why were you supposed to nab me?"

Beatty shook his head. "I don't know. He didn't tell us much."

"He who? The man who hired you?"

An eager nod. This Beatty was obviously not the brains of the operation. "Yes."

"What is his name?"

"I don't know. He didn't tell me and I didn't ask."

"Of course you didn't. What did he look like?"

"It was dark when we met. He wore a hat."

"Surely you saw something?"

"He had paint on his hands."

Paint. A painter. Torrent. Grim, deadly satisfaction tightened Saint's lips. "And he told you to go to that alley and wait for me?"

"I was supposed to get you. It's got something to do with the girl."

"The one I was with when you showed up?" Did that mean Eliza was supposed to be another victim? Had Torrent chosen her?

"No, the other girl. The bitch who shot me. It's all about her."

Saint's entire body went frigid, followed by a wave of heat so intense it felt as though he were on fire inside.

"What about her?"

"I don't know. I got the idea that she's special somehow. The gent who hired us won't be 'appy that Ned hit her."

Saint cocked his head to one side, a sardonic smile twisting his lips. "Poor Ned. But I think you're holding out on me."

The man shook his head, but there was something in his gaze. He was withholding something—something that might very well mean Ivy's life.

Then Beatty showed a surprising display of balls—unfortunately for him. "I hope they get her too. I hope she suffers."

Saint lifted the damp wad of cloth and shoved it back into the man's mouth. Then, he took one of Beatty's fingers in his own and snapped it, like he was snapping a twig. The gag absorbed the scream. Saint waited to the count of five before crouching and removing the gag once more. Tears streamed down the man's dirty cheeks. Saint was unmoved.

"Now," he said. "Let's try that again, shall we?"

"Where have you been?" Madeline demanded when Saint walked through the door two hours later. He was too tired to sneak through the tunnels this time. "My daughter pitched a fit when she found you gone."

"No doubt she found my room empty two seconds after sunset." He tried to smile as he sagged against the foyer wall, but his lips wouldn't do it. Spending an evening torturing a man who genuinely seemed to know nothing—including when to stop wishing death upon Ivy—had a way of sucking the humor right out of him.

"She was livid that you went out without telling her." Her shrewd gaze raked over him. "I take it you didn't find out much?"

"No." He ran a hand over his face. "I could use a drink, Maddie. Will you join me?"

"Of course, but do you really think a drink will have any effect on you?"

"It might if I drink a bottle or two."

"Good enough, then." She took his arm and steered him down the corridor. "I have a request of you, my dear."

Saint sighed. "This has to do with Ivy, doesn't it?"

"It does." His old friend gifted him with a faint smile—the first he'd seen on her face in days. "She's more fragile than she looks, Saint. Please don't break her heart."

"It's not her heart in danger of breaking," he replied, patting her hand. "She's an unfeeling wench, you know."

Madeline's smile grew rueful. "It's my fault she thinks of love the way she does. She's never seen real love and growing up here . . ."

"I brought you here. If you're going to blame yourself you may as well blame me too."

"You saved my life."

"And you gave your daughter the best one you

could. You do not have to see the air to know you breathe it. You do not have to see the truth to believe it and you do not have to have witnessed love to feel it. Ivy is just afraid."

"I don't think I've ever heard you speak so passionately before."

Somehow, he managed to keep a straight face. "Passion is what I do best."

She laughed at that. "You try so hard to play the rogue."

"Used to be a time when it wasn't playing."

"And now?"

He shrugged. It wasn't that he wanted a house or a wife or even a dog, but he wanted the feeling that came with that. He wanted . . . He wanted a home. He wanted a place to call his own and he wanted someone to share it with—forever.

They stopped just outside the parlor door. Madeline turned to fully face him, her lovely face marred by a frown. "Before we go in, you should know that Justin Fontaine is in there with Ivy."

Saint swore. "You might have mentioned that earlier."

"I'm mentioning it now so if Ivy tries to use Justin to make you jealous you won't kill the poor boy."

"Why the devil would Ivy do something so foolish?"

Madeline gave him a look that made him feel

incredibly stupid. "Because you abandoned her to-night and she needs to know you care about her half as much as she cares about you."

Sarcasm took over before he could stop it. "Only half?"

She pinched his arm. Hard. "She's my daughter."

Saint smiled at her. "And I adore her, Maddie. Very much."

She brightened like a newly minted penny. "Good." Then she opened the door and practically dragged Saint into the parlor behind her.

Ivy and Justin were standing together in the middle of the room. So close that a growl rose up in Saint's throat at the sight of them. When his gaze met Ivy's her eyes widened like saucers.

So much for hiding his feelings.

"Oh, you're back." Ivy's disapproval was as obvious as Fontaine's appreciation of her cleavage. And her cleavage was very impressive indeed in a heather-gray evening gown. It didn't make Saint think of mourning, not at all.

"So it would seem," he replied smoothly. "Good evening, Mr. Fontaine."

The young man bowed. He smiled at Saint, all youthful health and golden good looks. "A good evening to you as well, sir. I called on the ladies this evening because I heard about how you saved one of the girls from being kidnapped this morning. It seems you are a hero."

Saint didn't care why Fontaine was there and he certainly didn't give a flying frig if the boy thought him a hero or not. "Someone's been exaggerating, Mr. Fontaine. It wasn't nearly that fantastic."

"If you say so, but I feel compelled to thank you for all you've done to keep Miss Dearing and her mother safe."

Saint ground his teeth. "Well, Maddie and I are old friends."

"Yes, I know." A quick grin at the siren on his right and then, "You're practically an uncle to Ivy, are you not?"

Madeline coughed and Ivy looked as though she might laugh or scream, or both.

"I'm having bourbon," Saint announced. "Can I get something for anyone else?"

Madeline recovered enough to request a glass of wine and Saint went to the bar to pour it and his own. He had just taken the top off the crystal decanter of bourbon when Ivy joined him.

"Where have you been?" she demanded.

He really wasn't in the mood for this. It wasn't that he thought her wrong in her anger, but rather that he hadn't the energy to be the target of it.

He downed the bourbon in one gulp. "Questioning the man you shot this morning." He refilled his glass.

Ivy's cheeks paled as she glanced over her shoulder to make certain neither her mother nor

Fontaine had heard. "Keep your voice down!"

"Perhaps you can wait until later to flay me alive," he suggested. "We wouldn't want Fontaine to know that you shot a man rescuing the vampire you've been shagging, would we?"

Their gazes locked and he watched as her face became pinker and pinker.

He lifted his glass. "God, I want you."

Ivy blinked. And then she grinned at him—that sultry curve of her lips that she seemed to save just for him.

Before he could say anything else, Emily came into the room, followed by two constables.

"Begging your pardon, Miss Madeline," she said. "But these gentlemen would like to speak to Mr. Saint."

Ivy's stare was a confused and heavy weight, but Saint kept his own gaze fixed on the police. "Of course. May I ask what this is about?"

One of the men came forward. "Sorry to bother you, sir, but there was a young woman killed in the Covent Garden area earlier this evening and a witness saw you near the scene."

A witness, his arse. "That's impossible."

"You weren't in Russell Street this evening?"

Shite. That was where he had interrogated Beatty.

"You say a woman was killed?" he asked, avoiding the question.

The constables traded uneasy glances. "Like the other unfortunates of late, sir."

At Madeline and Ivy's twin gasps, Saint set his glass aside and quickly strode toward the men.

"Am I a suspect?" he demanded.

More uneasy looks. "I'm afraid so, sir."

"You'd better take me to the Yard then," he informed them. "It seems we need to talk."

Chapter 14

❦

It was true what they said about Hell and good intentions. Saint's had made him a murder suspect.

He sat at a little table in a little room where there was little light. What light there was was hazy and filtered through a fine fog of smoke. When one of the constables—the skinny one, MacKay was his name—offered him a cigarette he refused. Even if he enjoyed the habit, he didn't breathe like a human and smoking would just call attention to that fact.

"This won't take long, Mr. Saint," MacKay informed him in a thick Scottish accent.

Saint affected a careless shrug. "I have nowhere to be." So long as they were done before dawn—and he would make certain they were—he would be fine.

"Could you tell us what brought you to Covent Garden this evening?" It was Smythe, the plumper of the two, who asked. He coughed and shot his companion a dirty look. Obviously not a smoker.

"I was questioning a man I suspected of being involved in the murders." There was really no reason to clarify which murders he meant.

Smythe seated himself across the table from him, fixing him with an indignant glare. "Are you a constable, Mr. Saint?"

Saint smiled at the constable's not so subtle tone. "No need to get your knickers in a twist, son. I'm doing this as a favor to Miss Dearing."

"Ah, yes. The whoremonger." He watched closely for Saint's reaction.

Saint merely cocked his head to one side. Maddie had been called much worse. "Maison Rouge is a quality establishment, but then you know that, don't you?"

Smythe's cheeks reddened as the other constable turned to stare at him. "How would you know, Henry?"

The larger man didn't respond, but there would be plenty of explaining to do later as to just how familiar Smythe was with Maison Rouge. His name had appeared in the books several times.

Saint couldn't resist adding, "I'm not sure Madeline will be so hospitable the next time you stop by, constable."

Now the husky man's expression was positively devastated.

Leaning forward, Saint rested his forearms on the table and linked his fingers together. "Look, boys, we all know that when the first girls were killed, the Yard wasn't too concerned with two dead whores. It was the actress who got your attention—and the whispers that ole Jack had returned."

The constables traded guilty glances.

"I appreciate that now you want to find this bastard, but five women are dead." Five, the same number Jack the Ripper killed a decade earlier. Others were sometimes suspected to have been killed by Saucy Jack's hand, but not like those all important five.

A faint chill settled in Saint's chest. "And if I'm correct, he's done now."

"You mean *you're* done, Mr. Saint?" Smythe suggested.

Saint scowled at him. "Don't be an ass."

"Eh, now," MacKay interjected, stubbing out his cigarette in a saucer near Saint's elbow. "Watch your mouth. You were in London in 1888 weren't you, Mr. Saint?"

He fixed the constable with a bored stare. "I do not remember."

MacKay wasn't cowed. "I think you do. You would have been a young man then, but old enough to know how to gut someone."

Young? Saint almost laughed out loud. "The

first of these killings took place before my arrival in London. And the Ripper continued to kill after I departed London that summer eleven years ago."

"You seem to know a lot about these killings," Smythe remarked.

He turned his head to face the stocky detective. "And you do not."

Hands braced on the table, MacKay leaned down so they were eye level. "Why don't you enlighten us, Mr. Saint? That is your real name, isn't it?"

Saint rose to his feet, tired of this. They had nothing on him and they knew it. They couldn't hold him—unless they had a silver cage somewhere.

"The strongest suspect I have is a man by the name of Jacques Torrent."

MacKay scrunched up his face. "The painter?"

"Yes. I'm going to pay a call on him now." He smiled amiably. "Feel free to accompany me if you like. Unless you plan to lock me up?"

The constables traded surprised glances. Obviously they weren't used to suspects getting up and leaving in the middle of an interview.

"Don't think this means we trust you," Smythe informed him as the three of them left the room, the two constables flanking him tightly. "I know you're guilty of something."

Saint allowed himself a thin smile as he fought the urge to laugh. "Aren't we all?" he asked with mocking gravity.

Traveling to Torrent's lodgings with the constables proved an exercise in patience for Saint. He could have gotten there so much quicker on his own—and in a much more silent and stealthy manner. Six centuries had made him forget how noisy humans could be, even when they weren't trying.

They went by coach—with him sandwiched between the two men—as if the quarters weren't tight enough already. It was all Saint could do not to dig his nails into the scuffed roof and tear it open. After all these centuries one would think these old fears would have gone away, but they hadn't. Every time walls closed in around him—little walls such as these—he was reminded of what it had felt like, cramped in a box on a ship crossing the ocean, rats scurrying around him.

And then the ship had been shot out from under him and sank. And he, trapped in that box had gone into the cold, dark abyss in the fading daylight, sinking so far he hadn't known which way was up. He had been stuck in the box till nightfall. Only the fact that he didn't have to breathe saved him—that and the fact that the crate was fairly watertight. Then he had struggled to the surface, dark water crushing him. Thank God he had found a cave before the next dawn. A small dark cave that had been almost as bad as the crate, but it had kept the sun from killing him.

"You all right, mate?" MacKay asked him, an

expression of genuine concern on his narrow face. "You don't look so good."

"Feelin' guilty?" Smythe suggested.

Saint shot him a bored gaze—or rather, he hoped it was bored. It might have been one of pure panic. "I don't like small spaces."

"Then a jail cell is something you'd like to avoid, isn't it?"

"Fuck off, fatty," his voice was so low it was practically a growl.

MacKay laughed. Smythe did not. Saint closed his eyes and waited in tense silence for the torture to end.

Torrent lived not far from Covent Garden, in Russell Street. No doubt this had been convenient for his relationship with Priscilla Maxwell. Had it made it convenient for him to kill little Opal Gardiner—the girl found murdered that evening—as well? Opal had been killed in the same manner as the other victims, but so far she seemed to have no connection to Maison Rouge.

The landlady let them in as soon as she saw the uniforms Saint's companions wore. She even gave them the location of Torrent's rooms, but Saint already knew it. He could smell paint and brush cleaner drifting down from the second floor.

The constables followed him up the stairs, a fact that made him shake his head. As far as these two were concerned he was simply a normal human

man. They were the authorities—and should be in charge, but they were happy to leave all of that to him.

Wouldn't Temple—the undisputed leader of their little vampire brotherhood—get a chuckle out of that? The only time Saint had ever led was when he unlocked the door to the cellar hiding the cup that changed them all. That was why he worked alone, even as a thief. Having others depend upon him for their safety terrified him.

Upon reflection—and it was a bloody poor time to be reflecting on anything—that was probably why his love life always ended up in shambles as well. And why Ivy had made the wrong choice in asking him for help.

He would have no more reflection this evening.

When their little trio reached the second floor, Saint became aware of other odors—ones that were so commonplace they generally escaped his detection unless they were overpowering. They worsened as he approached Torrent's door.

Urine. Feces. The smell of death.

Saint cursed as he turned the doorknob. The door was locked, but one good shove opened it, gouging the frame in the process.

Smythe and MacKay followed him into the room, slipping around him when Saint stopped just inside the threshold.

"Christ," MacKay whispered on one side of him.

Smythe wretched on the other.

And straight ahead, Jacques Torrent's lifeless body dangled from a makeshift noose.

The painter was dead.

This development should have solved all their problems, but as Robert Burke, Baron Hess sipped his brandy at a secluded table at White's, he felt anything but satisfied.

"You are very quiet tonight, Robert. Are you troubled by the painter's death?"

Burke chose his words carefully. Hamilton, the man sitting with him, was an old friend, but he was also a Magus in their order, and therefore as much his superior in that world as a duke was in this. "His death was necessary. The situation was getting . . . out of hand."

Hamilton lifted his glass. In this light, with the shadows as they were, the man's eyes looked black as coal and just as stony. "The impulsiveness of youth," he lamented softly. "If only we could have the wisdom of our years and retain those bollocks."

Burke chuckled at that. "Amen."

"That is the end of it, then?" Hamilton reached inside his coat and withdrew a slim cigar case. "No more . . . unpleasantries?"

What a wonderfully polite way to put it. "No."

"Were we successful? It's not like last time?"

Burke shuddered at the thought of what had happened ten years before when that member of their order made himself a butcher of whores in Whitechapel. "Five were taken, just as the scripture calls for." One for each of the Sons of Lilith, as the Order liked to refer to the vampires who drank from the Blood Grail.

"Excellent." A match flared and was set to the tip of a long cigar. Smoke wafted, warm and fragrant. "A distasteful business, really."

Burke nodded. At least he wasn't the only one in the order who hadn't the stomach for bloodshed. Once upon a time their ancient brothers had studied thaumaturgy and alchemy, concerned with power of the magical and spiritual sort. Blood was part of it, yes, but not like this.

There should be honor in a kill, and blood should come from such honor, or a willing sacrifice.

No one could tell him those girls had been willing. They hadn't been willing ten years ago when he had to clean up the "Ripper's" mess. Of course, he hadn't thought that far ahead when he impregnated Madeline Dearing.

"You're thinking about the girl, aren't you?" Hamilton asked, giving Burke the eerie sensation that the old mage could read his mind. "Your daughter?"

Another nod. He saw no purpose in concealing the truth. "I was so proud back then, knowing I was offering so much to the Order. Now . . . well, now it's too late."

Shrewd eyes narrowed. "Would you change things if you could?"

This was the time to conceal the truth. "Of course not. The good of the Order is all that matters. If I could go back, I would do things properly this time, instead of going against the Order's wishes."

Hamilton nodded, pleased by the answer. "Soon we will have all the power we could ever dream of, Robert. It would not have been possible without your seed, and you will reap the reward for all you have given us."

At the cost of Ivy's life. Wisely he did not say this aloud. Years ago he had made Madeline Dearing his mistress with the intent of begetting a child with her. He had been chosen for the task by the Order, who needed the girl child of a fallen woman. When his feelings for Madeline made him question his devotion to the Silver Palm, he cast her aside because he did not want his child to be a pawn in the Order's quest for power. But she had come looking for him later. He offered to keep her, protect her if she only turned her back on her life and started a new one, where the Order couldn't find her. She refused.

And then the Order had found her and there was nothing he could do for her now. Even if he warned her, she was too close to the vampire to ever be safe now. And while he truly coveted the power she would bring them all, and was proud that his daughter was the chosen one, he wasn't so much a heartless cad that he didn't regret that the process would destroy the woman she was inside.

At least Rose, his other daughter, was safe, having a different mother.

Hamilton tapped the ash from his cigar into the crystal dish on the table. "What happened to the idiots who tried to take the vampire?"

"Dealt with, sir."

"Including the one Miss Dearing shot?"

He nodded, angry as the memory came back. That had been a close thing, that attack. His young friend had made a seriously bad error in judgment by trying to have Saint captured. "The vampire hadn't finished him, but I saw his corpse with my own eyes."

"Good. We cannot afford mishaps like that again."

"The impulsiveness of youth, as you said."

Hamilton exhaled a thin stream of smoke. "Huge bollocks, little sense, yes."

"The vampire will go where we want him. All we have to do is offer the right incentive." The words were bitter and sharp on his tongue. He took a long swallow of brandy to wash them away.

Hamilton turned his head, tapping the ash

from the end of his cigar. "Is everything in place, then?"

"Yes."

The other man smiled, thin and wide as the cat in that bizarre children's story by Lewis Carroll. "Very good, Robert. You know, I believe there just might be a spot among the magi for you after this."

Burke smiled, guilty that only a little of it was forced. "I would like that, very much."

And all he had to do to get it was watch his daughter go to her destruction.

"They're saying it was suicide." Ivy poured a cup of tea from the delicate china pot sitting on the low table before the sofa. "That Jacques left a confession."

Her mother shook her head as she lifted her own cup to her lips. They were in the parlor with some of the girls and Saint, who had brought the news of Jacques death upon his return from Scotland Yard. It was not quite midnight, early yet for Maison Rouge.

"I simply cannot believe Jacques killed my girls."

Ivy couldn't believe it either.

"Bastard," Emily muttered from her spot at the card table where she played at whist with Gemma, Anna and Mary. "I hope he rots."

Saint smiled. It was humorless, but not malicious. "Apparently Emily has no trouble believing it."

Her mother said something, but Ivy didn't hear it. She was watching Saint. He looked tired and drawn and she wanted nothing more than to go climb into his lap and hold him. Kiss him. Make him promise to never leave her side again.

Which was why she hadn't done exactly that.

When the constables had taken him she had almost gone mad with fear. What if they kept him until morning? What if those lunatics who had tried to take him before returned?

Justin had stayed with her for a while, but she felt oddly vulnerable pining for Saint in front of the friend who had made his own feelings quite clear, so she sent him away. When Saint finally returned she'd been so happy to see him she hadn't spared a thought for Justin, or poor Jacques.

But her sympathy extended only to the Jacques Torrent she had known—the temperamental but kindhearted artist with a penchant for lewd jokes and opium. Who never seemed the kind of man who would do something so horrible as he was now blamed with doing.

"Thank you for all you've done for us," Madeline told Saint. "It means so much to me."

Saint inclined his dark head, obsidian eyes glittering. "Anything for you, Mads."

The spider web of scarring on his cheek and temple didn't detract from the beauty of his face, it only made him look more dangerous. How odd that this man, who looked every inch a pirate, a rogue, was so very sweet and gentle and so open with himself.

At least, he was sweet, gentle and open with her.

She watched as her mother reached over and patted Saint on the thigh. It was an innocent gesture, but Ivy wanted to slap her mother's thin fingers. Saint was hers. Since his arrival he hadn't looked sideways at any of the girls there, despite their allure and openness to the idea. All of the Maison Rouge girls knew about the vampires—and knew that feeding them was a requirement. Saint never demanded it of any of them, even though he could have done so easily.

Why hadn't he? Out of respect for their grief, or because of her? She wanted it to be the latter and it scared the hell out of her.

She felt so . . . needy where he was concerned. In his arms she never gave that any thought, but these past few days made her see the ugly truth. She had almost lost him—twice—and it had revealed the weakness in her.

She had only wanted to seduce him and he had taken so much more than her body and her blood. Ivy didn't know how to get it all back. Didn't know if she wanted it back.

"I suppose you'll be leaving us now that Jacques . . ." Madeline paused. "Now that it's over?"

Ivy hadn't thought of that. She turned to Saint for his answer, trying to hide the horror she felt in anticipation of his answer.

He didn't look at her, but kept his gaze on her mother. "I suppose. To be honest, I have yet to give the matter much thought."

And then her mother glanced at her and Ivy knew the older woman saw what she sought to conceal. "Ivy, Saint, you will excuse me, won't you? Emily and I need to go over the menu for tomorrow."

And Emily, even though she seemed surprised by this new twist, didn't say a word. She simply rose to her feet when Madeline did and followed her to the desk on the other side of the room.

Well out of earshot.

Amusement twisted his lips as he shifted in his chair to face Ivy. "She never was very subtle."

"No," Ivy agreed softly, not sharing his amusement, though trying very hard to fake it. "You will be leaving soon though, won't you?"

Did she sound as dispassionate as she hoped? Somehow she doubted it.

He regarded her closely, carefully. "I suppose I will."

Ivy's heart broke.

"Unless," he continued quietly. "I've reason to stay."

She wanted to tell him yes, to stay, but she couldn't seem to make the words come out. They felt too much like begging.

Instead, she changed the subject. "Did you find any evidence linking Jacques to our mysterious order?"

He sat there for a second, still as a statue, watching her with an expression she couldn't read. It could have been sadness, regret or even relief.

"No. That is partially why I haven't thought of leaving just yet. Torrent might very well have been our killer, but I don't think he was alone in his actions."

So he wasn't staying just for her. That was good, wasn't it? It had to be better than it felt.

She pushed her own feelings aside. "It does seem a bit convenient that Jacques killed himself when he did."

"And that we found no evidence of his guilt at his lodgings." Saint shook his head. "What did he do with his treasures?"

Ivy arched a brow. "Treasures?"

"Yes," he replied, lowering his voice. "Those which he stole from his victims."

"Oh." *Those* treasures. Dear God. What would he have done with five wombs? It made her shudder with revulsion to even contemplate the possibilities.

"What do you suspect?" she asked, once the rolling in her stomach had passed.

He shook his head, a lock of sable hair falling over his tanned brow. "If Torrent did belong to the Silver Palm then he probably wasn't alone."

"Do you think they killed him?" If so, that meant they might still be in danger.

He leaned his elbow on the arm of the chair and set his cheekbone against his finger, supporting his head as he pondered the question. "Or they simply might have come in and cleaned up after him. Taken the evidence with them."

"Why would they do that?"

His gaze locked with her. "Perhaps they wanted his treasures."

Ivy prided herself on being fairly stoic, but these women had been her friends. "I think I might be sick."

Saint sat up and leaned toward her. "Drink some tea. We won't speak of it anymore tonight."

She took a sip, then put the cup down again. "I think I'll go to bed." She hated being so spleeny, but she needed time alone. Time to think and . . . think some more.

He took her cold fingers in his. "Shall I come to you later?"

The husky timbre of his voice, coupled with the neediness inside her sent a shiver down Ivy's spine. "Yes," she whispered, unable to meet his gaze for fear he'd see the desperation there. *Please*.

She stood then. She had to get away before she

did something stupid, like throw herself at his feet and beg him to love her or something equally humiliating.

But she did stop beside his chair—just for a second. Long enough to look down and meet his black gaze. "It will be nice to have you around a little longer."

Ivy didn't wait for his reply. She kept walking and didn't stop until she was in her room where she could feel like herself again.

It wasn't until she closed the door that she realized just how lonely feeling like herself really was.

Chapter 15

"**I** think I might retire."

Slumped in his chair, rumpled and wary, Saint looked up at Madeline's voice, but his mind was still on Ivy. "Are you tired, Strawberry?"

Ginger brows rose as she regarded him with obvious amusement. "Retire, Saint darling. From the business."

He straightened, watching her closely as she moved around him to sit in the chair her daughter had vacated not long ago. "But you love this place. The girls adore you."

"All that is true." She smiled, but there was no amusement in her face. "These murders—these losses—have affected me greatly, my friend. I don't want to go through this anymore. I just want to live a quiet life in a quiet cottage somewhere."

"But . . ." He had brought her to this place. It was true that years had passed since then, but he looked forward to her smile whenever he crossed the threshold and now she was going to leave?

"I'm not going to live forever." She smiled again, but with sympathy this time. "I want to spend what is left of my life doing all the things I want to do—not looking after other people."

The rest of her life. He didn't want to think about the fact that some day, Madeline Dearing would cease to exist.

"Have you chosen a successor?"

Her green gaze, shrewd and bright, stayed focused on his face. "Ivy."

"No." He made the command before he could stop himself.

Madeline didn't bother trying to hide her surprise. "I beg your pardon?"

He rubbed his eyes. "What about her photography? She's so talented."

"She's brilliant, but there's little money in that. At least with the revenue from the house she could afford to live while pursuing her dreams."

He couldn't argue that. "But, Maddie . . . the things she'd see. The men she'd have to deal with."

"She's seen me do it."

"But I don't—" He stopped. Just what the hell was he about to say? That he didn't think of Madeline the same as he did Ivy? That he didn't *love* Madeline as he did Ivy?

Madeline seemed very interested in what he was thinking as well. "You don't what?"

Saint shook his head, as much to shake some sense into it as to clear it of these thoughts. "Nothing. Ivy is the logical choice. She'll do you proud."

"Then I can tell Reign that I have your approval?"

"Reign doesn't care what I think."

"Of course he does."

He arched a brow in response. "He trusts your judgment."

She watched him for a few seconds more before asking, "Do you believe in fate?"

"I've believed in many things," he replied glibly, sinking lower in the chair as fatigue washed over him. "Immortality will do that to you."

"Answer me."

He rolled his head toward her. "I don't know. I haven't given it much thought."

"Don't you find it interesting that you brought me to this place, saving me and my daughter, never once laid a hand on me and then ended up sleeping with that same daughter?"

Good God, she knew about him and Ivy. He wasn't so old that he didn't feel as though he should apologize. "Interesting?" He hadn't given Ivy much thought when she was younger. He liked her, but as an adult did a child, never sexually.

"Yes. It's almost as though it was meant to

happen—you bringing us here so that you could be with her years later. It's as though you waited until she was full grown to return, and you do not have a sexual past with me to complicate things."

He stared at her. Fate? She had to be frigging joking. "I never slept with you because you were too good for me."

Ginger brows knitted fiercely. "Are you saying my daughter isn't?"

"No." Christ, why did women always have to jump to conclusions like that? "She is. But I can't say no to her."

"But you could to me."

He was such shit. "Yes."

Madeline didn't look the least bit offended. "I hear you gave money to Clementine's and Goldie's families. Daisy's too." She paused only for a second, not even time for him to reply. "Ivy would do much better running this place if she had someone to help her."

"I'm sure she'll have plenty of help."

"You could stay."

"And watch her grow old and die? No thank you." Why did he have to go and say that? He was so much like a woman—prattling about his feelings so easily. Why couldn't he just be a man and keep it all to himself?

"You could change her."

Now it was his brow that came together in a scowl that seemed as though it might cleave his skull in two. "Do you hear yourself?"

"If it's fate, how can you not?"

"Because it's not fate, Maddie. It's really fucking bad luck, that's what it is."

She was shocked. "How can you say that?"

"Because I'm still fool enough to believe in love. Love is the only thing that makes the risk of changing a person worth it, and your daughter—your very *mortal* daughter—doesn't believe in the emotion. To her this is nothing more than an affair."

"That's my fault." Madeline hung her head. "I raised her in this place and never taught her that this is not how it should be between a man and a woman."

"It's her father's fault for tossing you aside like garbage." It was true, but it also kept him from trying to blame himself for bringing Madeline to Maison Rouge in the first place.

Her lips twisted, her eyes bright with unshed tears as her bright gaze met his once more. "Perhaps he and I must share the blame."

Whatever irritation he felt with her evaporated. "You're a good mother, Maddie. Never doubt that. Ivy believes what she does because it keeps her safe."

"Safe?"

"She thinks it was love that got you tossed into the street."

"It was. He said he couldn't protect me."

Another frown—smaller this time. "Protect you from what?"

"I don't know. It was so long ago, but he told me I'd be better on my own. He even gave me money, but it was stolen along with everything else I had."

This was a side of the story he hadn't heard before. "Does Ivy know?"

The twist of her mouth turned bitter. "No. I was so angry at him that I wanted her to think the worst of him. It hardly seems worth it now, knowing what price she's paid for my pride."

"She's a good girl, Maddie. You raised her right."

"Do you love her?"

"I . . . could." It was the best answer he could offer.

"When you went missing she was frantic, do you know that? She had to bring you back here herself."

He smiled, puffed up despite his heart's warnings. "She's determined. I wonder where she gets that?"

Madeline smiled too and rose to her feet. "I think, if given the right incentive, Ivy could love you too. If she doesn't already."

And then she left him, with all the drama of a

Shakespearean heroine, to ponder that little tidbit on his own. He didn't ponder it for long—not sitting there at least. He jumped to his feet and left the room, needing to be away from these pumping hearts so he could think.

Ivy love him? Part of him actually wanted to pray for it to be true and another part wanted to pack his bag and run away as fast as possible.

He was passing the bottom of the staircase when he felt her. Her delicate scent flooded his senses. He could taste her in his mouth, bringing the familiar tightness to his gums—and to his groin.

Saint stopped and looked up. It was dark at the top of the stairs but he could see her standing there in the inky moonlight. She wore one of those ridiculously girlish nightgowns and her hair hung heavy around her shoulders. She was beautiful and vulnerable and he could no more walk away then he could make the sun stop rising.

He was halfway up the staircase before she even beckoned. And then she was in his arms and they were backed away from the stairs, into a little alcove that couldn't be seen from downstairs.

Barely an hour had passed since she left him in the parlor and it felt as though they had been separated for days. The sight of her, the feel of her igniting such longing inside him, such desperation. If he couldn't have what he wanted from her then he would take everything else—for now.

Her mouth was hot and lush beneath his, opening readily to the demands of his mouth. He tasted her, stroked her tongue with his own and let her explore the length of his fangs.

Backing her against the wall, he lifted the hem of her nightgown, running his hand along the satiny expanse of her thigh as soon as the garment was high enough to allow it. She trembled beneath his hand, her legs parting easily for his fingers.

Softly, he touched the soft, springy hair between her thighs, drawing his finger along the heated furrow.

"You're so wet," he murmured against her lips as he slid a finger into that tight, hot passage. "So ready." His other hand reached down to release the fastenings on his trousers, pulling the fabric aside so that his rigid cock was free.

Ivy smiled, more wanton and willing than any woman he had ever known as she moved against his hand, tugging on his finger with the tightness of her body. "I'm not the only one who is ready."

Reaching down between them, she gripped the length of him with strong fingers, pumping him with gentle, but firm strokes. Her thumb caressed the tip, teased the slit there until there was enough lubrication to moisten the head. She wasn't the only one trembling now. And when she lifted her leg to hook around his hip, drawing him closer, Saint withdrew his finger from her sweetly fragrant sex.

His hands cupped the soft mounds of her buttocks and lifted until she was at the right height for him. Then he watched, scarcely breathing as she guided his swollen length to the entrance of her body.

With one slow and easy thrust, he was buried to the hilt inside her, and they both groaned at the ecstasy of it. Saint glanced toward the stairs to see if by chance anyone had managed to sneak up on them while his senses had been overpowered by his desire for Ivy.

"You make me feel like a boy," he muttered, turning his attention back to the amazing seductress, squeezing him with the silken vice of her sex. "I could come already."

"But you won't." Her voice was a breathy whisper as her hips undulated against his.

Just the sound of her voice had him throbbing, but she was right, he wouldn't.

She moved again, wrapping her arms around his neck as she slid up and down on his cock. "You need to make me come first."

Oh, hell.

Saint shoved his hips, thrusting upward. She was so wet, so slippery and tight. And she made the most maddeningly arousing noises as she clutched at him.

"Then come for me," he urged, his voice little more than a hoarse rasp. "I want to hear it. I want to feel it."

Ivy gasped, her head falling forward as they moved together. Saint pulled her tight against him, controlling each and every movement with his superior strength. It wasn't long before he had her moaning in his ear, her sharp little teeth nipping at his flesh.

"Saint I . . . oh, God . . ."

"Say it," he growled. His finger slid between her sweet, plump cheeks, lightly stroking, delicately probing until he found another source of pleasure for her.

She gasped again and gripped him with her thighs. Then, she lifted her head so that he could stare into her heavy-lidded eyes. "I've never . . . felt like this before."

His heart leapt. His breath caught and inside her he pulsated so violently he knew the end was soon upon him.

He rubbed his cheek against hers. "Neither have I."

And then she shuddered in his arms, clenching his cock and finger. He turned his head, fastened his mouth on hers just as she came and swallowed the cries until they mingled with his own. It was only seconds after he realized he had pleased her that his own release tore through his body, robbing him of all thought except for how damn right it felt to be buried inside this woman.

They stood there for a bit, forehead to forehead as he held her off the ground. Her legs stayed wrapped around him, though not as tight and she clung to him like her namesake.

He was breathing heavily—something that amazed him. And there was a peculiar tightness in his chest that only worsened when Ivy feathered his face with soft, damp kisses.

"You're so lovely," she whispered, and his eyes burned. No one had ever said such a thing to him before. Never.

Saint didn't know what to say. He kissed her instead of saying anything. He withdrew from the warm cocoon of her body and set her on her feet, but only long enough to right his clothing, then he swung her up into his arms and carried her down the corridor to her bedroom.

Inside, he placed her on the bed and went to the bathing chamber to wet a cloth, which he used to bathe between her legs—as any considerate lover should.

"Why do you do that?" she asked. "Wash me, I mean?"

He shrugged. "So it is less messy—less distasteful for you."

She rolled her eyes—as he expected, of course. "I don't mind. I like feeling that part of you left inside me."

"You might not like it so much tomorrow morning when it's running down your leg."

She chuckled at his crass remark and he smiled as well.

When her smile faded, she gazed up at him from her pillows with eyes that were wide and a gaze that was painfully affectionate. Needy, almost. She stroked his arm. "Stay with me."

And he did. He lay beside her in her bed, holding her against him until dawn when he crept down into the safety and darkness of his apartments.

He was in his own bed for only a few moments before he heard her enter the room. She climbed into bed beside him, wrapping her warm slender arm around his torso.

"You can't escape me that easily," she murmured as she snuggled against him.

Saint merely rubbed his thumb across her knuckles in response, not trusting his tongue.

He didn't think he'd ever escape her at all.

"Are you going to take over Maison Rouge?"

Ivy hadn't expected Saint to ask such a question. "Who told you?" she asked, squinting up at him with sleep-bleary eyes.

He was sitting on the mattress, watching her with those unreadable dark eyes of his. "Your mother mentioned it last night. Are you?"

"I don't know." She struggled up to her elbows. "Does it matter?"

"Promise me that you will not give up your photography if you do take over."

"All right." Was this conversation real or a dream? It felt like a dream, but it seemed so real. "I wish she hadn't told you."

"Why?"

Her eyes widened at his vaguely suspicious tone. That and being awakened before she was ready made her snippy. "Because I wanted to tell you myself. What the hell is wrong with you?"

He sat back. "I just want you to be happy."

"You sound like you are saying good-bye. Are you leaving?" Her very soul screamed at the idea.

"I have to go out for a bit."

"That's not what I mean and you know it."

"I can't stay forever, Ivy. People will notice that I don't age."

She hadn't thought of that. She hadn't thought about "forever" either. Hadn't thought much beyond keeping him with her.

"Where are you going?" Better to talk about the immediate than the things she didn't want to face.

"Ezekiel's." He looked away. "He has something for me."

What "something" was dawned on Ivy like being doused with ice water. "You're going to feed. You're risking daylight exposure to go out to get blood instead of taking it from me."

He didn't deny it. "I think it's for the best."

"Because you have a need to cheat death on a daily basis?"

His gaze blazed with inner fire. "Because you've been through enough without me weakening you."

"I'm not weak."

He stood. "I'm not going to risk it." As he moved toward the entrance to the tunnels, she noticed that he was fully dressed. He could have left before this but he obviously wanted to speak to her before he went.

"Not going to risk me getting weak?" she asked as a suspicion occurred to her. "Or not going to risk getting attached?"

He didn't respond, just looked at her as though she should know the answer, stupid man. "I'll be back as soon as I can."

Some spiteful—hurt—part of her made her reply, "Don't hurry on my account." And she knew from his expression that her barb had done its damage.

Then he was gone.

Confused, hurt and seething, Ivy rose from the bed, cursing the male gender and immortal vampires for being so cryptic, thickheaded and cowardly. If Saint had something to say to her why not just come out and say it?

Why couldn't he just be honest like she was?

Because she was oh so very honest about *her* feelings. The thought was so caustic even she cringed at it.

She left Saint's room without bothering to make up the bed—let him do it and maybe he might spare a thought or two of how much he liked having her in it—and returned to her own bedroom where she bathed and dressed for the day.

No one said anything about her sour mood or remarked upon where she had spent the night. Everyone in the house had to know she and Saint were sleeping together, and yet in an establishment where sex was a business, no one dared mention the fact that Ivy was the only one not profiting by it.

"I was just coming to fetch you," her mother remarked as they met in the upstairs corridor. "Justin is here to see you."

Dear Justin. Lord, but she was in no mood to sit with him right now. She'd only be mean.

"Tell him I have a headache."

"I do not think that will dissuade him. He brought flowers."

Ivy's brows rose. "Flowers?"

Her mother nodded, looking less than impressed that her daughter was sleeping with one man and being courted by another. Of course, that could be Ivy's guilty conscious talking. "Roses, I believe. You had best find out what you've done to deserve them."

She wasn't immediately moved to action. "Did you tell him you wanted me to take over the house as well? Maybe the flowers are a premature congratulatory gift." It was meant to be a scathing remark, but her mother merely smiled.

"In a snit because I told Saint, are you? Well, I'm sorry darling. He's an old friend and I didn't think you'd mind."

"I don't mind you discussing it with him. I just would have liked to tell him first."

"Hmm. How very intimate of you. If I didn't know better I'd think you were falling in love with him."

Oh, not this again. "Where is Justin?"

"In the parlor of course. Where else would I put him?"

Her mother never allowed anyone who wasn't part of the house into the private rooms. Only the vampires were allowed to go wherever they wanted—mostly because no one could stop them.

"Then I will go see what I did to 'deserve' those flowers." With that, she picked up her skirts and hurried down the stairs, more eager to escape her mother than to see her caller.

Sure enough, he was waiting for her in the parlor, dressed in a dark blue coat and trousers that set off the gold of his hair and complexion. His hair was neatly combed, his jaw freshly shaven and slightly pink. And in his hand was the largest bouquet of fresh yellow roses Ivy had ever seen.

She'd never been a big lover of yellow, but she smiled anyway. "Hello, Justin. Are those for me?"

He grinned. "Ivy, you look beautiful this afternoon. And, yes, they are."

She accepted the flowers as graciously as she accepted his compliment and gestured for him to sit on the sofa where she joined him after ringing for Emily to put the roses in water.

"Now tell me, what have I done to deserve roses and you all trussed up in such finery?"

His blue eyes were bright as he gazed at her. So bright that it made her a little uneasy. He was looking at her as though she was some kind of gift from God—something precious and rare.

"I had thought to try to impress you with the flowers and maybe some pretty words about your eyes or your smile," he confessed, turning his whole body toward her. "But you're far too sensible for such nonsense."

She didn't know about that. She rather liked it when Saint told her how good she tasted or how her eyes reminded him of a jade statue he once stole.

"Why don't you just say what you came to say?" Even as she made the suggestion, she knew it was a bad one.

"Ivy," he took one of her hands in his much

larger ones, "will you do me the honor of becoming my wife?"

It was a little like being hit in the stomach with a pillow. It didn't hurt, but it knocked the wind out of her all the same.

"Justin, I . . ."

"I know it's sudden, but we're a good match, Ivy. I adore you and we have similar interests and many of the same friends."

"Yes, we do."

"I'd be a good husband. I don't mind if you continue with your photography, in fact I'd love it if you did. And I don't mind if you want to some day take over for your mother. I just want you to be happy, Ivy."

Oh, lord. Two men had expressed that same sentiment to her within a couple of hours of each other. And while Saint made it seem heavy and sad, Justin made it seem perfect. Too perfect.

And he went on to make it more perfect, "I don't care if we have children, that's up to you. As far as intimacy goes, I want it, but only if you are ready. I don't want anything you aren't willing to give."

"J . . . Justin," she stammered when it seemed that he was done. "I don't know what to say."

His fingers tightened around hers, warm and secure but not overpowering. "Say yes."

Ivy stared at him, unable to say anything at all. Here was this golden, beautiful man offering her everything she could ever want in a marriage, so why wasn't she saying yes?

She knew why—and the realization terrified her.

Because the one man—the one *im*perfect man— with whom she could imagine spending the rest of her life seemed positively determined to walk right out of it as quickly as possible.

Chapter 16

❧⟨✦⟩❧

The bottled blood Ezekiel gave him was stale but it satisfied Saint's hunger. He wanted Ivy, wanted the taste of her in his mouth, the strength of her in his veins, but he didn't dare risk it. He was already so addicted to her, giving in to the craving would only make it worse.

He wanted her. She wanted him. It should be so easy, and in a way it was. He had all the time in the world to win her heart. Unfortunately, time would eventually run out for Ivy and he would be alone again. Was it worth the risk of the pain that would follow? Yes. She would be worth every aching minute of it.

"I haven't heard anything, my friend," Ezekiel said, drawing Saint's attention as he lit a cigar. "Either the painter truly was your killer, or the real culprit has moved on."

Not moved on. Stopped. What purpose did killing five women serve? And there had to be a purpose because real killers didn't just stop. Real killers couldn't.

"Maybe it was Torrent after all." He took another drink from the bottle. Ezekiel discreetly looked away. "But it just all seems so neat, so convenient."

Ezekiel shrugged. "He could have been doin' it for someone else and they killed him once he was done."

"True. And that person or persons might not be in England at all."

Shaking his head, the old man ran a polishing cloth over a silver spoon he'd taken from a chest on the counter. "If that's the case, you'll never find out who was behind it."

That was disappointing. Saint didn't like disappointment.

"It's over." Ezekiel placed the spoon aside. "Where do you go from here?"

"I thought I might pursue this Order of the Silver Palm for a bit. They're in this deep and I want to know the reason." Whether by design, or by accident the lead was worth following.

Ezekiel frowned. "Torrent was probably one of them."

"I haven't found any evidence to support that."

"Maybe someone took it. Or maybe you're trying to make up a reason to stay in London a little while longer."

Maybe he was. "I promised Madeline I'd find the killer. I want to be certain the right man was punished for these crimes."

Ezekiel shrugged. "And here I thought you were doin' it for her daughter."

The empty bottle came down on the counter with a clatter. "I have to go. Thank you for the blood." He was tired of talking about his relationship with Ivy. And he didn't want to think about it anymore. He thought too much.

The old man eyed him shrewdly. "You'll be back before you leave town?"

Saint clapped him on the shoulder. "I wouldn't dream of doing otherwise." He didn't add that he didn't have any plans to leave just yet—not without Ivy.

He left the shop the same way he'd come, dropping into the dark tunnels below. Tonight, when he dared risk it, he would go to Torrent's apartments and search it again. His last attempt had turned up nothing, but it had been rushed what with the police about. He might find something Scotland Yard had missed, though it was highly unlikely. Either Torrent had a secret place where he kept the bits that he hid of his victims, or Ezekiel was right and he had been hired to do the job.

That brought him back to the original question— why go to such lengths to protect the deaths of five women—four of whom were prostitutes? What could they have possibly known? The last woman hadn't been part of Maison Rouge and she hadn't posed for Ivy, though it had turned out that she was an actress who was known to offer her company to rich gentlemen—for a fee.

Had Opal Gardiner posed for Torrent? That was something he would have to ask the constables at the Yard. Smythe would give him information, if for no other reason than that Saint had helped the constable clean up his vomit and hadn't told anyone that Smythe had been sick at Torrent's apartment.

He ran through the tunnels, twisting and turning beneath the city, crossing train tracks and ducking under sewage lines. It was a damp, rainy day and he had the damp feet to prove it. By the time he reached his room at Maison Rouge he was dirty and smelled of things he'd rather not smell of.

By the time he had showered and changed it was almost dinnertime. Food might not be necessary for his survival, but he enjoyed sitting at the table and engaging in conversation. He enjoyed being with Madeline and Ivy and the others. It made him feel as though he belonged, as though he was a part of this house.

That was a feeling he hadn't enjoyed for a long time.

The ladies of the house were already seated when he entered the dining room, all of them somberly clad in gray and black—and in some cases, lavender. Drab-feathered little doves who strove for some brightness by painting their faces and wearing colorful jewelry.

A chorus of voices rose in greeting at his arrival. Madeline rose and gave him a peck on the cheek and bade him to sit at the head of the table. Only Ivy didn't greet him. She didn't even look at him.

Saint frowned. He hoped she wasn't still sore about him leaving earlier.

He took the seat offered to him and flipped the snowy white tablecloth up so it didn't catch on his trousers as he slid into the chair. The air was warm and heavenly with the smells of succulent, pink beef, gravy and potatoes, sweet vegetables and rich wine. His mouth watered a little—mostly at the beef. Perhaps he'd have a little after all.

There was an energy to the little group that he hadn't sensed since his arrival. The girls were chatty but Madeline, and especially Ivy, seemed edgy—nervous.

"Mr. Saint, you won't believe what happened today," Agatha, one of the girls chirped from far down on his left.

Since Agatha hadn't spoken to him during his stay there unless he spoke to her first, Saint should have realized that something awful was coming.

"Oh?" He helped himself to the rarest slice of beef he could find. "What?"

"Justin proposed to Ivy!"

The girl had no idea how malicious she was being—that was obvious from the way the other girls were shooting daggers at her with their gazes. Agatha was simply excited; happy for her friend, and totally ignorant of the fact that Ivy and Saint had been having a relationship. But that didn't alter the fact that it felt as though she had stuck a silver fork between Saint's ribs and was twisting it as though trying to cut through a steak.

He kept the pain from his face and turned to Ivy with a gentle smile. "Are congratulations in order, Miss Ivy?"

Of course every set of eyes at the table were watching this exchange with interest.

She met his gaze, the wretched creature. Her jade eyes brimmed with . . . regret? And her cheeks were stained with blotches of bright crimson. Would she have told him on her own? Or would she have kept this little announcement to herself a while longer?

Ivy cleared her throat. "I have yet to accept." She sounded as awful as she looked. Good.

"Don't keep him waiting too long." He stared her straight in the eye as he spoke. "He won't wait forever." Not like Saint could. But he wouldn't. Perhaps Justin could be happy with sex and friendship, but Saint wanted more.

He demanded more. From her he refused to settle for less than everything.

The flush in her cheeks deepened as she looked away, driving that invisible fork a little deeper into his gut.

Saint raised his chin, glancing around the table with a forced smile that seemed frightening only to Madeline, who actually looked as though she thought he might go feral at any moment. "This calls for a bottle of wine—a good one. I'll go down to the cellar and find one for us."

He didn't wait for anyone to speak, he simply pushed back his chair and left the room, his body stiff with emotion—most of it rage.

He had no right to be angry. He had no claim on Ivy. He could tell himself these things, but he couldn't make himself believe it. She was *his*.

But underneath the anger was the pain of knowing that if Justin was who she wanted, he would let her go. He would always want for her what she thought best, even though it hurt like hell.

But Justin Fontaine was not what she wanted, the little idiot. She wanted *him*. The only thing that kept her from admitting that was her fear of being abandoned. As her father had abandoned her mother. As her father had abandoned her.

In the cellar he kept himself from punching holes in the walls by reminding himself that the women would feel the house shudder. So he stood in the darkness and closed his eyes, willing himself to be calm.

"Are you all right?" asked an all too familiar voice from the stairs.

She had an awful way of sneaking up on him. Or perhaps he had been hoping that she would. Opening his eyes, he turned his head to look at her. "Any reason why I shouldn't be?"

She stiffened at his tone. "I wanted to tell you myself."

"Then you might have waited before telling Agatha."

"I didn't tell her!" Her eyes were wide with insistence. "I think Emily did. My mother told her."

"No secrets in a whorehouse," he muttered as he turned to peruse the racks of wine, and almost laughed at his own absurdity. "My apologies." He rarely allowed anyone to refer to Maddie or her girls as whores, he would not allow himself.

Ivy stepped off the stairs and came toward him. "I haven't accepted him." She looked at him as though wanting his approval.

"Tell him no."

"Why?"

Face impassive, he turned the full force of his gaze on her. "You know why. Because you belong to me."

Her delicate jaw tightened. Not quite the declaration she had been expecting, obviously, but what kind of declaration did a man make to a woman who claimed not to believe in love? "Belong to you? You ass."

"Perhaps." Finding a suitable vintage, he pulled it from the rack and wiped the dust off. "But it's true. The only reason you'd marry Fontaine is because you're afraid of what you feel for me."

Some of the color left her face at that remark, but she neatly sidestepped it. "At least Justin won't remain young while I grow old. I won't have to worry about him running off with someone younger."

A sardonic smile twisted his lips. "Because mortal men never stoop to such behavior?"

She looked away, proving that there was more to this than her flimsy argument intimated. "I would stay by your side until the end," he informed her, the words cutting him to the quick.

Her gaze whipped back to his. "We wouldn't last that long," she said bitterly. "Your interest would wane as soon as I lost my youth."

"Don't presume to know what I would do." She was pissing him off by lumping him with every arse she had ever known, by comparing him to her father. "And you could have eternal youth if you wanted it."

"And be a vampire?" As though he could mean anything else.

"Yes." It was not an offer he made lightly. In fact, it terrified him. He was offering her forever if the change took. But he knew all too well the consequences if it didn't.

She brushed the gravity of what he offered aside

with a shrug, callous wench. "You'd grow bored eventually. Men do."

"And yet you'd marry Fontaine."

"I don't know. Perhaps." How could she look him in the eye and say these things? "Justin would make a good husband. We'd have children together. Grow old together. He'd never claim to own me."

"You're not afraid that he would leave you?"

She shook her head. "No."

It made sense then. She wasn't afraid of marrying Justin because she knew there was no risk to her heart. She wasn't doing this to hurt him, but to protect herself. "Fontaine won't make you feel like I do."

"You don't know that."

He chuckled mockingly as he placed the bottle of wine in her hands. "Yes, I do. And so do you. He won't love you or demand love in return. If that's what you want, then you'd better accept his proposal." He started to move past her, but stopped long enough to whisper near her ear, "Because I, my dear Ivy, won't settle for anything less."

Ivy didn't see Saint again after he placed the bottle of wine in her hands and turned his back on her. He went into his apartments and when she tried to follow shortly after, she found the rooms empty. He was gone, leaving her to face the dinner table alone, feeling like a barrel of trash that had been kicked until it was ready to burst. But she went back, and she gave the table some excuse about Saint having to go out. A few pitying looks were shot in her direction, but no one said a word, and she was left for the remainder of the dinner with little else but her own thoughts to plague her.

Justin was the better choice—at least he should be. Life—eternity—with Saint was impossible to contemplate. If she allowed him to make her a vampire she would have to drink blood and would never see another sunny day in Hyde Park again.

But she would be with Saint. Forever. There was a terrifying thought. What if he didn't want her after a few years? What if she didn't want him? What if he made her so dependent upon him that she was lost without him? What if she finally figured out how to give him her heart and he tossed it back to her?

She would have to trust him not to hurt her. She would have to give in and make herself vulnerable to him. She didn't know if she could do that.

She didn't know if she *wanted* to do that. Saint made her feel like no one ever had before. She loved being with him, loved his sense of humor and his romantic nature. She loved the feel of him, the scent, the taste. A night without him in it was . . . well, just another night. When she was with him she never thought about the sun, never thought about Hyde Park. She thought only of how right it felt to be with him.

But he asked for her love. How did she give him that, when she didn't even know if she was capable of feeling it?

Justin was the better—no. Justin was the safer choice. She should just tell him yes, but she couldn't.

There were so many changes happening in her life right now—so many choices to make. At least there was one she was certain of.

She made the announcement after dinner the following evening, while she, her mother and the girls were in the parlor having wine and talking. Saint hadn't joined them that night. In fact, she hadn't seen him in over twenty-four hours.

Ivy stood and smoothed the front of her gray gown. "Ladies, I have something to say."

Voices died to a hush as all eyes focused on her. She smiled at every one of them—her friends. Her sisters.

"You all know that my mother has been entertaining the notion of retirement." A soft chorus of disappointment met this statement. "She has asked me to take over management of Maison Rouge, and I've accepted."

This time the girls were more enthusiastic with their voices. One by one they rose from their seats and came forward to congratulate her and Ivy's smile grew with every hug.

It was amazing. Not one of them seemed upset that she had been chosen over them. It was as though they had all expected that this was how it would be a long time ago.

Only one seemed less pleased than the others, and that was due mostly to the look of confusion on her face. Agatha turned to Ivy with a small frown. "If you're taking over the house, does that mean Mr. Fontaine will live here as well?"

Ivy shrugged. "I haven't given him an answer to his proposal yet, but that is something we will have to discuss if I accept." It wasn't something she wanted to discuss in front of everyone, so she resolved not to say anymore on the subject.

And then Matilda spoke, asking the question that Ivy suspected everyone else wanted answered as well. "What about Mr. Saint?"

"What about me?" Saint entered the room like a pasha entering his harem.

Heat climbed Ivy's cheeks at the sight of him. "We were just wondering where you were."

It was obvious from the look he gave her that he knew that was a lie. "I checked with my friend to see if he had learned anything new that might help with the murders, but he hadn't. It's looking more and more like Torrent was indeed the killer."

That started murmurs among the girls. Mary started to cry. She had always like Jacques and Priscilla. Poor thing.

"Do you believe he did it?" Ivy asked him. She didn't care what Scotland Yard thought. If Saint believed then she would as well.

He rubbed the back of his neck. "It seems rather neat to me, but it hardly matters. There won't be anymore murders."

"How do you know that?"

Another glance—shorter this time. "Torrent wouldn't be dead if there were going to be more."

He had a point. If Jacques really was the killer then he certainly wouldn't be hurting anyone else, and if he was just a patsy, then the job must be done.

"What about the Order of the Silver Palm?"

"It's over, Ivy." The glance he tossed her was tired, so very tired. "Whatever it is they were do- ing, it's over. Torrent is dead. I checked every lead I could while I was out, there's no trace of the Palm left here in the city. They've either left the city or are very good at hiding. There's nothing more I can do."

"So it doesn't matter if Jacques was innocent?"

"Torrent is dead," he reminded her harshly. "He either committed the murders or was meant to take the blame for them."

"That might be good enough for you, but not for me."

Saint looked at her as though he could see inside her. "He painted all of them. We thought you were the connection but you weren't. You can absolve yourself of that guilt."

Damn him for knowing her so well. "I suppose if this is all over, then you'll be leaving London soon."

His gaze broke from hers then and moved around the room, meeting each inquisitive stare. She had forgotten where they were, and that they had an audience.

"How long I remain in London hinges on several things."

Ivy wanted to ask what, but it would be rude. Not only that, but she was afraid of what he might say in front of the others. She remained silent, however, even when he joined them for dinner. He talked to her mother and to the girls, but he left her alone and she hated it.

But she hated wanting his attention even more.

After dinner she excused herself from the table without having dessert—normally her favorite part—and went to her studio. It was quiet there, the smells comforting. The memories were anything but. All she could see when she looked about that tiny room was Saint. She remembered taking his photograph, remembered him kissing her. Remembered the night they'd made love for the first time.

At one time she thought that was all love was—the joining of two bodies. Now, she wasn't so sure.

Whatever it was, it was awful. She would never feel this terrible with Justin. She would never want Justin this badly.

Behind her the door creaked open. She knew who it was without turning.

"It's not like you to run away," Saint remarked.

"I'm not the one running." She turned to face him. "You're the one who's going to be leaving soon."

He closed the door and walked toward her. "Shall I stay?"

She shrugged. "If that's what you want."

A dry chuckle escaped him, but there was little humor in it. "You cannot bring yourself to ask me to stay, can you?"

No. She glanced at her feet before returning her gaze to his. He deserved her honesty, if nothing else. "When I was a girl I would have given anything to have you want me as your own. In fact, when you first came back I hated having those feelings resurface."

"And now?"

"Now I'm scared."

"Scared that I will behave like your father did, or that I won't?"

"I don't know."

He came closer, overwhelming her with his heat and his scent and his presence. It would be so easy to just melt into his arms. Too easy.

"Tell me to stay," he urged as his arms closed around her. "Tell me and I'll risk wondering if some day you'll grow tired of a man who cannot go out in the sun. I'll risk watching you grow old and die. I'll do this if you ask me to."

Good God, how could she ask that of him? It sounded so awful! And yet, it sounded so terribly inviting. "That's not fair to you," she whispered against his chest.

His arms fell from her back and his fingers came up to grip her shoulders. He pushed her away, so that she was forced to meet his gaze. Black eyes bore into hers, so earnest and bright it hurt to look. "Tell me you don't want me."

Ivy gazed at him with blurry eyes, defiance driving her as her heart slowly broke. She was such a coward. She opened her mouth to respond, but no sound came out. She couldn't lie to him. She couldn't say that she didn't want him.

His hands came up to cup either side of her head, pulling her to him for a kiss that robbed her of speech, of breath. His lips bruised hers as she struggled to match his movements. She clung to his arms, throwing everything she had into the kiss, teasing his mouth open with her tongue. She thought for a moment, when his body pressed against hers, that he was going to do more than kiss her. She wanted him inside her, wanted that connection.

He wasn't going to give it to her and the realization left her empty inside as he let her go.

"You want more than I am prepared to give," she told him, nearly choking on the words.

He flinched as though she had slapped him. Ivy forced herself to stand still as the distance between them grew physically and emotionally. All she had to do was let him know just how very, very much she *needed* him with her and she could have him. So why couldn't she do it?

But for all his talk of feelings, Saint hadn't told her that he needed her and she was too terrified, too determined to not be weak and vulnerable to make the first move.

He paused at the door, and threw her one last glance over his shoulder. "I can love you for the rest of your life, Ivy Dearing—mortal or immortal. Remember that when you give Fontaine his answer."

Then he opened the door and went through it, leaving Ivy standing there. She couldn't move. She couldn't speak. If she could, she might have been able to stop him. Instead, all she could do was stand there and weep as he walked out of her life.

Chapter 17

❦

"**Y**ou're not going out again?"

Saint closed his eyes at the sound of Madeline's voice. *Merde.* He should have gone out through the tunnel, but he needed to feel the night on his face.

He flashed her a tight smile. "Yes."

She stopped him with a hand on his arm as he tried to leave. "Did you speak to Ivy?"

Sighing, he turned fully to face her. "Yes. And then I spent twenty minutes pacing my apartments trying to work out whether or not I should go back out to her cottage and kill her or kiss her."

Faint amusement shone in his friend's eyes as she made a point of visually inspecting his person. "I see no weapon, so shall I assume you're going to kiss her?"

"I don't need a weapon," he reminded her sourly. "And no, I'm not going to kiss her. I'm going out." The kiss he and Ivy had shared earlier would have to do.

Madeline's good humor faded. "To do what? Feed, fight or fuck?" He winced at the sharpness of the word. "Saint, you're not going to do something you'll regret are you?"

"I usually do, Strawberry." He rubbed his neck. "I'm going back to the city—see if I can't find out anything more about the killings so Ivy can have peace of mind."

Pleasure softened her face. "You love her. I knew it."

Saint sighed. There was no use in denying it. "That doesn't mean I'm not still tempted to kill her."

"She loves you too."

He moved closer to the door. "No offense, but you have no way of knowing that."

She stopped him again. "I'm her mother. I know how my daughter thinks and feels."

"Then perhaps you might enlighten her as to just what those thoughts and feelings are." He pulled free of her grip. "Mads, I really need to get out of here. You can lecture me all you want later."

A mixture of sadness and understanding shone in her eyes as she nodded and pulled her hands back to fold in front of her. "Be careful."

They shared a glance and then Saint nodded. "I will."

As he reached for the doorknob, there was a knock from the other side. The door opened to reveal Justin standing on the step, finely dressed and freshly shaven, carrying a wrapped canvas under his arm. He looked surprised to see both Madeline and Saint standing there, but he managed a smile regardless.

This was the man who would spend his mornings waking up next to Ivy. This was the man who would give her children and a normal life.

All it would take was one quick swipe and Saint could rip his throat out.

"Good evening," Saint said instead, gritting his teeth.

Fontaine kept smiling, oblivious to Saint's murderous regard. "Good evening to you, Mr. Saint. Mrs. Dearing. I've come to see Ivy. Is she home?"

"Come in, Justin," Madeline said, holding out a hand in a gesture for him to enter. "I will check on Ivy for you." As she turned to leave she spared Saint one last glance and a pat on the arm. "Give my regards to Ezekiel."

It was an exchange Fontaine didn't miss. He closed the door behind him, a curious expression on his fair face. "Are you leaving?"

Saint lifted his head and forced a small smile. "For a bit. Business that can no longer wait."

"I've said it before, but I do want you to know how grateful I am for all you've done for Ivy and her mother."

The boy was so gracious it was next to impossible to hold on to any real hatred for him. That didn't stop Saint from wanting to remind the idiot that he didn't owe him any thanks. Saint had done what he did for Maddie and Ivy and no one else.

He should just go, but he couldn't bring himself to leave, not just yet. "Speaking of Miss Dearing, I hear there may be wedding bells in your future." If only one of the bells would fall on the idiot during the ceremony.

Fontaine grinned again. "I hope so, sir."

This was about all Saint could stand. Fontaine was probably older than Saint had been when he drank from that cursed cup and became a vampire, and yet Fontaine talked to him as if he were an old man. If Saint remained there any longer he really would kill the foolish bastard. "Well, good luck, Fontaine."

Justin offered his hand. "Good evening, Mr. Saint."

Saint accepted the handshake—with a little more force than he should have. Fontaine's hand was saved from being damn near broken by a sharp burning sensation on Saint's palm. The boy's ring. He had forgotten Fontaine had silver on his finger.

Saint didn't flinch even though his flesh was seared. He withdrew his hand from the other man's with a faint smile. "Good night." There was nothing else to say. Fontaine didn't know what he was and wouldn't be offering any apologies for burning him and Saint really didn't want to be there any longer. Not when there was a good chance that Madeline might return with Ivy in tow.

He was closing the door behind him when he heard Madeline return to the foyer. "Ivy will meet you in her studio, Justin."

Saint closed the door. As he walked away he didn't wonder what Ivy was going to say to Justin when the young man proposed again. He already knew what her answer would be.

"I'm sorry to have kept you waiting," Ivy told Justin when he walked into her studio. After her mother left she had dried her eyes and splashed some water on her face. It improved her appearance somewhat, but it was obvious that she had been crying. Her mother had offered to send Justin away, but Ivy didn't want to make him wait for her answer any longer.

Justin's smile faded as he drew closer. He was dressed as he always was—impeccably. He looked smooth and warm and golden and Ivy was struck with the craving for rough, dark and swarthy.

"Seeing you is worth the wait," he told her. Ivy's stomach roiled at the sincerity in his words. "But Ivy, whatever is the matter?"

She tried to smile as she stepped farther into the studio. As of their own accord, her hands nervously smoothed the front of her gown. "I'm fine. Please do not concern yourself."

Her gaze fell upon the chair where Saint had first made love to her and she remembered his mouth on hers, his velvety gasp as he slid inside her. She remembered feeling so full of him, physically and emotionally that she thought she might burst apart.

"Ivy, my dear. You do not look fine."

No, she wouldn't if her cheeks were as flushed and her eyes as bright as she thought them to be. "I suppose it must be the stress of the last few weeks."

He came to her, put a comforting hand on her arm. His fingers were firm and warm, but they didn't make her tingle. Didn't make her want to curl into him and hide from the world.

"That's all over now," he said soothingly. "You do not have to be afraid anymore."

"But that won't bring my friends back." Tears burned her eyes as her gaze met his and she didn't care. "It doesn't change what happened."

"Shh." Justin took her in his arms, resting his chin on her hair. It felt nice to be held. Nice to be comforted, but that was the extent of the emotion Ivy felt at his embrace. "They're in a better place now. Nothing can hurt them anymore."

His words gave some comfort. "I hadn't thought of that. Thank you." Then she straightened and he released her.

"I have something for you," he said, once again breaking what might have grown into an awkward silence. She had no idea what to say to him; her mind was still reeling from Saint's departure. It seemed as though she was incapable of thinking of anything but him for any length of time.

"You shouldn't have," she replied weakly, but she meant it. She didn't want or deserve gifts.

What she wanted was Saint. Ever since he had left her alone in the cottage she had felt as though she was hollow inside. She kept thinking of what he said to her; that he would have loved her for the remainder of her life.

Did that mean he loved her now? Why could he believe in such an emotion and not she? He didn't seem weakened by it at all even though admitting such things to her surely made him vulnerable.

God, it made her head spin.

"Open it."

Her head jerked up. Justin was standing before her, holding out a wrapped, flat package. Woodenly, Ivy took it and untied the string that held the paper closed around it.

The paper fell away to reveal a painting. She recognized it instantly because she was in it. She remembered posing for it as clearly as if it were only yesterday.

"It's the painting Jacques did." Brow knitted, she lifted her gaze to Justin's. How had Saint missed this one when he explored Jacques's apartments? "How did you get it?"

He looked almost apologetic. "I got it from Jacques shortly before he . . . died. The paint wasn't completely dry or I would have given it to you then. Didn't you notice that I walked around for days with paint smudges on my hands?"

Ivy shook her head, dazed and frowning. "No."

"I wasn't certain whether I should give it to you after that, but I thought you might want to have it."

Her scowl grew as she handed it back to him. "I'm sorry, Justin, but I don't want it."

Justin looked surprised, but he took the painting from her, glancing at the image there. "Why ever not? It's beautiful."

"Jacques was involved in the murders. I don't want anything of his."

Now he looked hurt. "But you and I are both in it, Goldie too. Remember? He asked all of us to pose in the garden that day?"

All she could do was shake her head. She didn't want it anywhere near her. Saint would know what to do. What to say.

Justin set the painting on the bed. "My apologies. I never meant to upset you."

Now it was she who hugged him. He smelled so clean and proper. There was no spice to his skin as there was to Saint's, no hint of danger or darkness. "I know. It was a lovely thought and I appreciate it, really. It's too fresh for me right now. Too painful."

He was stiff as he nodded. "Of course." She released him then, realizing that he didn't want her to comfort him as though he were a child.

Ivy sighed and rubbed at her eyes with her palm. "I'm sorry, Justin. I'm not good company tonight."

The weight of his gaze fell upon her. "It has to do with Saint, doesn't it?"

She wasn't going to lie. He deserved better than that from her. "Yes."

Some of the brightness left his eyes. "You love him."

She turned away, hands pressed against her stomach to quell the fluttering there. "I don't know."

"Does the thought of never seeing him again make you hurt inside?"

Ivy closed her eyes, not at the roughness of his voice, but at the way his question struck the very quick of her. "Yes."

"Does the thought of him with another woman make you ill?"

Her stomach clenched and rolled. "Yes," she whispered.

"Would you do anything to have him with you right now?"

"Oh yes." She almost choked on the words. Anything—her soul, even her pride. Damn him.

"Now, let me ask again, Ivy. Do you love him?"

The answer came, like the opening of the heavens for a heavy rain. She thought it and knew it for the truth deep inside. No fear, only certainty.

"Yes." She turned to face him. "Oh, Justin. I'm so very sorry."

"Do not apologize for your feelings." He smiled ruefully. "I realize they cannot be helped."

Only guilt for hurting her friend kept Ivy from shouting her jubilation from the rooftops. It was as though finally admitting the depth of her emotion for Saint set her free from a prison she hadn't been aware of. She loved him and she knew that he loved her too. She could think about it and dissect it forever, but she knew it in her bones. And now that she made herself admit it, it didn't scare her anymore.

She had to tell him.

"Justin, I truly am sorry for misleading you, but I have to go." Hiking her skirts she sprinted toward the door.

"He's not here," Justin called behind her.

Ivy stopped so quickly she actually slid a few inches before stopping. "What? Where is he?"

Justin's handsome face hardened a little, as though he was making a difficult decision. "I know where he went."

Hope blossomed in her chest. "Where?"

He stood in the center of the room, shaking his head. "I wasn't going to tell you. I was going to wait until your pain lessened and try to woo you again, but I can't do that to you. I care for you too much." He lifted his gaze to hers once more. "I'll take you to him."

Ivy stared at him. It was just as well that she hadn't accepted him. He was obviously too good for her. "You would do that?"

"For you? Yes. I would do anything for you."

More tears, but happy ones this time. "Oh, Justin!" She threw her arms around him. "You truly are the best person I know. Someday you will find the right woman for you, I just know it."

He touched her cheek, his face full of regret. "So do I."

Another search of Jacques Torrent's apartments yielded nothing more substantial than dust and a few blond hairs. Torrent had been dark, so the hairs weren't his, and they were too short to be a woman's. There was also a portrait of Opal Gardiner. How Saint had missed it before he didn't know, but it was there among the others, with the title "Rahab"—the prostitute who helped the Israelites conquer Jericho—on the back.

After leaving Torrent's he went to a couple of pubs around Whitechapel, trying to sniff out any

mention of the Silver Palm. There was nothing.
He went to Ezekiel's after that. He needed to put
as much distance between himself and Ivy as he
possibly could. Otherwise he was likely to go back
to Maison Rouge and beg her to love him. And if
anyone would have heard something, it would be
his old friend.

"You look like hell," Ezekiel said as soon as he
saw him.

Saint merely smiled. "I feel it. Do you have any
information for me?"

He shook his head. "You still riding that horse?
I am sorry, Saint, but I haven't heard anything new.
The Silver Palm has disappeared like a whore's
cherry."

So it seemed. All evidence of them ever having
a chapter in the city seemed to have evaporated.
Saint wasn't used to being duped so thoroughly, in
fact he despised it.

All that was left was for him to return to Maison
Rouge then. If he was wrong about Ivy's feelings
for him and she had accepted Fontaine he would
pack his belongings and leave London as quickly
as possible.

Or, he could rip Fontaine's throat out and give
Ivy no choice but to be with him. Somehow, he
didn't think the latter would work, although it was
by far his favorite of the two.

"This may be the last time we meet for a while,"

he told Ezekiel. "I will send word once I've moved on." If he moved on.

Ezekiel offered his hand. "Take care of yourself, my friend."

It wasn't until Saint put his hand in the other man's that he remembered the burn from Fontaine's ring—or rather the sting in his palm reminded him.

He looked down when his hand was free, investigating the mark on his flesh. Then his chest tightened and the entire world pulsed and blurred around him.

Burned into his skin was the perfect outline of a chalice. Just like the one left on Daisy's cheek the night she was murdered.

Justin Fontaine was a member of the Order of the Silver Palm. He was part of the group who had killed Ivy's friends, who had violated the sanctity of Maison Rouge and tore Daisy apart in her own bed—where she should have been safe.

The blond hairs he found at Torrent's could belong to Fontaine. If so, then Fontaine had killed Torrent. Not just Torrent, but the women as well.

He was also with Ivy at this very moment. Alone.

"I have to go," he said to Ezekiel, as he bolted for the door. Outside he hurled himself into the sky, not caring if anyone might be watching. Normally he was more cautious, but not tonight. Normally he was thankful for his gift of flight. Now he simply wished he could fly faster.

When he touched ground at Maison Rouge he went straight to the back of the house to Ivy's studio. The door was unlocked and he walked in without knocking.

"Ivy?"

There was no answer. There was no sign of life in the little cottage. Only the sweet scent of Ivy on the air alerted him that she had indeed been there. And so had Fontaine.

And despite the dark circumstances, he had to admit to being relieved that the studio smelled of photography chemicals rather than sex.

And then he saw it. Sitting on the bed was a painting. The same one Fontaine had under his arm when he came calling earlier? Saint crossed the floor to look at it.

It depicted a seductive woman in a gauzy dress being ordered from a paradise by God. Behind her stood a man, looking all too satisfied to see her go, with another, meeker woman on his arm.

Only because he was familiar with the subject did Saint recognize the work for what it was. It was Lilith being ordered from Eden for refusing to accept Adam as her superior. She was the mother of vampires, the original fallen woman. It was her blood that ran in Saint's veins and had made him what he was.

And she had Ivy's face. And Adam was Fontaine, looking smug and arrogant as Goldie clung to him as a timid Eve.

He didn't need to look at the signature to know who painted it, but he did anyway. It was one of Torrent's and it literally stopped his heart.

All of the dead women had been either photographed or painted as seductresses—fallen women. Fontaine had to know this and now he had Ivy.

Fontaine was the killer and he wasn't done.

Ivy was next.

Chapter 18

"Will we be there soon?" Ivy asked Justin as they jostled along the darkened road. He didn't look at her. "Soon."

Perhaps it was just nerves, but it seemed to Ivy that they had been driving forever by the time they finally stopped. They were in Justin's motorcar, which he claimed would get them to Saint quicker than a carriage, and Ivy had suffered every rut and bump in anticipatory agony. She'd suffer more if it meant Saint would return to her.

She looked around when they finally stopped. They were in Hertford, just north of London, at a lovely but small isolated estate that looked as though it had been built during the Tudor reign.

"*This* is where Saint is?" There were so many windows, it didn't seem a practical lair for a vampire—unless he was in the cellar.

"Yes." Justin exited the automobile and came around to her door just as Ivy had her hand on the handle. She wasn't accustomed to being treated like a lady.

"He's inside," Justin continued as Ivy brushed past him to scurry up the walk.

She glanced over her shoulder. "How do you know this?"

He didn't look at her. "I arranged for it."

Well, that was unexpected. Why on earth would Justin want to help Saint? There was something so strange about this situation. Had she stopped to ponder all the facts, Ivy might have satisfied the niggling in the back of her brain, but she was too distracted by thinking of what she was going to say to Saint when she saw him again.

It was all she could do to wait at the door and allow Justin to open it. When he did open it, she bounded inside.

The hall was small but open. The paper on the walls was cream colored and the wood trim was dark and rich and shone with polish. Oil lamps burned in shiny brass sconces and the air was fresh and inviting—not musty or stale.

Someone had to be living there then. She walked to the center of the floor. "Saint? Saint?"

No one answered.

"Upstairs," Justin told her. "Check upstairs. Second door on the right."

Hiking her skirts, Ivy ran up the winding staircase, to the first floor. Sconces burned up there as well, lighting her way down the narrow corridor.

Her heart was pounding heavily when she reached the second door on the right. Her hand trembled as she reached for the knob. She never thought to knock first, she just barged right in.

"Saint, I—" The words died on her tongue. The bedroom was of a comfortable size and obviously recently prepared for a guest, but the small canopy bed had not been slept in and the curtains were wide open, allowing the light of the moon to stream inside, mixing with the glow from the lamps as it pooled on the carpet.

There was no one there. But in the center of the floor, there sat a stiff-backed wooden chair with skinny legs and flat arm rests.

There were manacles attached to those legs and arms.

Ivy gasped and stepped backward, colliding with a solid frame. Whirling, she half-thought it might be Saint, but it was Justin. He smiled.

"Ivy, there's no need to be afraid."

She didn't like this. Not at all. "Where's Saint, Justin?"

He shrugged. "I have no idea, but I'm sure he'll be here soon."

A sigh of relief welled up in her lungs.

"Don't worry, once the vampire realizes I've taken you, he'll come to us."

Ivy nearly choked on her own breath. "What?"

"You heard me." The smile grew. "It might take him a little while to sniff us out, but his kind have incredibly keen senses. He'll find us eventually."

It felt as though all the blood in her body had poured itself into her feet. "How did you know?"

He held out his hand and showed her the silver signet ring he wore. She had seen it before—it was engraved with the image of a hand, palm up. Only now when she looked, it didn't have a hand on it at all, but a chalice. Just like the one on Daisy's cheek.

Ivy's blood whooshed up from her feet, filling her limbs once more—filling them with the fire of a rage she had never felt before. She stared at Justin for just a second, sick at the thought of having been so deceived.

Then she launched herself at him, kicking and punching with all her strength. She even tried to smash his face with her head.

"Ivy! Stop this," he cried. "Let me explain! You don't understand."

She didn't heed, she simply fought. She would tear him apart with her bare hands if she could.

And then there was a sharp explosion of pain in her face and her head snapped back. Justin had punched her and the force of it knocked her off her feet. She hit the floor with a bone-jarring thud that knocked the breath from her and felt as though it caved in the back of her skull.

Then the blackness came and there was nothing.

Saint tore London apart.

He followed Ivy's scent, mixed with Fontaine's and that of his horses to town, then to a decent upper-class neighborhood in the West End. When he arrived at Fontaine's townhouse, he forced his way inside, but found nothing. The frightened servants gave up several places where he could be. And Fontaine's valet remarked that his master had taken a small valise with him.

The scent died there. The horses were in the stable and the groom told him that Fontaine had taken his automobile when he left. And yes, he had a woman with him matching Ivy's description.

Desperate, Saint went to Fontaine's club but no one there had seen him or knew where he was. He went to two other clubs and a house party. Nothing. No one knew anything.

By this time, a gray light was spreading across the horizon, signaling the coming dawn. Impotent against the ever moving hands of time, Saint fled to Maison Rouge, barely escaping being reduced to smoldering ash.

He didn't take his frustration out on his apartments—that would be too easy. Instead, he went into the catacombs and put his fists and boots through solid rock, pounded iron and steel until he actually felt enough pain to dull the ache in his heart. Until the raging helplessness inside him eased somewhat.

Damn. Why did she go with Fontaine? None of her clothes were missing so it couldn't have been an elopement.

It was his fault that she was gone. He should have suspected Fontaine. Anyone that agreeable had to be up to no good.

If he had paid more attention to finding the killer and less attention to bedding Ivy, she might still be there right now. It didn't matter how many people tried to tell him it wasn't his fault—and everyone present at Maison Rouge had done just that—he could only blame himself. It was either that or blame Ivy and he missed her too badly for that.

He'd blame her once he got her back. Then he'd make sure she never ran away with a killer again.

Had he truly just thought that? The absurdity of it almost made him smile.

"She's made me into an idiot," he muttered aloud to the dank dark of the tunnel. Oh, yes, when he got Ivy back—when, not if—he was going to make sure she never left his sight again. He didn't care if it took a hundred years, he'd *make* that woman love him.

Because it seemed that he was hopelessly in love with her.

It was that realization that brought him out of

the darkness and back into his room. It then drove him upstairs to where everyone else was—or at least those who weren't out looking for Ivy. Covered in an old quilt, he dodged what little sunlight there was between the servants stairs and the corridor and dove into the only room suitable for a vampire.

Madeline's office—Ivy's office now—was often used by Reign during his visits and was suitably equipped with extra thick drapes that blocked out all traces of daylight. This was where Madeline came to have tea with him, and where Saint paced and raged and contemplated risking sun exposure to bring Ivy home. Madeline put up with this behavior for about an hour and then she went off to do something she referred to as "useful." She was obviously aggravated by his behavior, but that didn't stop him from envying the fact that she could leave the room.

There was no way he could think of to protect himself thoroughly enough and long enough to find Ivy. Risking his own skin was only worth it if he found her—saved her. Otherwise he was killing himself and leaving her at the mercy of a madman.

By nine o'clock he was ready to kill someone himself. His men checked in as often as they could, and even the girls, bless them, had joined in the search, contacting friends and going to places Justin frequented. Meanwhile, Saint remained helpless and useless, like balls on a mare.

He rearranged the shelves of books that lined the walls so that they were in alphabetical order. He even rearranged the furniture to better suit his own liking. Keeping occupied kept him from going insane and destroying everything he laid his hands on.

And then, at five minutes before two that afternoon, a visitor came calling. Madeline, so tired and scared, joined Saint in the office as Emily brought the caller in. Apparently this person had information concerning Ivy's disappearance.

He had no preconceptions of who this person might be, but he was still surprised when Ivy's sister—he recognized her from the photograph Ivy had showed him—entered the room.

Madeline stared at the girl with her mouth slightly agape. Given the difference in their social spheres, it wasn't surprising that they had never met before. No doubt Ivy took pains to keep them apart so her mother wouldn't be reminded of the man who betrayed her.

"You're Robert's daughter," Madeline said so softly it was almost a whisper.

The girl nodded, her lips, so much like Ivy's, curving into a soft smile. "Yes. I'm Rose."

Saint took over then, introducing Madeline and himself. "Emily says that you may know something about Ivy's disappearance?"

The girl nodded. "Yes."

"I'm curious—how did you know she was missing?"

She hesitated, as though gathering her thoughts. "My father has these friends that come 'round on occasion. It's as though they're some kind of club."

"Does your father have a signet ring with a chalice on it?"

Her eyes lit. "Yes! These men have been coming about very often as of late. One of them was in the park with Ivy when I last saw her. A handsome blond man."

"Fontaine," Saint muttered.

"I didn't think much of it, then," Rose continued. "But not too many nights ago I overheard my father and one of his friends—a very scary man—discussing those awful murders. I'm ashamed to admit this, but my father seemed to know something about them."

Saint didn't look at Madeline. No doubt this revelation was damn near killing her, thinking that Ivy's father might have something to do with her disappearance and the death of the girls.

"I haven't gone to the police," Rose told them. "I don't know if I will. I cannot turn against my father, who has been nothing but loving toward me."

Saint nodded. "I understand. What else can you tell us?"

"This morning I chanced to overhear . . . blast, there was no chance about it. I listened outside the door to my father's study while he and the scary man were in there. They were talking about the fact that someone named Fontaine has become a liability. I assume this is the same man you just spoke of. The scary man told my father that Fontaine had taken Ivy to complete some ritual."

A chill crept up Saint's spine. Rose kept talking. "The man said all their hard work was about to come to fruition. He said that they would overcome the failure of eleven years ago, especially since they already had someone named Temple in custody."

The chill turned to solid ice. "Temple? They said they had Temple?"

She nodded. "They didn't say where. Do you know him?"

Saint nodded. Temple was a vampire and one of Saint's oldest friends. He had been the leader of their ragtag group, and if the Silver Palm had Temple, they were not the kind of people to fuck around with.

He wasn't about to let them have Ivy.

He focused his attention on Rose. "Did the man say where Fontaine took Ivy?"

"Yes. I'm so sorry, I should have told you already. He took her to his country estate in Hertford. It's called Redstone Park."

For the first time that day, Saint felt as though

there was real hope of getting Ivy back. So much so, that he actually hugged Rose. The girl stiffened in surprise, but she didn't pull away.

Saint turned to Madeline. "I'll put together a group. We'll go as soon as the sun sets."

"That's hours from now," Rose remarked. "Can you not leave now?"

He gave her a quick smile. "Element of surprise. They won't see us coming." Not to mention he'd fry like bacon if he tried to go now. There were times when it was damn frustrating being a vampire.

That answer seemed to satisfy her. "What can I do?"

"You can go home," he told her. "And keep an eye on your father. Do you have a telephone?"

She nodded.

"Good. Telephone us if he leaves or if anything else happens that we should know about." He turned to leave.

"Mr. Saint, there is one more thing."

There always was. He glanced at her. "What is it, pet?"

"The scary man mentioned that once Fontaine 'initiated' Ivy that someone they called 'the vampire' was welcome to him. Do you know what that means?"

This time Saint out-and-out grinned. "Yes, my dear. I certainly do."

* * *

Ivy woke with an awful ache in her face and head and a horrible stiffness through her neck and shoulders.

Through the haze of pain she forced herself to look around, to clear her vision. She was still in the bedroom in the house where Justin had brought her and she was alone, shackled to a chair in the center of the room.

She was in a house in the middle of nowhere with a madman who knew Saint was a vampire and was hoping he would come for her. Justin was part of the Order of the Silver Palm, the people who were responsible for so much death and pain.

Had Justin been the one to do the slaughter? It made her sick to even think it, and yet she knew in her heart it was true and that somehow, she herself was expected to play a major role in all of this madness.

Was he going to kill her too? Oh, God, she prayed that Saint would never find them if Justin killed her. She didn't want him to find her like that. She would rather his last thoughts of her were of anger rather than that kind of pain.

The thought of Saint, coupled with the myriad pain in her body, filled her eyes with hot, stinging tears that trickled down her cheeks, scalding her bruised flesh.

The door opened as she sat there, helpless, sore and weeping. Justin walked in. He was wearing the same clothes that he wore when they first arrived so not that much time had passed, but the light in the room was different. It was daylight.

Saint wouldn't be coming anytime soon.

"No," Justin said as he closed the door with his foot. "He hasn't come yet." His hands were full with a tray of food and what smelled like coffee.

"How do you know he will?" she demanded, wincing as even the simple motions of speech made her head feel as though it was splitting apart.

"Because he loves you," her captor replied, setting the tray on the bed. "He won't be able to help himself. He won't rest until you are safe."

"And you plan to keep me like this until he shows up?"

"Oh, no." He bent over her with a key and unlocked one of the wrist restraints. "You and I have a ritual to complete while we wait for your demon lover to appear."

Ivy scowled as she slowly lifted and rotated her freed hand. "Saint's not a demon."

Justin actually looked surprised. "Has he told you nothing of how he and his friends came to be vampire?"

Her silence must have proved answer, because he continued as he labored over the tray, preparing what Ivy assumed was her breakfast. She didn't want to eat it, but the practical side of her knew better than to allow herself to get weak.

"I will make the story as short and simple as possible," he began. "When Lilith—the very same our dearly departed friend Jacques painted you as, at my request, of course—was ordered from the Garden she became the lover of the angel Samael. Unfortunately, Lilith learned that Samael was plotting to destroy mankind so she told Eve to alert God to this plot. Samael and his followers were cast down from the ranks of angel into the lower orders of demon kind. Lilith and Samael didn't have far to fall as they were already cavorting with demons. Since the information came from Lilith, God made her queen of night demons rather than destroy her.

"Now, as you can imagine, this betrayal did not sit well with Samael and he put a powerful curse upon Lilith. He imbued her essence into thirty pieces of silver so that she might be passed from man to man as she deserved. That silver cursed all who touched it—a man named Judas for one—until the Knights Templar found it. They sought to protect the silver and hide it, so they melted it down into a chalice. What they didn't know was that Lilith's essence filled the chalice as well and all who drank from it became vampire."

Ivy stared at him. "You don't really believe this, do you?"

Justin laughed and set a small table in front of

her. "Of course I do. It's true. Now, there was a secret branch of the Templars who were dissatisfied with how things were run, and they used the cup in their rituals, eventually discovering its power. That's when the Templars stole it and hid it away. It's what King Philip was looking for when he sent his men out to sack the Templars in the fourteenth century. And his men did find it. They drank from it and it made them vampires unlike any the world had ever seen save for Lilith."

He set the tray on the table and motioned for her to eat. "And that, my dear Ivy is how your Saint came to be a vampire—and a demon."

She picked up a spoon. The hard-boiled egg before her wasn't the least bit tempting, but she was going to eat it, damnit. "I don't care what you say. Saint is no more a demon than I am."

Justin made a scoffing noise. "You're thinking of the Christian idea of a demon. It's hardly the same. I have a great deal of respect for Saint. He and the others are going to help our cause very much."

Ivy stilled. "How?"

Another smile—secretive and gleeful. "You'll see. You're going to play a part as well, Ivy. A glorious, wonderful part."

He was insane, he had to be. And yet, he seemed so sincere, so calm.

"I'm sorry I hurt you," he said, suddenly somber. "But you didn't give me much choice."

"Is that why I'm chained to this chair?" She took a bit of toast. It was like chewing sawdust. "Because I didn't give you a choice?"

He nodded. "I can't risk you running. I'm sorry. I've worked too hard for this to let you ruin it."

"Worked for what, Justin?" At least when she had him talking, when she was listening to his insane ramblings, she wasn't thinking about how stupid she was for not telling Saint she loved him when she had the chance, or how she might never have another chance to tell him.

He shook a finger at her. "No more of that. Eat. You're going to need your strength for the ceremony."

It was all she could do not to gag. He was going to sacrifice her. Use her for his unnatural urges. "What ceremony?"

He grinned. "Our wedding, of course."

Chapter 19

"Trying to fatten the lamb before the slaughter?" Ivy asked drolly when Justin brought her dinner just before sunset. How many meals was he going to bring? The only times she had seen him that day was when he delivered her food.

He shook his head, giving her a mildly chastising smile. "Of course not, you are perfect just as you are, but you need your strength for tonight."

It had to be her imagination that put those spots of color in his cheeks, but the sun was sinking fast and so she had to ask, "For the wedding?"

Justin smiled as he fussed with the tray. "That's part of it."

The rest wasn't going to be anymore pleasant, of that she was certain. "Is Saint part of 'it'?"

That brought his head up, but he looked out the window rather than at her. "Possibly. I hope the first part of the ceremony will be completed before he arrives."

Ivy made a mental note to eat as slowly as possible.

As though reading her thoughts, Justin turned his head so that their gazes met. He smiled indulgently, as though she was a child. "Do not even think of dragging your heels, Ivy. I have a schedule to keep and you'll be downstairs in twenty minutes whether you've finished your supper or not."

Downstairs. "You're moving me?" He would have to untie her and once he did she'd level him with a knee to the groin and run. If she could she'd steal his automobile and drive it back to Maison Rouge—even though she didn't know how to drive one of the blasted things. It was the perfect plan.

Justin waggled a long finger at her. "I know you, Ivy. You're planning your escape, but it won't happen."

She lifted her chin, irked that he did indeed seem to know her very well—better than she ever knew him. "Oh?"

He shook his head. "You'll be free to walk, but your hands will be tied behind your back."

She could still run.

"Oh, and I've had some friends join us. There are two guards at every exit." He grinned. "You're not going anywhere."

"Why are you doing this to me, Justin? I thought we were friends."

His grin faded a little. "I thought we were more than that until you started fucking that vampire."

"Is that what this is about? You're angry about me and Saint?"

He laughed then. "No. I understand the vampire's appeal. No, this is about something much, much more important than me and my feelings."

Time to try a different approach. "You underestimate yourself."

Another chuckle. "You are so transparent, Ivy. If you want to know what this is all about, all you have to do is ask." He set the tray before her, once again on a small table. "Eat."

Hadn't she tried asking him once already? "What is this all about, Justin?"

"Power," he replied easily. "I can tell you that it is about power and privilege. You've been chosen, Ivy. I've been chosen."

"I don't want to be chosen, Justin. I want to make my own choices."

He nodded. "If things had gone as they should have, you would have been prepared for this. You would have made this choice on your own."

"No, I don't think so. I would never choose to be shackled to a chair."

"If your father hadn't had a slip of faith before

you were born, you would have been raised knowing your destiny. There would be no need for restraints."

His words chilled, cut and angered her all at the same time. "My father? What does that son of a bitch have to do with this?"

Justin's face darkened. And for a moment, Ivy was actually afraid that he might beat her. This was not a side of him she had ever seen before.

Then, as suddenly as it came, the darkness left his face. "I can understand why you feel as you do, Ivy, but you shouldn't call your father such names. He deserves your respect."

"He doesn't deserve anything from me but contempt."

Justin looked as though he pitied her. "I find it so sad that you think that way of a man who has given you an amazing birthright. True, he has stumbled in the past, but he is a great man all the same."

She said nothing. It was only making her angry and she needed to keep a level head if she was going to get herself out of this. She couldn't trust that Saint would come for her—he might not make it in time, or worse he might think she eloped with Justin.

Her captor, however, took her silence as an excuse to keep talking, "The baron made the mistake of falling in love with your mother. I don't blame him, she's a beautiful woman, but that was his big mistake. He thought he could send her away and that the Order would never know that she bore him a daughter. He thought he was protecting you. He was very confused."

Ivy stared at him. Confused? Her bastard father? "He knew exactly what he was doing when he tossed my mother aside."

"Yes," Justin agreed, kneeling before her. "He thought he could prevent your destiny, but he couldn't. He's not that powerful."

Her father had been trying to protect Ivy and her mother? Impossible.

He had unshackled her wrist so she could eat and Ivy drew that arm back and lashed out, catching Justin off guard. He saw the blow coming at the last second and managed to move, but she still caught him in the mouth with a tight fist, knocking him onto his arse. He took the table and her dinner with him.

He sat back on his hands, scowling at her as a drop of blood beaded at the corner of his mouth. "You want to act like a child? Fine. I will treat you accordingly. No supper for you."

Ivy watched, silently fuming, as he rose to his feet. He brushed the remnants of her meal off his clothes and went to the door. "I think it's time we got started. The sooner we're done the sooner you might start to appreciate your circumstances."

He knocked on the door and a few seconds later, two burly men entered the room. They were dressed entirely in black, with masks on their faces, obscuring the upper half of their faces.

"These are two of my *brothers*, Ivy." The way he said it made her realize they weren't blood, but members of the Order of the Silver Palm. "They will escort you downstairs."

She could have fought them, but what was the use? One of them alone could squash her like a bug. Better to save her strength for when the odds were more in her favor.

They released her feet from the shackles and then her arms, only to then tie her arms behind her back. Then each took an arm and dragged her out the door. Justin followed behind.

The corridor was so narrow they had to move in single file. While one gargantuan pulled the other pushed and several times Ivy thought her feet actually left the floor. It was amazing that she didn't trip going down the stairs.

They took her down even more stairs—a staircase off the back kitchen that led to what had one time been the original kitchen or a creamery of sorts. The air, though a little dank, still smelled of salt and butter, the essence of each having soaked into the stone walls.

There was a bed on a dais in the middle of the room. It practically dripped in lace, and all around it were pure white candles, each burning a small golden flame. On the bed, rose petals were strewn about. And, on a table to the side, there were five jars sitting on what appeared to be an altar.

"Take her to the bed," Justin instructed and the men did as they were told. They had to untie her hands once there, and one of them fiddled with leather straps on the posts of the bed.

They were going to tie her there.

Now was her only chance. If she didn't make a move now, Justin would do whatever it was he planned to do to her. Quickly, she looked around for some kind of weapon.

And her gaze fell upon the altar and the jars.

"We want to go with you."

The sun was just a fiery smear on the horizon as Saint made his final preparations that evening. He was sharpening the blade of one of his daggers he kept for just such occasions when the little band of harlots and henchmen burst into the office.

He looked up, then at each and every determined face. "What a brave lot you are," he remarked—and he meant it. "But no."

Gemma, a plump little thing with a head of blond ringlets and a will that would cow a mortal man, stepped forward. "Ivy is our friend. You cannot expect us to simply sit here while you go off alone."

Mary, a thin redhead, stepped up as well. "No offense, Mr. Saint, but what if something happens to you?"

"Never m . . . mind that," stammered a short brunette—Agatha, he thought. "That bastard Justin made friendly to all of us and he . . ." Tears filled her eyes. "We want to be there to see him die."

Saint couldn't condemn them for their blood thirst. He felt the same way. He had every intention of tearing Justin Fontaine apart—slowly. The bastard would suffer for his crimes, especially where Ivy was concerned.

How could he deny them the satisfaction he so craved? He could if it put Ivy in even more danger.

"I can't take you with me because I'm going to be traveling too fast for you to keep up." Before they could protest, he continued, "But you can meet me there."

That seemed to please them.

"You all realize how dangerous this is?" he asked as he slipped the dagger into a sheath inside his boot. "You risk your own safety, possibly your very lives."

The girls nodded as the men looked upon them with concern. Then, the men turned to Saint and nodded as well. Honorable and gentlemanly in their own ways, these common men would not allow women to go into danger without offering themselves as protection.

"Then make haste," Saint commanded. "I'm leaving at sundown, whether you are ready or not."

They scattered then, briefly. Obviously they had given this a lot of thought and preparation because they returned within minutes with weapons, the women wearing split skirts and trousers instead of their usual gowns.

He couldn't help but smile at the sight of them. "You know where to go?"

This time it was George who answered, "Yes, sir. I have the carriage and several horses waiting outside. We just need the word from you."

Sneaky little bunch had planned all of this. Saint's smile faded, but his respect for these people increased immeasurably. "You were going to go whether I said yes or no, weren't you?"

Gemma again, "Yes."

There was no point in anger—he couldn't spare the energy. All of his focus was on saving Ivy. She was the only thing he cared about.

"Then let's go." He felt the setting of the sun in his very bones—some kind of built-in clock that his kind possessed.

They filed out of the room before him, streaming into the foyer and out the door into the awakening night.

Madeline was there—Emily as well. Both clad in coats and trousers, each armed.

"You're not going," Saint told his old friend. "Ivy will kill me if anything happens to you."

"And I'll kill you if anything happens to her," came the quick reply. "I don't take orders from you, Saint."

He rolled his eyes. Heaven save him from stubborn women. "Fine. Get going."

The two women preceded him out the door and as soon as he stepped outside, the most amazing sense of calm washed over Saint's entire being. The night embraced him, fed him power with its darkness, strengthened him with its shadows. He was secure in his abilities, confident in his own success.

He was afraid for Ivy, yes. Terrified even. But that fear was overpowered by the sheer certainty that he would defeat Fontaine and whatever forces he might have behind him. The demon in him cried for vengeance, for blood and Saint meant to see that desire assuaged.

He propelled himself into the cool, blackening sky with a single-minded purpose.

To bring the woman he loved home.

Justin wasn't prepared for Ivy's attack, and so when she jumped on him, he went down. She went with him, somehow managing to stay on top as they hit the hard floor. She smashed her knee but the pain only fueled her rage.

Fingers curled into claws, she raked at him—not as a cat, scratching and spitting, but as a madwoman, trying to rip out a throat with her bare hands.

"Butcher!" She cried as she tore at his flesh. He raised his arms to fend off her attack, but she was like a wild animal. "You bastard! I'll kill you!"

And she would have, had his two henchmen not interfered. The noise brought two more tromping down the rickety stairs. They grabbed her and hauled her up, and when she couldn't use her hands, she started kicking with her feet. She caught Justin in the jaw with her heel, but since she was wearing flimsy little slippers, she doubted it did much damage.

"Tie her to the bed," Justin ordered roughly, gingerly touching his neck with his fingers. They came away bloody from where she had clawed him. "And knock her the hell out."

Ivy struggled even harder as the men hauled her to the bed—closer to those *things*. It was no use. The men were barely breaking a sweat and she was panting and exhausted. She trembled with rage and disgust.

"I hate you," she snarled at Justin. "I will see you dead for what you've done."

He wiped at his wounds with a handkerchief. "Ivy, I'm willing to forgive you because you have no idea of the honor that has been bestowed upon you."

"Honor?" She spat at him, and jerked her head toward the jars. "Like the honor you gave them?"

He truly seemed confused. His gaze—not so friendly now—went to the altar and then back to her. "Even more. They will help bring the prophecy to fruition, but you . . . you will bear the fruit."

The talk of "bearing" anything with those . . . those . . . pickled wombs sitting behind her was more than Ivy's stomach could tolerate. Bile rose and she gagged, then retched.

Justin wiped her mouth with his bloody handkerchief. "There, there. Feel better?"

For the first time since he had taken her, Ivy didn't feel angry. She was too scared. Plain and simple, Justin terrified her. She wasn't sure he was insane, though his thinking certainly was. He truly seemed to believe that he was offering her this wonderful gift.

"What are you going to do with me?" At least her voice didn't tremble—much.

He smiled. "First we'll be married and then we'll consummate the union there." He pointed at the bed. "My brothers will serve as witnesses."

"You mean . . . ?" Oh, God.

And Justin just kept smiling, but there was a touch of something new there—something that made her shiver deep inside at the thought of being at his mercy.

"Don't worry, my darling," he said. "I'll be gentle."

Chapter 20

～◇◇～

Saint landed on the roof of Fontaine's Hertford estate as silent as a cat, surprising the man standing there.

Saint tilted his head. "What's wrong, son? Never seen a man drop from the sky before?"

The man shook his head, frozen with fear as he clung to his weapon. He didn't have a silver signet ring, but the top of his left hand sported a tattoo of a chalice.

Seems Fontaine had his own henchmen.

"You have silver bullets in that rifle, don't you?" A nod this time.

"First time actually meeting a vampire?"

"Yes."

"Leave this place. Do yourself a service and get as far away from here and these people as you possibly can."

"I can't. I'm supposed—"

Saint cut him off. "I could have killed you twice by now."

The man's face was white as a sheet as he handed over his rifle. He hurried to the side of the roof some distance away and lowered himself over the side.

Misguided human. He was going to be a little ashamed of himself in the morning for not at least trying to fight Saint, but he would be even more glad to be alive and that's what would matter most.

Saint tossed the weapon aside before stepping off the roof. He dropped a few feet to a balcony on the back. The terrace doors were locked. Saint popped them open with a slight push.

How long had Fontaine known what he was? Saint wondered as he stepped inside. He had to have known almost from the beginning, and he had certainly been aware of Saint's true nature when he burnt him with that damn ring. He had wanted Saint to know what he was.

He wanted Saint to come here.

That gave Saint pause as he moved across a deserted bedroom. As much as he wanted to tear the place apart looking for Ivy, he would do well to exercise a little caution. If this was a trap, he wasn't about to make it easy for the Order. They had captured him once with their silver and he had the scars to prove it.

He wouldn't be any good to Ivy if he was incapacitated. But he was un-fed, on edge, and filled with rage. That in itself would make him more difficult to take down. His demon self craved blood and he intended to bathe in it.

He left the little bedroom cautiously, easing into the lamp-lit corridor. The scent of Ivy overwhelmed him. He smelled her anger and her fear—and he smelled Fontaine's blood. A small smile curved his lips.

There was an armed guard at the top of the stairs. Saint rendered him unconscious and tossed his body inside one of the bedrooms. He wasn't interested in killing these men—not unless he had to. The only man whose death appealed to him was Fontaine.

Down the stairs he crept, extinguishing the lamps as he went. Darkness was his friend, his advantage over the Order. He followed Ivy's scent and the distant voices his keen hearing picked up. They were under the ground, beneath the house.

Four more guards got in his way before he found the stairs leading down into the cellar. He took care of them as quietly as possible, and stuffed them into the pantry with a chair against the door should they wake before they expected.

He peered through the crack of the open door. Two more masked men waited for him at the bottom of the stairs. There would be no element of surprise if he went this way. There was no telling what Fontaine might do to Ivy while Saint fought his men.

There was no knowing what Fontaine had already done to her.

A spike of rage almost had him smashing through the floor with his fists. Then, he spied it. The dumbwaiter. He could enter the basement that way if it went all the way down.

Quietly, he opened the small door and peered down the shaft. It did go down, and his luck was good enough that the actual shelf was stopped at the floor above, so the passage down was clear of impediment.

He slipped into the narrow opening—just squeezing his shoulders through.

A wave of panic ripped through him as the walls encased him like a tomb. It felt too much like being trapped, crushed. Sweat beaded on his brow as he forced himself to take several deep, calming breaths.

He wasn't trapped. He was trying to get to Ivy. Ivy's safety, her very life, depended on him being able to do this and by God he would do it.

He opened his eyes and stared hard at the wall. It was just a wall. He could break through a wall if he needed to. He could breathe. He knew where he was going. He knew where he was. Ivy was depending upon him. He was her only chance.

Panic drifted away, replaced by resolute determination.

Feet and hands braced on opposite sides, he began easing himself downward, down into the darkness toward the small sliver of light near the bottom that marked his exit.

The voices were louder now. He could hear Fontaine and at least three men. And he could hear Ivy. The sound of her voice cursing Fontaine blue brought a smile to his lips. She was alive and she was angry. This was good.

Both swiftly and silently as possible, he maneuvered himself down the narrow shaft. Near the bottom he twisted his body so that when he dropped to his feet he was crouched facing the door.

"Did you hear that?" he heard a man ask.

Then Fontaine. "What?"

"I thought I heard something."

Saint put his eye to the space between the door and the wall. He could just barely see Fontaine and the other man. They were standing beside something low and flat like a table or . . . he saw a flash of female leg . . . or a bed.

It was Ivy. The bastard had Ivy down here on a bed. God knew what he had in mind and he was going to do it with an audience.

It would be a pleasure to kill this man.

"Get upstairs and check in with the others," Fontaine commanded. "The vampire might descend upon us at any moment." He had no idea just how accurate that statement actually was.

Saint waited until the guard left then eased the dumbwaiter door open. Fontaine's back was to him as he stood facing the bed and the woman on it. There were four guards in the room counting the two at the bottom of the stairs.

Easy.

Instead of trying to climb out, Saint merely rolled forward, palms out. He hit the floor, flipped and came up in a crouch. Then one of the guards glanced in his direction, and he and his companion were unconscious before they knew what hit them.

Fontaine looked actually surprised to see him.

The other guards lifted their rifles and took aim, waiting for their master's orders.

"Saint!" It was Ivy who cried out his name, and it was as sweet to him as any music.

"Mr. Saint, you're a little early," Fontaine remarked easily, gestured to the bed. "I was just about to give my bride her wedding night."

Something froze in the vicinity of Saint's heart. "Ivy, are you all right?" he asked.

She shifted on the mattress, craning her neck so that she might look at him. "I'm fine. He had someone perform a wedding ceremony, but I never consented."

Fontaine shrugged. "It hardly signifies." Then

he fixed Saint with a friendly smile. "Now that you're here all that's left is the completion of the ritual and we can leave for Rome."

The man was obviously insane. "Sorry, Fontaine, but I'm not into a *ménage à trois*."

Another smile. "Oh, you won't be with Ivy and me."

"What makes you so sure that I will agree to just go along with you rather than ripping your heart out?"

Fontaine lifted his hand—the one partially concealed from Saint's view. In it was a pistol—which he pointed directly at Ivy's head. "Because I'll kill her if you don't."

That moment was one of the few times in Saint's immortal life that he knew real fear. He had felt it when Marta died and he felt it now, facing the very real possibility that he might lose the woman he loved more than he had ever loved before. He knew this because he would do anything Fontaine said just to keep her alive.

"You son of a bitch," Ivy swore at her captor. "You coward!"

Fontaine didn't look at her. "Not a coward, my love. I'm being smart. I'm sorry, but he's as important to my plans as you are. And since I don't stand a chance against our friend in a physical contest I must use any means available to me."

"You don't stand a chance against him, period,"

she retorted. "And I'll never love you the way I do him."

"That's fine."

Saint blinked, his mind and heart reeling. She loved him? Or was she simply saying that to distract Fontaine?

"If you kill me," she reminded him. "You won't be able to complete the ritual. How will you explain that to your brothers?"

Fontaine faltered then, taking his attention off of Saint to glance at Ivy. It was all the time Saint needed. He pounced on Fontaine, taking him to the floor with a crash. The guards opened fire, but Saint rolled the pair of them behind the bed where they were safe from the bullets. They wouldn't risk hurting Ivy, not after what Saint had just heard. Fontaine would have made it clear to them not to hurt her. It was evident on his face as he had looked at her that he had forgotten that he couldn't use her as leverage.

One punch was all it took to knock Fontaine out. Saint added three more for good measure. Then the guards were upon him.

"Get off him, vampire," one of them instructed. "Or I'll fill you full of lead."

Saint smiled. "No you won't." Whipping to the side he grabbed Fontaine's limp form and threw it at the guard. The man fell to the floor, dropping his weapon as he was pinned beneath Fontaine.

This happened so fast the other guard couldn't react. Saint wrapped his hand around his throat and squeezed until the guard passed out, then he let him drop to the floor as well.

The other guards would no doubt soon return so he had to work quickly.

"I didn't think you were going to come," Ivy told him as he snapped her restraints. "I thought you would believe I went with him willingly."

"I knew you'd never take him over me," he replied with a grin as he offered her a hand up. "You do know how to make life interesting."

The next thing he knew she was on her feet with her arms tight around his neck and her full, soft lips pressed to his. He had never been kissed quite so . . . joyfully in all his life.

"I want you to stay," she told him, once she'd had her fill. "If you'll still have me."

"I will." His heart was full to bursting at the moment and they weren't out of danger yet. "You need to get out of here."

Her smile turned to a scowl. "Don't be an idiot. I'm not leaving without you!"

"Ivy." He peeled her arms from around his neck. "I need to take care of Fontaine and I don't want you to see it."

She pointed at a series of jars on an altar that he hadn't noticed before. "That's what he did to my friends. If you're going to kill him, I'm going to watch."

One look was all the persuasion he needed. "Fine." Picking up a rifle from the floor, he handed it to her. "If anyone moves, shoot them."

As he moved toward Fontaine there was a clamor upstairs. Saint stopped and listened. It was the group from Maison Rouge storming in to help save the day.

"It's your rescue party," he informed Ivy with a grin.

They tromped down the stairs like a herd of elephants. Unfortunately they had the police with them.

Saint stopped where he was. There would be no killing Fontaine tonight. Damnit.

Oddly enough he wasn't too concerned with that. Fontaine would be brought to justice for what he had done and Ivy was safe. That was really all that mattered.

Smythe and MacKay were two of the police present, so it was to them that Saint spoke.

"Miss Dearing needs to be taken home," he informed them. "You may come by Maison Rouge later to speak to her if you like. We will give our full cooperation, but we're leaving. Now." He couldn't force them into allowing it, couldn't charm them or play with their minds like so many sources claimed vampires could, but still, the end result was the same.

Or perhaps it was simply the fact that neither

constable could resist the chance to visit Maison
Rouge.

Once they were in agreement, Saint turned to
Ivy and held out his hand. "Let's go home."

By the time the constables from Scotland Yard
left, Ivy was so tired she could scarcely move.

The police assured her that they had enough
evidence against Justin that he would surely hang
for his crimes. He had confessed to all of it apparently with an arrogance that sickened Ivy. He
also claimed to have been working alone, so as far
as Scotland Yard was concerned, they had their
killer and there would be no more death at Maison
Rouge. They knew nothing about the Silver Palm
and they didn't seem to care.

Ivy couldn't help but wonder if they had seen
the last of the Order of the Silver Palm. Saint had
asked to be allowed to speak to Justin. He wanted
to ask about Temple. The police wouldn't allow
him access that night, but since he had been the
one to apprehend Justin, they agreed to let Saint
question him the next night. Saint planned to ask
about the Silver Palm as well. Justin would no
doubt find him a tad more persuasive than the
police.

The meeting with the police, along with her
mother's tears at having her home, and all of the
girls wanting to know every last detail exhausted

Ivy. The whole ordeal felt as though it had taken years off her life. It was amazing to her that she had any energy at all.

But she found that she did, when Saint took her to his room—where he could watch over her and protect her, he said. Ivy knew better. She had confessed to loving him earlier and her swarthy vampire had plans for her that required a soundproof room.

In the quiet, golden darkness of Saint's bedroom, Ivy turned to him, eager to put all of this behind them. "Yes, I'm truly fine. No, Justin didn't hurt me. Yes, I meant it when I said I love you. Now tell me you love me back and take me to bed before I scream."

He was smiling that little lopsided smile of his as he took her into his arms. "I love you," he confessed, his gaze soft as it locked with hers. "I always will."

It struck her then just how awesome his love was, because she believed it when he said it would last forever. And then his smile faded, only to be replaced with something that looked uncomfortably like sadness.

"What is it?" Her heart thumped into a pounding pace.

He released her. "There are some things we need to discuss."

"You would rather talk than make love?" She

didn't want to talk at all, because he was right—there was a lot they had to discuss and none of it had to do with what happened that night.

And she was afraid of what he was going to say when she told him she wanted to be with him—forever.

Taking her by the hands—at least he was still touching her—he guided her to the bed and sat beside her on the cushiony mattress.

He got to the point right away. "I won't force you to do anything you don't want to do."

"I know that. I'd never do that to you either." He seemed to find that amusing.

"What I mean, is that I don't want you to think that I want you to become a vampire."

Her heart fell a little. "You don't?"

He shook his head. "Not if you don't want to."

"What if I want to?"

His black gaze brightened a little, but there was a strange light there she didn't recognize. Was that fear she saw? "Don't be so quick to make that decision. There are risks involved, Ivy. Risks I would have you think long and hard about before you decide."

"I have thought long and hard. I had a lot of time to think when I was locked in that room at Justin's estate. You know what I thought about? You. And how much I wished I could be with you again so I could tell you how I feel. I promised myself that if you came back to me I would never let you go—ever."

"I'm not going anywhere."

"But someday I will. I don't want to grow old and leave you, Saint. I don't want to put you through that."

"Ivy, don't do this for me . . ."

"I'm not!" She laughed a little in frustration. "Justin made me realize how I feel about you. I want to spend the rest of my life with you and I want that life to be at night, in the dark, beside you."

He was strangely silent and she wasn't sure what that meant, so she kept talking. "We do this together as equals. We do this sharing the same risks or we don't do it at all." It was a risky gamble, but one she was ready to take.

Their gazes locked for what seemed an eternity in itself. "All right," he said finally.

She raised a brow. "All right, what?"

"I will bring you over, if it's what you want."

"It is."

"It can be dangerous, Ivy. Some . . . some don't survive."

The pain in his expression was almost too much to bear. "I'm not Marta."

He looked offended. "I know that!"

She smiled, not the least bit jealous of a ghost. She knew that Saint loved her more than he had ever loved any other woman. She knew this because he was willing to give her a human life rather than spare himself the pain of her death. But above all, she knew it because she saw it every time he looked at her.

"It will make you a demon."

That's what Justin had told her. "You're not a demon, and even if you were it wouldn't matter. You are everything that is beautiful and good to me." Reaching out, she gently touched her fingertips to his cheek. "I'm willing to take a chance on eternity with you, my lovely vampire. Are you ready to do the same?"

And then he was on her, on top of her, pressing her into the bed as his mouth devoured hers. His fingers, usually so sure and deft, fumbled with the buttons on her clothes as she tore at his.

When they were both naked, he laid her on the bed, kneeling between her splayed thighs. His burning black gaze seemed to drink in every inch of her.

"Will I satisfy you forever, do you think?" she asked coyly.

He smiled. It was a pirate's smile, a thief's smile. "You'll do."

Then he leaned down and touched her breast with the tip of his tongue. She gasped and that was only the beginning. That hot, wet tip circled her nipple until her flesh puckered and ached. He stroked the other breast with his hand, squeezing until she cried out.

His hand slid further, nudging her legs apart. Her body jumped as his fingers stroked the curls there, teasing the cleft between. Ivy gasped, her hands clutching at his hair as his mouth drew insistently on her breast.

One of his fingers parted her, moving with tortuous slowness between the slick folds of her flesh. Jolts of pleasure flared deep within her, rolling into one tight, pulsating ache that demanded release even as she wished it would go on forever.

His teeth nipped at her breast, drawing a cry from her. Lifting his head from her swollen, glistening flesh, he gazed down at her, his ruthless fingers still stroking the wetness between her legs. The bright flame of his eyes made her heart thump with excitement.

God, the way he made her feel.

"Do you want more?" His voice was low and thick. Ivy nodded, unable to speak.

Saint held her gaze as he positioned himself at the entrance to her body. Dry mouthed, Ivy watched with greedy eyes as the long, thick width of him brushed the swollen flesh of her sex. The head of his cock nudged against her and she opened her legs even wider for him.

He was so beautiful, so wanton and seductive, her vampire. His shoulders were broad, hollowed and sculpted by the lamplight. The muscles of his torso were taut, dusted with a fine, dark hair. One of his hands was between his legs, stroking himself as he rubbed against her soaked cleft. The tease.

"Do you want me, Ivy?"

Raising her gaze to his, she met the burning of his eyes without flinching, without shame. "Yes. I want you. All of you."

Slowly, he fitted himself against her. He pushed—not hard, but insistently all the same. Ivy gasped as he slowly filled her, stretching her. He lifted her legs, held her ankles with his hands so that she was open to his thrust.

He moved inside her with deep, gentle thrusts, churning his hips more than pushing. There was very little discomfort now, and whatever was left, was nothing compared to the sheer pleasure of being joined with him.

But it wasn't enough. She wanted more of him, wanted to give more of herself. Slowly, she pushed herself upward, wrapping her legs around his waist as she rose into a sitting position.

"Ah!" A brief sting as his fangs penetrated her, and then a rush of pleasure as she felt him draw her into himself. Liquid heat flowed through her veins, flooding her with the most intense of sensations. His mouth worked at her throat as his hips pushed against her, his rhythm increasing.

Ivy clung to him, her body writhing into his embrace, pliant and so terribly aware in his arms. The tension between her legs grew, bringing her closer and closer to a second climax.

Gripping him with her thighs, she arched upward, pushing her pelvis against the delicious thrust of his body. The suction at her throat deepened and she knew he was as close to release as she.

Suddenly she was no longer simply close. Suddenly she was lost in the maelstrom of ecstasy his mouth and body wrought. She clutched at his head, holding him tight against her throat as orgasm tore through her, convulsing with mind-numbing pleasure.

Dimly, she was aware of Saint stiffening as his own climax struck. She felt him groan against her throat, felt the hot swipe of his tongue against her punctured flesh, and then a tingling, and she knew that come morning there would be no evidence of his bite.

That was the first step in making her his forever.

"Do it," she commanded, when he looked down at her, their bodies still joined.

He didn't ask if she was certain. The time for that had passed. She was anxious, maybe even a little fearful, but she had never been more certain of anything ever.

Saint reached down and took something from the floor—it was one of his daggers. And then he lifted her, so that she straddled his thighs as he knelt on the bed. The blade of the knife shone wickedly sharp in the golden light. Ivy flinched when he raised it to his chest, but she did not look away. She held his gaze, wanting him to see how committed she was to this—to him.

He made a small incision just above his collarbone. Blood welled to the surface and slowly trickled downward. Ivy stared at it, unsure of what to do next.

"Drink it," he told her. "A few swallows will be all you need."

Drinking blood. This was part of being a vampire she hadn't really thought about, although Saint had told her that blood tasted different once the change was complete.

Mentally she shrugged, she had tasted him in all kinds of other ways, what was one more? Lowering her head, she ran her tongue over the wound with one firm stroke. He shivered beneath her and she realized that this was a very intimate thing for him. That realization made her bold and she fastened her mouth on his flesh, drawing his essence and strength into herself. She drank greedily, but only succeeded in swallowing four or five times before dizziness overtook her.

She fell backward on the bed, the room spinning around her. She felt so . . . odd. So hot and strange and light.

Ivy looked up and saw Saint hovering above her, his brow knitted, his sharp features tight.

"Saint?" Her voice was distant to her own ears. "Why do you look so frightened?"

She never heard his reply because that was when the darkness came up from below her like a yawning chasm and swallowed her whole.

Chapter 21

"You almost let me die." Ivy's voice was firm but her eyes shone with merriment.

"Let you?" Saint laughed at the absurd remark. "Woman, you try my patience."

"And after all that talk of how I belonged to you," she teased, running her hands down his spine as a warm night breeze flowed over them. "You would have let me go."

"Never." Saint tightened his hold on her, as all good humor left him. "I would never let you go. I'd break into Heaven to bring you back to me."

He was rewarded by a glitter of wetness in her eyes. "When the change was happening I heard you. I heard your voice and it kept me here."

The change almost killed her. The convulsions lasted for what seemed like hours as Ivy's body tried to fight the powerful blood taking it over.

"Stay with me, Ivy," Saint had pleaded, wiping her brow with a cool cloth. "Stay with me."

Eventually the spasms eased and her skin cooled. And when she looked at him, there was clarity in her jadelike eyes. "You're not g . . . getting rid of me that easily," she retorted with surprising humor.

For Saint, it was one of the most terrifying experiences of his life. Helpless, he could only watch and pray that Ivy would accept the change. And then she had. The whole ordeal had taken less than twenty minutes, and when the process was complete, she curled up and fell into a deep and peaceful sleep.

Saint had stayed awake and watched her. Just in case. He was still afraid she might die.

Thank God that hadn't happened and now he was watching her thrive.

They were outside in the garden behind Maison Rouge, watching the stars twinkle in the night sky. A warm breeze drifted around them and the air smelled of flowers and coming rain. It was Ivy's first full night as a vampire.

"So tell me," she said, nestled in his arms as they reclined on a blanket on the grass. "What did you find out from the police today?" She hadn't been able to go out with him because she wasn't strong enough—not because of her ordeal, but because it was often difficult for new vampires to stay awake during the day. The first few days were very tiring as their bodies changed and adapted.

"A lot." He stroked the hair back from her face, enjoying the feeling of her round bottom pressed against his groin. "I have something for you."

She arched a brow. "What?"

He fished from his pocket the ring he had gotten from Ezekiel. It was the same one he had noticed her admiring that day they'd met in Ezekiel's shop.

The amethyst glittered and danced in the moonlight as Ivy's cool fingers wrapped around the jewelry.

"Why, Mr. Saint, are you trying to make an honest woman out of me?" Her tone was light, but he caught a slight tremor in it.

"You're honest enough as you are." He gave her a squeeze. "Think of it as a token of my love and adoration."

She grinned at him over her shoulder. "A lengthy engagement?"

He returned her smile. "As long as you want." He didn't have to marry her right away, they had all the time in the world. Whenever she was ready, he would be waiting.

Clearing her throat, she met his gaze. "Thank you."

He smiled, pleased that she meant it. "You're welcome." He started to lower his head but she turned hers instead.

"What of my father?"

He didn't want to tell her everything, but he couldn't keep it from her either.

"Your father and his family have left town."

Her brow puckered. "What do you suppose that means?"

"I'm not sure, but it could be that he didn't wish to be implicated in the murders as part of the Order."

"What else?"

"Scotland Yard was robbed just before dawn this morning." That was perhaps the most difficult thing he had to tell her.

She closed her eyes. "The jars."

His arms tightened around her. "I'm afraid so."

"Do you think the Order has them?"

"I would be surprised if they didn't."

"What do they want them for, Saint? Why did they want me? Why you?"

"I don't know, but I won't let them near you again. And once you're able, we'll find the others and we'll put an end to this scheme of theirs."

She linked her fingers through his as they rested on her abdomen. She didn't seem to mind that she would never know what it was like to feel a child growing there. Or perhaps, now that she was also a vampire, there was the chance that they might breed. He had never heard of it happening before, but that didn't mean it was impossible—did it?

"There's something else you're not telling me." Already she knew him too well. "What is it?"

"Justin Fontaine is dead."

She stiffened. "How?"

"Apparently he hanged himself in his cell."

This time she twisted around to face him. "You don't believe that?"

"I don't."

She pursed her lips. "I should feel guilty, I suppose, but I'm glad he's dead. I hope he burns in hell for what he's done."

"He will." A slow smile curved his lips. "I've found proof that there is a heaven, so there must be a hell as well."

She returned the smile. "Heaven, eh? And where's that, pray tell?"

"Right here," he replied, pulling her closer. "With you."

He was just a breath away from kissing her when there came the sound of a clearing throat on the terrace behind them.

"Damnit," Saint swore. "I can't concentrate on anything else when I'm with you."

Ivy chuckled and sat up to face their guest. It was Ezekiel. Saint rose to his feet to greet him, and helped Ivy to hers as well.

Ezekiel smiled a little self-consciously as he came toward them. "Forgive the intrusion, but I had a package arrive for you earlier that I thought you might want. Looks like it got sent to your Paris address first."

Saint took the battered parcel. He thanked Ezekiel and asked if he wanted to join them, but the man just grinned and said he wouldn't dream of it.

When his old friend was gone, Saint and Ivy sat down once more; she looked over his shoulder as he opened the package. It had indeed been first addressed to the contact he used when in Paris who then forwarded it on to Ezekiel. But it wasn't the address that had his heart skipping a beat, it was the contents.

Inside was a small heavy box, and inside that was an amulet made of silver—silver that seemed to call to him and glow under the light of the moon.

He knew instinctively that if he picked it up it would not burn him, and it didn't.

"*Merde*," he whispered.

"What is it?" Ivy asked.

It wasn't the whole thing, and it had been etched with the symbols that had come to mean something to him and his four brothers. It was a sword, with a chalice on one side and a cross on the other—the same cross that had been burned into their backs.

"It's part of the grail," he told her. "The cup that made us vampire."

He felt her gaze, but he couldn't tear his own from the amulet. "Who is it from?"

"Temple. He must have sent this before they took him." He knew Temple couldn't be that easily taken. He knew his friend would have a plan of some kind. If the Order knew that Temple had sent pieces of the cup to the rest of them, then that could very well explain why they had been after him.

"There's something else in there," Ivy remarked, leaning so close their cheeks were almost touching.

She was right. There was a key and a slip of paper with a Rome address on it.

"What does it mean?"

Saint grinned. "I think Temple wants us to go to this address."

Ivy's eyes widened. "Do you think it has something to do with the Silver Palm?"

He nodded. "Yes."

"Who is the letter from?"

He looked at the envelope, at the familiar handwriting. "It's from Bishop."

"Another vampire?"

"Yes." He could go months, even years without talking to one of his brothers. To receive contact from two on the same day was astounding.

He tore open the letter, his breathing stuttering to a stop as he read words that made his fingers tremble and his heart soar.

"She's not dead," he whispered hoarsely.

"Who?" Ivy demanded. There was real fear in her eyes. "Marta?"

He grabbed her hand to silence her anxiety. "Her

daughter. The baby she was carrying when I tried to change her. She's alive and she's with Bishop. She's one of us now."

Ivy gazed at him with wide-eyed wonder. "How did she survive?"

"The change made her a dhampyr—half vampire. She's been alive all these years."

"You have a daughter—sort of."

A daughter. Yes, he supposed he did. "They're going to Italy as well. In fact, they're probably already on their way."

"We should send them word that we're coming."

His gaze jerked to hers. "You want to go?"

She swatted him in the arm. "You're not getting rid of me that easily. Of course I'm going."

"What about your responsibility to Maison Rouge?"

"My responsibility is to *you*," she corrected. "Besides, my mother isn't going anywhere just yet and Emily can run the place. Seems that all you guys are running off to Italy anyway."

He looked back at the amulet. Had Chapel and Bishop and Reign received these as well? They must have. The only reason Temple would melt down the cup would be to keep it from falling into the wrong hands. Had he known that the Silver Palm was coming for him?

Saint was actually excited. Even though it was

bound to be perilous, he was looking forward to this new adventure—this danger and intrigue. And he knew why.

He grinned at Ivy. "I love you."

She grinned back as she straddled him, the amulet forgotten for the moment. "I love you more."

He laughed, and she kissed him. And then he forgot about the amulet for more than a moment as she adjusted their clothing so that he was inside her and her fangs were in him.

And as they rocked together toward climax, Saint realized that his opinion of this pretty little house had changed after all. It was no longer just a house, it was his home, and in it he had found everything he ever wanted. Ever needed.

And she'd found him.

Next month, don't miss these exciting new love stories only from Avon Books

Untouched by Anna Campbell

An Avon Romantic Treasure

When Grace Paget is kidnapped, she believes it can't get any worse—until she finds herself imprisoned with a mad man. Declared insane and at the mercy of his uncle, Sheene trusts no one. But to escape this deadly web, he and Grace must put their fears aside; for their only chance at survival is each other.

Satisfaction by Marianne Stillings

An Avon Contemporary Romance

Georgiana Mundy has everything: fame, fortune—and a stalker that she would do anything to defeat. As long as "anything" doesn't include former detective Ethan Darling. The man sees too much and Georgie isn't sure how far she's willing to go in this dangerous game of life, death . . . . and love.

To Wed a Highland Bride by Sarah Gabriel

An Avon Romance

James MacCarran, Viscount Struan, must marry and sets out to find a wife of his own choosing. Elspeth MacArthur is beautiful, intriguing, and delightful—but not nearly as biddable as he had hoped! Will these two strong-willed people continue to butt heads . . . or will they find that they have the strength to embrace what they have been given?

One Knight Only by Julia Latham

An Avon Romance

Anne Kendall is a lady's maid impersonating a countess at the request of the king. Traveling with Sir Philip Clifford for safety, Anne is protected from everything—except when it comes to matters of the heart.

Avon Romantic Treasures

Unforgettable, enthralling love stories, sparkling with passion and adventure from Romance's bestselling authors

Avon Romances

the best in
exceptional authors and unforgettable novels!